FATAL SCORE

John Baird Rogers

Copyright © 2018 by Gotuit Publishing LLC

Cover design by Danny Media

ISBN 978-1-7322262-0-3 (trade paperback)
    978-1-7322262-1-0 (e-book)

Library of Congress control number: 2018904521

For Beverly

fortem posce animum mortis terrore carentem

Ask for a brave soul that fears not death.
    - Juvenal

FATAL SCORE

Mayfield-Napolitani #1

ONE

"SO YOU'RE THE DUMBASS."

The woman plopped into the booth across from Joe Mayfield. The bite of over-easy egg halfway to his mouth dripped a spot of yolk on his pants.

"Pardon me?"

He set down his fork and tried for an offhand smile, which he knew came off as a grimace. He had watched her enter, out of place here in North Dakota farm country. She was tall, not quite stick-thin. She wore cargo shorts, an MIT T-shirt and an untamed mop of chestnut hair. Certainly not the thug he'd watched for since he ditched Big Louie and Snake back in Florida.

"Plenty of people think I'm a dumbass. You're the first person to say it to my face."

The woman grinned and picked up a menu.

The diner was warm with the smell of bacon and coffee in thick cups served with honest-to-god cream. Forks clicked against plates and conversation flowed, a pleasant backdrop punctuated by an occasional laugh. The early crowd was finishing up now, people standing, nodding to friends, leaving. Not the place he expected to be caught.

Joe's pulse slowed toward normal.

No way this was official. Florida Consolidated Energy wouldn't send someone to North Dakota. Particularly not a pretty woman who looked barely old enough to buy beer, must shop at Goodwill, and hadn't met a hairbrush in a couple days. Neither would the FBI.

She turned her attention from the menu to Joe, big brown eyes serious. "I've been tracking you and your avatars ever since New Orleans," she said with a shake of her head. "This RazorBlue website thing you're doing exposed you. A great idea, but every time you add to the blog, you show your position. Pretty easy to connect the dots. You must know that. And that old guzzler with a Louisiana plate? In North Dakota, yet? I suppose you might have been easier to spot if you had a tractor with wings, but not much."

She tilted her head, examining him like a specimen in a science experiment. "I don't expect you to open right up, Joe, or should I call you Mr. Mayfield?" she paused, but continued before Joe could answer, "or Sarcosy? John Maxwell, maybe? Or Chester Burnell or Stevie Ray Morse? They're your avatars, right?"

She'd traced his avatars? After all that work? His breakfast turned leaden in his stomach.

"Who are you?"

"Let's not get ahead of ourselves, Joe. If you need something more than 'Hey, you', call me Weezy. But to answer your question, I'm either your worst nightmare or your last best hope. That's why you have to start at the beginning and tell me what you're doing and why."

Her look softened. "You're a smart guy. What you have done so far is way beyond what most hackers achieve. But consider: I know your real name. I know your wife Cynthia died in February. Ovarian cancer, I think it was. I know you used to work for Florida Consolidated. I know you've been on the Yak, rotating through those avatars I mentioned." She ticked off each point as she made it.

"You checked into the Florida Consolidated network last week as Nicolas Sarcosy. Clever, to spell it wrong. Then you hit it again yesterday as Stevie Ray." She cocked her head. "French politics and blues music, huh?"

Joe felt like a skunk must feel staring into the headlights of an oncoming semitrailer, strongly inclined to spray.

"It almost worked," she continued, "but the Yak firewall is sophisticated. You established a pattern, I recognized it, and here I am." She shrugged. "I don't know why you're driving around the countryside. I don't fully understand why you stuck your nose into Florida Consolidated medical records. You're either just plain nuts or onto something."

She slapped the menu closed.

"My regular go-to-the-office-and-get-paid-for-it job back at IAC headquarters—the Yak to you—is to protect the national database from people like you. I may be here to help you. I don't know that yet, because ever since CyberWar One, it's a federal crime to hack the Yak. But you know that, don't you?"

She pursed her lips and looked at him expectantly. Joe's thoughts were a tangle of questions, piling on each other, whirling toward nowhere. Finally, she gave a little puff of irritation.

"While you think about how to be forthcoming with me, I'm going to order breakfast."

She looked over her shoulder at the waitress, who eyed them from behind the counter. "Ma'am, I'm ready to order."

The waitress smiled at Joe as she approached. They had bantered about nothing much a few minutes earlier. She took the woman's order for the American breakfast with eggs scrambled, bacon, toast, hash browns, coffee, and a piece of apple pie. To Joe's raised eyebrows, this woman who called herself Weezy said, "Well, the pie looks delicious. Besides, this place has real food. I was brought up on real food. Now I live in the D.C. metroplex. I can get fast food, or something lumpy and glutinous a vegan thinks is good for the environment, or a fifty-dollar meal with a foreign name served with an attitude. Hard to find real food where I live."

The waitress brought pie and coffee. She looked at Weezy warily and said, "Breakfast's coming up."

Joe told himself to look unconcerned, overcome the fear, and assess the situation. He picked up a triangle of toast, realized his hand was shaking, quickly set it down. So much for unconcerned. But was this real or some distraction to get him to...what? Run?

Confide? Give up? She knew about his hack of Florida Consolidated, but maybe not the details. The reference to IAC might be a red herring. Why not have him arrested? Or send out Snake and Big Louie to finish their work?

He drew himself up into what he hoped was an authoritative posture.

"Alright, Weezy. I don't know you, and I don't know what you're talking about. I did work for Florida Consolidated for almost fourteen years. An exemplary employee until suddenly, I wasn't. My wife's dead." A hitch in his throat. "My life's gone to hell."

He stopped to draw a slow breath.

Her face was unreadable.

"Let me ask you...have you ever lost somebody you love? Ever wondered what to do with the rest of your life when most of what you care about is taken away?"

Weezy's mouth was taut, but her eyes seemed to reflect his pain.

"Until a couple of weeks ago, I was on a trip my wife had always hoped to take up the Blues Highway in Mississippi, visiting places where the music she loved was born."

He got up from the booth.

"All I know about you makes me think Florida Consolidated has decided to indulge in more harassment of a former employee. You need to stop threatening me."

He gave her a look he hoped was intimidating.

"I will leave you now to enjoy your breakfast."

Weezy spoke around a mouthful of pie. "Yes. Well, you did hack the Yak."

Joe turned toward the door.

"Sorry about your wife."

A wall of rage stopped him like a big hand slammed to his chest. He turned, choking on his words. "Pardon me?"

She froze. He retraced his steps, leaned down, face close to hers.

"You're sorry about my wife? My wife! Listen, you tell whatever fucking bureaucrat you report to back at whatever the hell agency you really work for that the fine folks at Florida Consolidated can think whatever they want, but you bastards killed my beautiful—" Tears flowed. "My beautiful Cynthia." He continued in a hoarse whisper. "If you want to do something to me, just do it. Go write your report. Send out your bozo security guys. Let them erase me like they promised. They scared me the first time, but not anymore."

He drew a ragged breath.

"It's not what you think," Weezy said. "Don't walk out."

Joe straightened up, jaws working to bite off a response. He turned, went to the counter and slapped down three tens. The door complained as he shoved it open.

***

Weezy watched Joe Mayfield cross the street to an ancient, dark green Honda Element, get in and drive away too fast.

Elbows on the table, she massaged her forehead. She had been so confident when she asked for the travel chit back in Bethesda. After all, she had studied Mayfield backward and forward. He was smart, and his dossier pointed to a happy, reasonable man. She had no doubt that logic and humor, spiced with a little of her trademark sarcasm, would prevail.

When she entered the diner, she had recognized him right away. Handsome, or close to it. Dark hair, receding a bit. Big but not imposing. Denim shirt, sleeves rolled up. Pretty much the same as the pictures in the dossier. When she sat down across from him, she started with her patented snappy repartee—intimidate him, then turn on the quirky charm. It worked most of the time, but here, she realized she hadn't factored in what happened since those carefree pictures were taken. Now there was pain, anger, and loneliness in his eyes.

And she blew it, got defensive.

She stared out the window, taking in the little town. Hand-written advertisements for chicken feed and antifreeze taped in the dusty window of the hardware store across the street, "Available" signs in empty storefronts. Old and tired. Maybe this whole project was a mistake. Maybe this man had become more than a case of a moderately capable hacker whose mission made no sense.

The waitress brought breakfast, setting it in front of her too firmly.

"The guy paid," she sniffed, turned and returned to her post at the end of the counter.

Weezy ate. She chewed and swallowed, thinking over the situation. Finally, she pulled an e-pad from a pocket in her shorts, found a phone number, and tapped out a message.

***

Joe kept his anger bottled up until he hit the edge of town. Then he jammed the accelerator to the floor. The four-cylinder engine groaned.

He read somewhere that the uncontrollable physical response to anger—the adrenaline rush, the ringing in the ears, the heightened sensory awareness that makes everything seem to move in slow motion—is purely chemical and lasts for ninety seconds. The rest is all on you.

Joe welcomed the anger that rose up hot and nearly choked him. He replayed the conversation with the woman who called herself Weezy, jumping back to scraps and phrases from the officious denials by the insurance company, the smarmy bullshit about what Cynthia would or wouldn't have wanted and the threats from Snake and Big Louie at his 'exit interview.'

A ring. A friendly synthesized female voice said, "Phone 3 wants your attention." *What?* All four phones were in vibrate mode. They were generic disposables he bought in Florida,

Alabama, Mississippi and Minnesota. Phone 3 was registered to his avatar John Maxwell. No privacy settings without giving out too much information. As a result, each day brought a dozen or more ads on each phone claiming to have latched on to some personal preference. He needed to stay sweet and clean, shave effortlessly, save energy, have a chance for free intercity passes to Spokane/LA/ Butte, enjoy a happiness massage, meet someone wonderful. A pause, then from the phone, "John Maxwell, you have a message."

Joe pulled off the road and got out. A wheat field stretched west. Redwing blackbirds argued in the distance. Through the warmth of morning, the earthy scent of summer. Wouldn't it be nice just to enjoy it? Wouldn't it be beautiful to be on this road, in this place, with Cynthia?

Phone 3's text said: One more chance. Lake Morain Park, 10 miles west of town. Second entrance, picnic area. I'll go there and wait 15. Otherwise, I upload my report & go home.

Damn it. Joe turned back to the car and reached into the front seat for the ditty bag. He shut off the phones. His gut told him to go silent and get away, keep moving.

One foot in the car, he hesitated. He'd made a habit of studying maps of places he passed through in case he needed to make a quick exit. If he continued west, it was forty miles with no major crossroad. She had tracked him to Underhill, could probably do it again. He imagined the road ahead, wheat and soybean fields, farmhouses every mile or so.

It wouldn't be hard to run him down. If he were to disappear, life would be easier for them. Maybe that was it. This Weezy was trying to lure him to some place they could erase him like they promised.

He checked over his shoulder. Nothing.

But if she was who she said she was ...

A line of Robert Johnson's "Cross Road Blues" Cynthia had loved looped in his mind. He was at a cross road, too. He looked back toward town. Run some more? Or face down the evil he had found?

The song wound through his mind, Johnson's tenor carrying a tinge of fear.

He shivered.

Was Cynthia calling him? What would she want him to do?

He blew out a long breath and got into the Element.

TWO

LAKE MORAIN PARK ANNOUNCED itself to be one-quarter mile away. Joe slowed and started to turn in at the first entrance, which had a building tucked away from the road. A small sign said *Main Entrance - 500 Feet* with an arrow pointing left. He drove on. The second entrance promised hiking, picnicking and swimming. The picnic area was partly visible, empty as far as he could see. He drove another half mile, watching the rear view. Nothing.

He made a U-turn, went back to the first entrance. The building set back from the road was unmarked except for a No Trespassing sign. No vehicles. Padlock on the roll-up door. Joe parked in the shadow next to the building. He opened both front windows and waited. The heat was not yet oppressive, and an occasional breeze brought the scent of clover and alfalfa. In a short time, a blue mono drove by. Nobody in Dakota farm country drove a one-person car. Plenty in the cities, but mostly pickups out here. Must be the woman. He heard the crunch of crushed rock as it entered the park.

Joe waited five minutes, then another five. A pickup passed, driving toward town, then quiet again. He strained to hear any sound from the picnic area. At twenty minutes, Joe began to sweat.

The crunch of tires.

Joe gunned the Element and pulled into the road. Sure enough, the little blue car was coming right at him. No one else in evidence.

The woman slammed on her brakes, coming to a stop a few feet from the Element looking furious, maybe scared.

Her window was open, and she shouted, "What. Thefuck. Are. You. Doing?"

Joe stepped out of the car and said across the hood, "Making sure this wasn't a trap is what the fuck I was doing."

She crossed her arms, fixed him in a pitying look and exhaled. "You didn't read my message carefully, did you?"

"In other words, you've uploaded the file. Is that right?"

Joe watched her face change and said, "I didn't think so."

"So, you decided to talk to me? Maybe you're not such a dumbass after all."

"I haven't decided to talk to you yet," Joe said. "I just haven't decided not to."

She gave a quick shake of her head, exhaled, and put the mono in reverse. She backed to the main entrance, slammed the little car into Drive and entered the picnic area, crushed rock pinging on the undercarriage. Joe followed. He backed into a parking space up against trees, covering the single Louisiana plate, and set the brake.

The woman was making for a shaded picnic table. He caught up with her.

She spun and confronted him. "Why all the cloak and dagger bullshit?"

"Look, Weezy or whatever your name is," Joe said. "The last person who was interested in talking to me on this subject was a big ugly guy who wants to make me go away, and he wasn't offering a dream vacation. I have no reason to believe you're not working with him."

The woman aimed a hard stare at him. "I already told you. I work for the IAC. You know, the national cyber security system. I'm not a black ops person or a special agent. There are no such people at the Yak, in spite of what you hear on the Net. I'm what the agency calls a tracker. I spend most of my time in the National Ops center near Bethesda. I do my work through algorithms that I design and run right from my extremely comfortable chair."

She went to the far side of the picnic table and sat down. "I'm going way out on a limb in your case, but for a reason. I'm not sure why you've been crashing around the Florida Consolidated system. You might be the person who appears to be siphoning off substantial money from the company. You may have hacked in to the company's system, but you used a sledgehammer when a scalpel would have worked better."

Joe grimaced. "And let me see, you let this 'dumbass' get into your system. This guy without special training waltzed right in and —"

"Yeah. You're right, Joe. I did catch you, though, and I would have caught you sooner if you were doing the predictable, boring things most people try to do. No apparent monetary motive, no interest in protected military information. Stomping around like a bull in a china shop, using laughable aliases. But you did get in. And because you made so much noise, it looks like there are some not-so-savory people after you."

She furrowed her brow and went on, "I don't quite understand why MedRecords are so important to you, except you kept hitting 'em over and over. If you'd killed your wife for the insurance— yes, I know about that, too—you wouldn't be trolling through the Yak risking being found out by someone like me. Doesn't make sense, Joe. Tell me what's going on so I can get away from this beautiful, healthy place and back to my comfortable office furniture."

She waited, tapping her foot. "Now it's your turn."

***

Joe felt himself beginning to relax. No cop cars or black SUVs swooping in to arrest him or worse. Nothing but the quiet North Dakota morning. Maybe she was for real. Finally, he started talking, intending to give this confusing, impatient woman a brief, dispassionate review of what he had discovered.

What came out was different.

"My wife died almost seven months ago from ovarian cancer. She had just turned thirty-three and was in great health, or so we thought. Right after she was diagnosed, her HealthScore changed. Dropped from 84 to 62. Do you know what that means?"

"Not really. I know the scores exist, but they're only probabilities."

"Well, Weezy, or whatever your name is, I would have agreed with you before last November, but they use those probabilities to decide what kind of treatment a person gets."

Joe stared at the ground, watching a column of ants conduct logistics on what must once have been a cheese curl.

"At a score of 84, Cynthia would have gotten targeted chemo, the Prism machine, consults at Mayo, maybe epigenetic studies, the whole works. With all that, she had a good chance of making it. At 62, she got palliative care. Hope, prayers and painkillers at the end."

He stopped for a moment to breathe.

"You know the hard part? I knew something was wrong right away, because I work...worked...with those numbers at Florida Consolidated." His voice quavered, but he continued, "You know the even harder part? I couldn't make anyone believe the MedRecord was wrong because, oh, yes, MedRecords are part of your IAC, and the IAC is the most secure, best-protected database in history. Of course, it couldn't have been wrong, could it, Ms. Tracker?"

He stopped again, trying to keep his voice steady.

"I was stupid enough to go through channels. Be polite, like I always have been. I played by the rules. I did not move mountains. I let my beautiful Cynthia, my funny, artistic Cynthia die."

He forced himself to go on.

"In the beginning, I just wanted to try to figure out what had happened. There's only one reason I can see to change the records. A lower score would reduce Florida Consolidated's insurance cost. Palliative care is cheap compared to the aggressive care Cynthia needed and deserved. I tried to get MedRecord history. It must be there, somewhere, but I couldn't uncover it. But I did find changes in her HealthScore and dozens of others. I finally identified a few of the people affected, and I took the evidence to my management. That was back when I thought Florida Consolidated stood by its Statement of Principles."

***

Weezy listened, watching Joe's pain and frustration play out. His story had the gritty feel of real people, mistakes made, dumb luck. Liars almost always have airtight stories. He might be lying, but his emotions seemed real. He was either a great actor or an honest man.

Finishing the story, he said, "I don't know what to do. I've got a few names, no details. Easy to explain as unfortunate clerical errors. I decided to go public on the Net. If Florida Consolidated figures out what I'm doing, they will bury me in a stinking, steaming pile of legal actions and PR releases. You know, 'A man led by grief to illegal acts.' I have a better chance of being arrested than exposing the MedRecords fraud. And what do I care, really? I failed when it mattered. Nothing will bring Cynthia back."

He rested his forearms on his thighs, eyes on the ground.

Weezy's mind raced. Check out his suspicions. Don't jump to conclusions.

"Okay, Joe. I think you've been candid with me, so I will be candid with you," she paused, knowing the next step put her farther out the plank she might be walking. "My name is Louise Napolitani. As I said before, I work for the IAC. You have violated several federal laws by hacking into the system, but you probably know that. The book of rules I run by is pretty straightforward. I should turn you over to Enforcement and watch them haul you off in government-issue bracelets."

She had been lulled by his candor and pain, but his expression made her suddenly wonder if she should be scared sitting at a picnic table in the middle of nowhere with a big guy that might not want to be arrested.

"I have an alternative," she added quickly. "It may not work. If it fails, it will be curtains for my career."

Weezy paused, considering the ramifications of her plan, and then said, "I want to flesh out your suspicions. There may be a larger problem for IAC here, and filling in some blanks will give us a better picture of what's going on. The downside is if you're lying to me, I'll find no evidence. You will have traded in your Louisiana pile-o-junk for something else and disappeared. If you're the thief they think you are—"

"I have never, never—"

"—I'll be left with a handful of nothing."

Joe seemed confused, like he wanted to say something.

Weezy continued, "So, here's the deal. I'm going back to the east coast to nose around. You need to keep moving. Maybe back toward Orlando. Carefully, in case those bad guys you mentioned are still tracking you." She cocked her head. "You've been on a well-needed break before going back home to find a new job. Your avatar Chester Burnell will call me once a day from his phone and leave a message. It's always going to be some variation on the same theme: 'Working on the L1389 anomaly. Will check in when I have more info.' It'll seem like a contract programmer giving a status report. If you're in trouble, say you're having trouble with L1389. I will be able to trace where you are, so don't mention that. The first day I don't get a report, I will turn your file over to Enforcement."

"How will I know what you're doing?" he said. "I need more than a check-in."

Weezy thought for a minute. She knew nothing about this man, but her gut said there was more to him than met the eye.

"Hold on." She stood and walked to her car.

Glancing over her shoulder, she saw confusion on his face. "I'm going to give you a new job, Joe."

***

Joe watched Weezy root around in the tiny one-person car. She returned carrying an e-pad like Joe's. She sat, opened it and tapped at the keyboard. As she concentrated, a single, straight line appeared between her eyebrows. She was good looking in an offbeat sort of way. Angular, pretty in the soft light filtering through trees. Looked about twenty, but now that he paid closer attention, surely older.

Finally, she said, "Open net. Olegarten Fabricating." A new window popped to life, went to the unsecured Internet and flashed up what seemed like a standard business website. Flat 2D, not much animation. One of those ancient sites that often stayed around past anyone caring.

"The world is going to see that you're now a sales rep for this fine firm, selling steel for manufacturing and construction. You're out of a job. You got a chance to do some selling online. Not like what you did before, but you gotta keep body and soul together, right?" She handed the e-pad to Joe.

"On the bottom right of the web page, there's a white flower. See it?"

Joe nodded.

"Punch on it, and you'll get a long string of html code. Roll over to the second comment …"

"Comment?"

"Yeah. See, right here...Bakkekløver," she said. "That's the name of the little white flower. Punch on that, and you will pass into a chat room. You will need a name …" She cocked her head. "You've used RazorBlue on that website you set up, so don't use it. Something you'll remember not associated—"

"luckymonkey."

"Meant sarcastically, right?" She cracked a grin and continued, "When you get in, you will see a whole series of threads. Go to 'Hotcakes' and you'll be talking to me. Olegarten has twenty members, all expert hackers and thus, very private. Stay on text only and only talk to me. No video with anyone but me. Understand?"

"luckymonkey, Hotcakes, right?"

"Now, let's switch pads," she said.

Joe fetched his e-pad from the Element, and Weezy said, "Mine's backed up. Is yours?"

Joe nodded. "Sure."

"How?"

"Some of it to cubes, but continuously to the secure Net."

She nodded and held out her hand. Joe gave her his e-pad, and she began tapping, concentrating, frowns and half grins crossing her face as she worked. Finished, she handed him a bright purple storage cube and said, "Okay, here's all your stuff. I turned off that 'secure' backup of yours. If anyone is tracking you, they may pick up on the fact that you discontinued it, but I can fix that when I get back home. You will have been dropped for nonpayment."

Joe grimaced.

"Really?" she said. "You're worrying about your credit rating? Really?"

"Yes, really. I've always been careful about things like that. It's hard to let go of that stuff. Makes me feel like a criminal."

"Well, dude," she said with a quizzical half-smile. "I hesitate to bring you up to speed, but almost everybody but a nice lady who used to work for you thinks you *are* a criminal. Following the epistemology embodied in 'walks like a duck, quacks like a duck,' you might as well act like one, no?"

She raised her eyebrows, but there was humor in her eyes. "Meanwhile, I need to get out of the fresh air, which I might get used to, and away from the clean-living people around here, who make me nervous. I'm going back to Bethesda." Her expression changed to serious. "If you mess this up, you will get caught and we will both be in much more trouble than you ever thought possible. Clear?"

"Clear. And thank you, I think."

She closed the pad and stood up. Joe, still seated, said, "One more thing you have to understand."

Weezy stopped, cocked an eyebrow, clearly anxious to get going.

"That bit about me stealing from Florida Consolidated is wrong. I don't know where it's coming from, but it's wrong. If I have money, it's only because I bought an insurance policy on Cynthia and myself to help a college friend." He dropped his gaze away from Weezy. "Never expected to collect on it."

Weezy gave him a sidewise glance, possibly skeptical. "Someone is taking money from Florida Consolidated, and it's connected to your department. I'll check that out, too. Keep in touch."

Her smile was sympathetic, almost friendly. Then she was on her way across the lot. All business. She slipped into the blue mono. A wave, and she turned east toward Fargo.

It was a hot day, insects buzzing and a hint of a breeze. Good growing weather. The field next to the park shimmered in the heat. Joe felt lighter. Telling this Weezy person his story lifted some weight from his shoulders. He could believe he was moving forward, not sideways.

In the months since Cynthia's death, he had come to think of his life as Before and After. He knew he romanticized the happy life they had in the Before. Sure, there were spats from time to time. Marry a creative free spirit to an analytical finance guy and you sometimes get friction, right? But the fights were rare, and the making up oh, so delicious.

He opened his e-pad, scanning the map. He'd intended to keep on the road going west but decided to backtrack through town to a state highway that would carry him south and east toward home, like Weezy suggested. He stood, stretched and went to the

Element, started it and turned toward town.

As he approached the outskirts, he slowed. The town seemed friendly now, the place where After might start getting better.

He rolled by the diner, remembering the pretty waitress, breakfast, and Weezy.

A shape caught his eye. A man sitting at the counter. Broad-shoulders, bald.

He gripped the wheel, almost stomped the accelerator, adrenaline pumping. He shook his head, trying to dislodge the fear. And realized he had passed a black SUV in a slant space across from the diner. He stared in the rearview mirror. Florida plate colors.

It couldn't be...could it?

He began to speed up. A black SUV with a Florida license. Maybe nothing, but...

Involuntarily, he started calculating. If it was Big Louie, he could go west or back east toward Fargo or on the state road going south. Probabilities spun through Joe's mind. He knew he needed to slow down, look at a map, make a plan. He turned off the main street at the SuperShop across from the motel he had stayed in last night. In back of the building, a dirt parking lot held a rusted-out muscle car and a dumpster. Joe pulled between them, wishing the car could conceal more of the Element's high profile.

He raised a map of the area on his e-pad and considered his options. Rather than run blindly, he realized he first had to be sure the guy he saw in the diner was Big Louie.

Joe walked the two blocks to the diner in back of the buildings fronting on Main Street. The breakfast perfume from the diner's exhaust fan let him know where to cut into a passageway between buildings.

The SUV across the street did have a Florida license. Joe took a deep breath and stepped onto the sidewalk.

From his angle, the morning sun made the glass front of the

diner into a yellow, opaque wall.

Joe took another several steps, hoping this was foolishness. The glare receded. The man was still at the counter, talking to the waitress, who shrugged. He turned.

Big Louie.

THREE

BY THE TIME JOE got back to the SuperShop, he was sweating. Not because of the warm morning or the near jog. He pulled his ditty bag out of the console between the seats and dug in it for his avatar phones. He selected Stevie Ray Morse and scrolled down the adverts it had received.

Ad for Asian massage? No, he needed something that would stay on for a while. Free high-speed rail? Ditto. Full Power Gospel Hour? That would work.

He walked around the building and peeked at the gas pumps. No SUV. Hoping to look nonchalant, he sauntered past two pickup trucks backed into parking slots in front of the building. Inside, a couple of weathered men were discussing hog prices. A teen-age kid with greasy hair and acne manned the counter.

Joe selected a can of pop from the cooler then turned down an aisle full of bagged snacks. The next aisle held auto supplies, lubricants and…duct tape. Joe grabbed a roll, thanking the gods of merchandising for their foresight.

The kid at the counter had his e-pad on his lap, playing an action game. His name tag announced "Dylan," hand-inscribed after an incised smiley face.

"If I'm going west, how far to the next gas?" Joe asked, turning to give the security camera a clear shot.

Dylan sighed, head down, swiped the pad several times, finally glanced up at Joe, one eyebrow arched.

"If you go west, you hit Lake Morain."

"I mean, going west, not driving into Lake Morain, how far?"

"Forty miles."

"Okay, I'll just take this," he said, pushing the soda toward Dylan while moving to block the roll of duct tape from the security camera's view.

He paid and retreated outside, around the corner of the building, thinking how risky, maybe what a waste of valuable time his plan was.

***

Leon Studt, 'Big Louie' to everyone but his mother, vectored in on the last bite of pie. These hick towns still had good food. As he raised the fork to his mouth, his e-pad buzzed. Zimmerman.

Target in Underhill at SuperShop. East edge of town. Finish the job.

Louie finished the pie.

It had been fifteen years since the KO in Vegas and the concussion that knocked him out of contention and out of a job. Since then, Louie's appreciation of food had moved him from light heavyweight through cruiserweight to heavyweight. He was bald now, and the roll on the back of his neck was no longer all muscle.

He stood from the stool, paid, and dropped a dollar tip on the counter. Then he was out of the diner and into the black SUV parked a few spaces down. He checked the map of the area on his e-pad.

He made a quick U-turn, then headed east on Main.

He saw the sign a block before he got to the SuperShop and slowed to a crawl. Couple of pickups. Lot empty otherwise. Nobody at the pumps. Mayfield must have stopped for gas and left.

Louie parked next to the pickups and went into the store. Kid at the counter, two older men talking at the coffee stand. Something about post-hole digging attachments.

Louie picked out a couple of pieces of jerky and waited as the two geezers left.

The kid, Dylan, was doing something on his e-pad. He glanced up between swipes, saw the jerky in Louie's hand.

"That all?"

Louie slid the Mayfield picture across the counter.

"Seen this guy?"

Dylan shrugged. "Might've."

Louie repeated the question.

Dylan gave him a smirk. "And you want to know...why?"

Louie reached across the counter and grabbed a handful of Dylan-with-a-smiley-face's overlarge smock, pulling the kid out of his seat. The e-pad clattered to the floor.

Dylan's face went white, throwing his acne into bas-relief.

Nose three inches from Dylan's, Louie growled, "I asked you a question, asshole."

"I...uhh...yeah, he was in a while ago."

Louie let Dylan slide back into his seat.

"What'd he say?"

"Not much. Asked where the next gas is goin' west."

Louie dropped a couple of dollars on the counter and turned toward the door.

Dylan inspected his e-pad and whined, "You mighta broke it."

Louie, hand on the door to leave, cocked his head. "Really? Kid, right now I'm bein' friendly. Piss me off, and I'll break more than your goddam e-pad."

***

Crouched behind a recycle bin, Joe had seen Big Louie get out of the black SUV and go into SuperShop.

Now or never. Take the risk or get in the Element and go like hell.

He bent down and scuttled by the two pickups and slid under the SUV, holding the Stevie Ray phone gingerly to keep the flaps of duct tape from sticking to each other or him. He felt around the undercarriage until he found a space on the inside of the rocker panel and attached one of the straps.

As he felt for a spot to attach the second flap, Joe realized there was a boot in the space between the neighboring truck and the SUV.

Holding his breath, Joe waited for a door to open above him and collapse his plan. The hackneyed phrase "life passing before your eyes" became painfully clear to him.

But then the door of the truck next to him creaked, the boot disappeared and the truck pulled away.

Breathing again, Joe slapped the second strap onto the frame. As he did, the Full Power Gospel Hour changed from barely audible to almost blasting just above his head.

He felt the phone, realizing he'd taped over the speaker button and then somehow activated it. A couple of fruitless pecks where he thought the buttons might be. Full Power Gospel still blasted. No time to fix the problem, though.

He grabbed the undercarriage of the SUV, pulled himself out, rolled a couple of times, looked toward the store's door. He saw it start to open and knew his plan had failed. He pushed himself up and sprinted toward the safety of the recycle bin. Breathing hard, he had a sudden vision of Sunday school long ago, Lot's wife and the pillar of salt. As he slid behind the bin, he turned back anyway. The pillar he saw was Big Louie, standing outside the SUV, brow furrowed.

***

Louie walked toward the SUV, concentrating on peeling the wrapper off one of the pieces of jerky. As he opened the SUV's door, he heard music.

Church music? On a Tuesday morning?

His train of thought was interrupted by a chime on his e-pad.

Got a hit on burner phone east edge of town. Might be him. Check out.

Louie sniffed. He didn't need Zimmerman's directions. He'd catch him on his own. Solo. No Zimmerman.

Louie closed the door, turned on the A/C and checked the map of the town. Motel across the street. The diner. Commercial buildings on Main. Houses clustering around the center. Grain elevator on the western edge.

He backed out of the parking place, craning his neck. Couple of cars at the motel, nothing like Mayfield was driving. He turned west on Main, checking the map, peering down each side street.

Another ping from Zimmerman: He's moving. Going west.

Louie checked the map again. Must be going out of town.

At the edge of town, low hills. No car ahead. Must be over the hill. Louie tore off a big piece of the jerky and put his foot to the floor. He pounded the disable button on the nav system when it began bleeping over-speed. He summoned his power, pumped himself up like he did back when he was in the ring.

A ping sounded on his e-pad. Zimmerman telling him something. As usual. Didn't need any more cop bullshit. The big SUV almost went airborne over the rise. Speedometer read ninety-five, and the SUV was juking and jiving on the old road. The prairie spread out flat ahead, no car in sight. Only a green tractor stopped where a dirt track crossed the road ahead.

Where's Mayfield?

Ping again from Zimmerman. Louie exhaled and looked down at his e-pad, which was bouncing on the passenger seat.

Stop. You're following yo…

Louie glanced up at the road. The tractor had started to move.

Dumb shit couldn't be …

The tractor continued onto the road.

Louie jammed the brakes. The anti-lock system chattered, telling him it was too little too late.

He wrenched the wheel, and the big SUV slewed down the road sidewise, teetering on its center of gravity. The tires finally caught. There was a gut-wrenching moment of weightlessness, and then the airbag hit Louie like a combination to the face and solar plexus.

Dazed, Louie fought with the bag and stumbled out of the car slow motion. The SUV was nose down in the ditch. The tractor had pulled across the road and stopped, chalk-faced farmer breathing hard.

In the quiet, music wound through the settling dust. Rich trill of a Hammond organ; double-clap rhythm driving the song forward. Call and response, a powerful baritone leading.

You know you gonna be saved.

(Saved! Yes Yes Yes.)

Louie, dizzy, stared at the source of the sound. A phone dangling from the rocker panel on a piece of tape?

I said, Saved …

(You right, brother. Gonna be saved. Saved. Saved.)

Shit!

Now you're crossing the river.

(Crossing, yes you're crossing.)

Crap!

To the Promised Land!

(Promised, yes promised land.)

Louie took in the car, the dangling phone, the exploded airbag, and the crazy angle of the front wheel.

Now you been saved, brother.

(You been saved, sister.)

Fuck!

Thank the Lord

(Thank the Lord)

You been saved.

FOUR

JOE DROVE EAST FROM Underhill to the state road that led south. After fifty miles, he relaxed. The land at the edge of the great western plain was flat, and there was nothing in his rear-view mirror. He tapped his e-pad into the Element's asthmatic sound system, and Cynthia's music filled the car. The mesmerizing sameness of the road, the fields passing by, the music made Joe pass over into the Before.

There are events that cleave a life, making a clean cut between Before and After. For Joe, it was a single tear.

He came home that Friday looking forward to the simple pleasure of a glass of wine, Cynthia's art show on Saturday, maybe the beach on Sunday.

He set his satchel next to the door and turned into the dining nook, making for the kitchen and that glass of wine.

Cynthia sat at the table, folding a scrap of paper into unrecognizable origami. Serious in a way he'd rarely seen.

"What's wrong?" Joe said.

A tear ran down her cheek.

"I'm sick, Joe." She folded the paper one more time.

"I have ovarian cancer. We probably won't be able to have children."

"C-Cancer?" The word stopped Joe in his tracks.

"Dr. Keating's office called me for a follow-up to the physical I had in October." The words spilled out quickly. "I assumed she wanted to talk about getting pregnant. You know, in private, because of all the controversy over genetic manipulation."

He heard her trying for a matter-of-fact tone.

"We have to see a specialist in Jacksonville on the Tuesday after Thanksgiving. Dr. Keating was optimistic. She said Dr.

Munoz at St. Bartholomew is the very best."

"Did she look up your HealthScore?"

"She did, and it's 84. She said that's very good and the science behind this is getting better all the time. I think she was trying to cheer me up."

He went to Cynthia, pulling her head to his hip, her arms coming up to circle his waist. He felt her tremble as she finally began to cry.

Cancer. *Not possible*. Her lustrous hair and golden skin. So healthy. *Not possible*.

***

On the Monday after Thanksgiving, Laura Raskin caught her analyst, Tom Shenko, in the hall at Florida Consolidated Energy.

"Tom, can you run that insurance projection you and Joe Mayfield developed last summer again? I want to get latest data for the budget. I asked BlueLight to update HealthScores. They think a rerun may cut our cost. I need final figures in a briefing package by tomorrow morning."

Tom scratched his head. "Why would a rerun at BlueLight help? Maybe a few Health Scores have changed, but there have been no huge claims since Joe Mayfield and I did the projection last summer."

Laura nodded. "You're right, but I need to be able to tell the Executive Committee I'm using the most current data. Can you do it by, say, four o'clock?"

"Sure. Joe designed the model we used, but he included pretty clear instructions."

Laura, hurrying toward the elevator, said over her shoulder, "Check with him if you run into trouble."

Tom returned to his workstation, wedged his lineman's bulk into the standard-issue chair and opened his data bank. The file from BlueLight was waiting, and he began importing it into the spreadsheet he and Joe had developed. He was tempted to call Joe, but six months out of Georgia Tech, new job, he wanted to impress Laura. With no interruptions and no problems with the new data, he'd finish in time. Halfway through the process, a muted tone announced a new file arriving. A duplicate file name, which Tom opened, puzzled.

"Same damn data. What the hell?"

The duplicated file was an irritation but not a surprise given BlueLight's complex protocols and frequent mistakes. Besides, time was leaking away. He sighed, muttered *assholes* under his breath, substituted the new file and restarted the budget run.

***

On that same Monday after Thanksgiving, Joe and Cynthia rode the train to Jacksonville, Cynthia with earphones in, listening to her music, eyes closed. Joe tried unsuccessfully to lose himself in a mystery.

At the clinic, Cynthia handed over her HealthCube, which carried her complete medical record. The clinic would update it, as well as the IAC database, with the results of the visit.

They were escorted to an exam room, and Cynthia was taken down the hall for the weigh-measure-blood-draw routine.

Joe flipped through year-old magazines, trying to hold anxiety at bay.

Cynthia returned, chatting with the nurse. Dr. Munoz followed them into the room. He was a young man, buzz haircut, white coat with "St. Bart's" inscribed on the pocket. He projected confidence, energy and optimism. He glanced at his e-pad, then smiled at Joe and Cynthia.

"Cynthia, I'm glad Dr. Keating recommended that you see me," he said. "This is serious, but there are some excellent options."

He sat down at the small desk, signed in on a monitor, and said, "Cynthia Mayfield, MedRecord 10113-4776e." Waiting for the file to load, he turned toward Cynthia and Joe. "You are in great shape, Cynthia, except for this cancer. I'm confident we can beat this."

As he said this, he glanced at the monitor, and his face fell.

There was a moment of leaden silence. Bits of conversation and the sounds of comings and goings in the hall filtered into the room.

"What?" Dr. Munoz mumbled, almost to himself. He scrolled through data, jaw working, and said under his breath, "We'll straighten this out right now."

"What's the matter?" Cynthia asked.

Dr. Munoz turned to them. Measuring his words, he said, "There is a problem with what the system said about your HealthScore for this condition. The formal record is different from what I have from your HealthCube."

Joe flushed. "D-different? How?"

Dr. Munoz took a deep breath and said to Cynthia, "Your HealthCube had 84 for MOC...uhh, the ovarian cancer you have. That's a very high score. But the IAC MedRecord said 62. Which means ..." He hesitated, kindness and pain breaking through his professional demeanor "...which means your DNA profile indicates high-level treatment is unlikely to help you."

Cynthia's face drained of color. "I thought, I mean, I expected we would come through this okay."

Joe took the initiative. "The HealthCube is right. Cynthia's young, otherwise healthy, and her HealthScore for ovarian cancer is 84. Always has been. I work with the scores at my job. Anything over 80 is a slam-dunk for high-level therapy. I don't know who changed that number or why, but it's wrong."

Dr. Munoz nodded, his face showing his frustration. "I'm very sorry. I know it's scary to have confusion about these important numbers. We'll fix this."

He stood and strode out of the room, not quite slamming the door behind him.

"He'll fix it," Joe said.

Over the next half-hour, Dr. Munoz and his assistant rushed in and out of the exam room several times, each time reassuring Joe and Cynthia that they would fix the score, checking the monitor. But each time, they sounded less certain. Finally, the assistant concluded that she needed to contact BlueLight Insurance. Her tone said that she did not hold out much hope.

After the hospital, Joe and Cynthia went for lunch at a little Cuban place. Cynthia picked at her food. Joe called Laura Raskin, Florida Consolidated's personnel director, and left a message explaining the visit and the need for a correction to the score.

"I don't see how the score changed," Cynthia said, "and I don't understand why it's so important."

Seeing the strain on Cynthia's face, Joe decided against a lecture about the score and repeated, "We'll fix this." He hoped she did not see the fear washing over him.

***

The day after the Jacksonville trip with Cynthia, Joe had gone to Laura Raskin to fix the error in Cynthia's HealthScore. .

"I want to see Cynthia's MedRecord in detail," Joe said. "I mean the whole IAC file, not just what she gets on the HealthCube. All the entries, all the changes, all the history."

"Joe, I can't do that," she said. "But let me see if I can get permission to have BlueLight show me the info. I will go through every detail and get back to you as soon as I can, but you must know these records are protected behind the Yak firewall. Aside from an occasional input error, they are almost never wrong."

Joe's jaw set. "Laura, remind BlueLight that Cynthia owns that data. And 'almost' is a pretty important word right now. Please do it quickly."

Over the next several weeks, BlueLight fought Laura at every step. Despite his optimism, Dr. Munoz couldn't fix Cynthia's HealthScore either. As far as anyone—Dr. Munoz' sweet and apologetic assistant, several automated voices on the "Healthy Help" line and some honest-to-goodness human beings at BlueLight—could see, Cynthia's HealthScore for ovarian cancer was 62. Always had been. After all, it came from the super-secure Yak. End of story.

Joe checked with Laura daily. Her patience was wearing thin behind her polite, "Nothing new to report today, Joe."

Finally, after a week of officious denials from BlueLight, an exasperated Laura told Joe, "This would never have happened in our parents' day. We'd have gone ahead and spent precious resources, way beyond our means. You would have bankrupted yourself and Cynthia. There was no way to know that all of our effort and expense were unlikely to come to anything. Nobody wants that. Cynthia wouldn't want that. This way, we do the right thing, but we recognize reality. I know that's hard. I'm so sorry."

Seeing the tacit assumption in her eyes that someone, probably Joe himself, had figured out how to improve the number on Cynthia's HealthCube, he said, "Laura, ask anyone in Treasury about me. You might hear 'boring.' You might hear 'plan the work and work the plan.' You will never hear 'imprecise' or 'loosey-goosey' or 'flies by the seat of his pants.' And you will never, ever hear 'dishonest.' I'm telling you...I review all of my family's important statistics at least annually. It amuses my wife and is perhaps the only thing her oh-so-traditional Chinese grandmother admires in me. I'm a numbers guy. I don't slip up on this kind of stuff, and Cynthia's HealthScore for ovarian cancer has always been 84. Now, suddenly, it's 62. Nobody...*nobody*...can see that it was ever 84. I have the data backed up, but it's poisoned because I'm the person who made the backup."

He realized his voice was rising. He tried not to show Laura that his hands were shaking, but she must have seen his anger in the set of his mouth and ended the meeting with a curt nod.

FIVE

CYNTHIA'S SPIRIT GREW STRONGER and brighter as her body weakened. More often than not, she bucked Joe up rather than the other way around.

After Christmas, the hospice became mandatory. Caring people, bright colors and fresh flowers—nothing muted the air of inevitability.

One afternoon, she said, "Come over here. Get in bed with me. Hold me." Joe slipped off his shoes, got in beside her, careful not to disturb the plastic tubes that snaked from her arms. They lay silently for a time. Joe cradled her head, felt her crying softly.

She pulled away. "I never gave you sons. I never gave you daughters. You should have sons and daughters, Joe, to teach them your wonderful, strong, quiet honesty. And your humor. And the value of good habits."

She smiled through tears, and they both remembered her needling him about his habits. "And the beauty of being a regular guy. You would teach the boys how to love a woman and set high expectations for the girls, who would all want to grow up and marry you."

Joe struggled not to be engulfed by the wave of pain washing over him. "But I have you," was all he could manage.

***

As her flesh diminished, Cynthia listened more and more to her music, rushing through songs as if packing treasured belongings to carry away to a new place.

She told friends who stopped by that she was tired and made the meetings as short as possible. She told Joe, "I love the people, but I can't stand the pity. I want to listen to my music, feel close to those old souls who sang to us about loss, and bad times, and good women and heartache. I want to spend all my time with them and with you."

She paused, and then said with a sad smile, "I always wanted to show you New Orleans. Listen to the music, wander around, drink some whiskey, eat some étouffée, listen to some more music and roll around in your arms in a big four-poster bed." She turned carefully onto her side, mindful of the tubes, and smiled into Joe's eyes.

"Then take off north on old Highway 61 to where those beautiful country blues came from. Go to Avalon, where Mississippi John Hurt lived. Then the Delta. Find the crossroad where they say Robert Johnson met the devil and traded his soul to be the greatest guitar player ever. Maybe stop in Memphis." She teared up.

"I'm not going to make the trip. But maybe you'll find another lucky woman and have kids—"

"No!" Joe reached to stop her.

"—Have kids and take them up Highway 61 and tell them about their godmother Cynthia. Tell them about the crossroads and John Hurt and Son House." Then, almost out of breath, hurrying the words because Joe was shaking his head No.

"— and Charley Patton and Memphis Minnie and Blind Lemon and —"

"Cynthia...Please! I can't think about that."

"Well, I can. Take that trip for me. Please. I can imagine my old soul seeing the thread of my life being carried on. It makes me happy. Really. I need to talk about my dreams, Joe. That's what I have left. Your love, and my dreams."

Later on, she touched his arm. *Must have fallen asleep.* A wan smile curled the corners of her mouth.

"Hey, baby."

"Hey."

"You've been sleeping. That's good," She said. He was

exhausted, torn between his need to capture every bit of her being and the terror of looking into her eyes. She had said a thousand times she didn't blame him, but he blamed himself. There were days when he wanted to avoid the hospice, only to be overcome by the want, the need to consume everything Cynthia. He felt like a man in a desert thirsting for the last sip of water in his canteen but wanting much more to have it not be the last.

He took her hand, closed his eyes. "I love you."

"Love you, too."

Finally, exhausted, he went home to bed. They called him at 3 a.m. Come quickly, they said. He did, but she was gone.

***

The Arts community came to the funeral in force, and Joe found that he had many more friends than he thought. He sat, shell shocked and staring at the pattern in the funeral home carpet, wanting to be alone. So many people, so much genuine grief. Joe couldn't help them. The formal ceremony seemed hollow. It wouldn't bring her back, wouldn't make any difference. The minister spoke of coming together; Joe wanted to be apart from everyone, from the world, maybe from his life.

Cynthia's parents were heartbroken. Grief radiated from Hu Wei, Cynthia's grandmother, though her face was a mask. Joe remembered her explaining when they met that Cynthia was born a Dragon in the Chinese calendar, as she herself had been.

"Dragons are full of vitality and strength," she said. "To us, life is a colorful, leaping flame." Her eyes—fierce, brilliant raisins in her wrinkled face—seemed to say she doubted that Joe was up to the task of tending Cynthia's flame.

She was right, he thought. Oh God, was she right.

Joe's mother comforted anyone who would let her and grieved for the grandchildren she would have adored. Joe's father was sympathetic but uncomfortable. Nothing black and white here, no rules to operate by. Nothing his engineer's logic could reduce to a simple solution. Guilty feelings, maybe? Had he secretly been relieved at the outcome? No long, expensive treatments. No entanglements, certainly not with that Oriental family. He never mentioned he thought the HealthScore was right. Didn't have to. Joe saw his father's polite, distant pity and remembered a TV report long ago. That same look on his face as he watched survivors of a catastrophe in the Middle East, shrugged and spoke about Darwin.

After several days, both families escaped to nurture their own forms of grief, relief, or self-centeredness. Joe was left alone.

SIX

UNABLE TO BEAR BEING in the apartment and uninterested in being out in the world, Joe returned to work after a few days. His analyst, Maggie McTillis, had kept things shipshape in his absence, but there was a full electronic in-basket waiting for him. He scanned the filenames and came to Laura Raskin's voice message. It was brief, to the point and too late to do any good. At least she didn't just send a text.

He listened stone-faced.

"Joe, I did finally get permission from BlueLight and IAC clearance to review Cynthia's file. I know it's too late now, and I'm sorry for that, but the MedRecord didn't shed any light on the situation (*The "Situation" Right!*). There was a change to Cynthia's file on the Monday before you came to see me, but it was only to recognize an update from gene base research. I talked with BlueLight, and they said it was part of a regular procedure. But it didn't appear to change Cynthia's HealthScore for MOC. I mean, well, the cancer she had."

She didn't have the guts to say metastasizing ovarian cancer.

"Anyway, I thought I'd give you a call to let you know. I know how hard this must be (Really? Do you?), so give me a call if you want to talk."

Joe pushed himself out of his chair too hard. He started out of his office, seething, telling himself to cool down. He knew Laura just wanted to close the loop, to be professional. But someone or some thing changed the record. He just had no proof.

His eye caught Lucky Monkey. Cynthia had fashioned the statuette from found office materials as a gift to celebrate his promotion to Treasury.

"It's a Lar for your office," she had said.

"A Lar?"

"Yeah," she said with an impish grin. "A good-luck god like the *lares* Roman households always had. He'll keep an eye on you for me."

Maybe he was watching. What would Cynthia want him to do?

"Mayfield!"

The dyspeptic foghorn of Milt James, Joe's boss and Assistant-By-God Treasurer, rolled over his privacy wall. Didn't bother to come to his door; just yelled. Typical.

"Mayfield!"

Joe leaned out his door. Milt stood outside his own office, twenty feet away, irritated as usual. He crooked a finger at Joe, his usual way of asking Joe to join him, then turned without waiting for a response and disappeared back into his office.

The crook of the finger. Reminded him of...HealthScore. Insurance. Some connection, but what?

He sighed and went back into his office to get his e-pad. Probably an assignment that had to be done Right Now, or maybe a small error he'd made that Milt could use to squeeze more juice out of him.

Joe's duties as Treasury Manager included short-term cash management and all the computational jobs too difficult, too time consuming, or too invisible to top management for Milt to bother with. Over time, Joe had come to realize how he intimidated Milt and so shrugged off the arrogance and small indecencies that Milt visited on him.

Milt was fond of saying, "I don't have stress and anxiety, but I'm a carrier." You had to wonder how the hell Milt got to be Assistant Treasurer. Certainly not talent. Most likely not hard work. When you thought about it, you knew Milt probably was willing to kiss pretty much any appendage that presented itself. And speaking of appendages, Milt was a dyed-in-the-wool Prick. With a capital P.

Knew it. Gloried in it. Maybe a psychologist would say he secretly harbored fears of competence or was brought up by overbearing parents. Milt didn't care. To top management, being a Prick carried a certain cachet.

Joe picked up his e-pad and went toward Milt's office. The image of Milt's crooked finger was picking at something in the back of his mind. Why did it suggest HealthScore?

***

As Milt James harangued Joe one floor below her, Laura Raskin's monitor chimed, bringing up an image of her boss, Frank Hoskins.

"What's with your message about medical insurance budget?" he said. "I thought we wrapped that up long ago."

"We did, but there is an issue with how we did it. We need to talk."

"Uh, okay," Frank was multitasking, sorting papers on his desk. "But I'm not tracking this. Is this somehow connected with an employee issue?"

"Possibly. We need to talk offline to protect employee confidentiality. Can we meet at Lequ Coffee? Ten-thirty?"

"Riiiight. Gotcha. You mean the place on Amelia, across I-4?"

"Yes. That's right. Lequ Coffee."

***

Lequ Coffee was busy, just as Laura had hoped. Privacy in noise and numbers.

Laura watched Frank Hoskins enter in a rush and peer around the small shop. She signaled him from her table in the back.

"Wasn't sure I had the right place. Never been here before. Not bad. Always thought people were going to a place called 'liquid coffee,' which sounded pretty dumb."

He sat.

Laura smiled, seeing Frank was uncomfortable out of his preferred environment.

"I bought coffee," Laura said. "You like it black, right?" Frank nodded. "The 'Lequ' is Mandarin for 'pleasure.' Pleasure Coffee," Laura continued. "My daughter is in a Mandarin pod at school, and she always wants to come here when she visits me at work. The owners are very sweet to her and correct her Mandarin so politely."

Frank snorted. "And here we'd convinced ourselves we'd all have to learn Spanish. Should have been Chinese. I'm grateful that most of us still speak English, too. But you didn't ask for a meeting off-site to expand my linguistic boundaries, did you?"

"No, Frank, I didn't." She glanced around the shop before speaking. "Do you remember that issue with controlling medical insurance cost for next year's budget? Our good friends at BlueLight estimated our costs would go up 14 to 18 percent, even after last year's benefits reduction. Janicek went ballistic when we showed him the numbers. I'm sure you remember that because he was screaming in your face."

Frank winced, no doubt remembering the CEO's tirade.

"Well, you told me to fix it." She sipped her coffee, peering over the rim of the cup at Frank. "We decided not to reduce benefits, so the only place I could go was medical insurance cost. You must have understood you were asking me to change the data we used to get bids, right?"

"No, Laura, I was asking you to solve the problem for me, which you did. Besides, the whole thing is only an estimate, right?

"Well, in a word, no. Not right, Frank. These days, the only way we can affect what we pay for medical insurance is to change the actual IAC HealthScores they use to make the estimates."

"So?"

"So, we did that."

"What do you mean, 'We did that?' HealthScores are part of the Yak, right? Super secure, right?"

Laura shrugged and said, "The IAC does have ironclad

control over your MedRecord and mine, except for HealthScores. A private company develops HealthScores. Their formulas are secret, so what comes out is, well, what comes out. That's courtesy of Congress, a platoon of lobbyists, and the hairball they coughed up as medical insurance policy."

"Okay, Laura. How is this relevant to us?"

"We gamed the system at BlueLight's suggestion. A temporary tweak to some scores to get a lower insurance bid." She curled her lip, as if smelling something spoiled. "All very hush-hush. But legal, strictly speaking, or at least that's what BlueLight said."

Laura paused and took another sip of coffee. "The idea was to get all the scores back to normal right after we did the analysis. So, no harm done, right? We pay for the two adjustments and save $500k on our insurance premium. Only it didn't work out that way."

"Why am I not surprised?" Frank said. "What happened?"

"Someone died."

"Pardon me?" Frank inhaled a mouthful of coffee and coughed.

"A person who originally had a high HealthScore got ovarian cancer, Frank. She should have had aggressive therapy, which probably would have saved her life. But her score was lowered and apparently didn't get reinstated. She got limited treatment, and she died."

She let the statement sink in. She watched Frank computing, recognizing the reason they were away from the office.

"It was Joe Mayfield's wife," she continued. "He's the treasury manager who helped us set the stop-loss budget. He doesn't know exactly what happened, but he does know something's wrong, and he's a smart guy. He might figure this out."

***

It had been several weeks since Cynthia died, and Joe still

wanted to be alone. Friends and co-workers had been kind. They didn't say "died." Usually it was "passed on" or "is no longer with us"—any euphemism to escape confronting the cold, hard, Anglo-Saxon four-letter reality. He had been given food, artwork, a couple of poorly written songs and one good one. Acquaintances had offered counseling, dinner invitations, and sex to help him heal.

He was eating supper alone. Chewing, swallowing. Sustenance, not pleasure. He stared at his e-pad, but the news of the world seemed like white noise. His mind cycled through Laura Raskin's message, sunspots of anger flaring then receding. Underneath it, something knocking lightly, picking at his mind.

If you push to recall something, you usually just get a headache. When you finally give up, sometimes the memory comes to you in a flash. In Joe's case, it came in pieces, interspersed with the events the e-pad's software concluded would interest him: Flooding in Turkey. *The HealthScore*. The Players Championship. *Milt's crook of the finger when he assigned Joe to help Human Services build the stop-loss model*. Wall Street rallies on the news of lower interest rates. *BlueLight and getting HealthScores*. Asian slowdown. *Tom Shenko fixing his first model*. MOMA New York show featuring "found objects" art. *The "corrected" estimate*.

Why was it corrected?

The next morning, Joe went directly to Human Services. The receptionist said, "Hi, Joe." Pity, but also friendship, in her eyes.

"I'm just going to see Tom." Tom was a nice guy, a straight shooter. He'd thought of asking him to join one of the Friday night get-togethers with Cynthia's artist friends. He might look like a dumb jock, but he was one of a few people from Florida Consolidated who would fit in.

Joe saw Laura Raskin, ensconced in her glassed-in director's office, focused on her monitor as she talked on her phone. Tom was in his cubicle, and Joe slipped into the chair beside his desk.

Tom turned to him, surprised, then friendly. "Hi, Joe."

"Hi, Tom. I don't want to get you in trouble, but I do have some questions about this MedRecord thing with my wife. I assume you've heard about it."

Tom's face told Joe he had.

"Joe, you can ask, and I'll tell you what I know, but I'm afraid it's not much." Hard for a man who played on the offensive line in college to look furtive, but Tom managed. "Laura is already on edge over this, so I'd rather have the conversation stay private, okay?"

"Sure, and I just want to fill some gaps." Joe smiled, trying not to let his desperation show. "I know the actual record is something only Laura has seen." Tom nodded.

"So, Laura said there were changes to the MedRecord, but none of them would have affected the MOC score. Then she said small changes occur all the time. Is that true, from what you see?"

"Sure. BlueLight told me it gets updates on a regular basis," Tom said. "That's why I wasn't surprised when we got a new set of numbers for the budget workup in November. Remember that?"

Pieces of a puzzle falling into place, but no picture yet. Except...

"Tom, now I'm remembering. Didn't that second list of scores produce a lower estimate of medical costs? What was the difference?"

"The estimate went down five hundred thousand under what we'd originally estimated," Tom said. "There must have been some important differences. Of course, we were happy. We were also up against the budget deadline, so we used the data."

"Can we check both lists again? I have the original, but I never saw that second file."

"Sure." Tom turned to his monitor, "Let's see. Insurance budget documents, data only." The screen displayed files with a BlueLight "confidential" stamp. Tom selected the list of employee HealthScores that had been the starting point for the insurance cost estimates.

IAC MedRecord Search, HealthScores 19:38:47Z

For: Florida Consolidated Energy subset: all employees

Record length: 8.2 Gb Employee Records: 8,319

Joe said, "Okay, let's see the original file."

Tom tapped the monitor. A second file opened:

IAC MedRecord Search, HealthScores 14:19:03Z

For: Florida Consolidated Energy subset: all employees

Record length: 8.2 Gb Employee Records: 8,319

Both men looked from one image to the other. Below the headers there were 110 columns of data for each employee, including the twenty HealthScores for each of the genetic vectors used to predict likelihood of common fatal diseases. The two files seemed identical. Tom squinted at the screen, concentrating.

"Joe...oh, jeez...the time stamp! I told you they were both done at the same time, but I read the "As of 29 November" date. Didn't look further. The older one was done at, let's see, just after nine in the morning, and the second...uhh...four-and-a-half hours later. Damn, I should have caught that! They said it was a minor update."

Tom stopped, thinking. "I don't understand why anyone would have known to ask for the second data set and tell me to use it. We should have had you check it, but by then, you know, your situation ..."

Joe's mind was spinning. The intercity to Jacksonville. Dr. Munoz. It was right after Thanksgiving. The Monday after Thanksgiving. The 29th.

"Tom, can I have copies of the two data series? I want to make sure my spreadsheets weren't wrong." Tom paused for a long second, then said, "Sure, Joe."

While the files downloaded to a storage cube, Tom said, "I've got a boat, and a day spent fishing relaxes my mind. We could go up to Sanford, catch some bass."

Nice of Tom to offer friendship, rather than sympathy. Hard to believe he would cover anything up.

***

At home, Joe opened the files. There were 8,300+ scores for each of twenty critical diseases the HealthScore system tracked. No employee names, just strings of numbers.

He separated out the ovarian cancer scores, lined them up next to each other and studied the columns until he saw a difference, then another, then another. It seemed as if they changed a high score every fifth row, starting with the thirteenth. So regular. A computer glitch? But there was an 84 score missing—got to be Cynthia's—and it wasn't a fifth person. Her score changed right before the Jacksonville visit.

Finished, he had a list of the thirty-four altered scores, all lowered.

The next day started with one of those beautiful, late winter Florida mornings. Lush, humid, but not yet uncomfortable. He sat on the small balcony where they used to have coffee, drink in the warmth, talk about their friends, her art, his job. He had taken to listening to Cynthia's music, holding onto things that defined her. Robert Johnson was on the sound system, singing about standing at the crossroad, jus' trying to flag a ride.

She'd bought a guitar shortly before they married. Joe remembered her sitting in the corner, looking up from a video showing how to play "Statesboro Blues" and giving him the sparkling smile that let him know she saw he was bemused. Most people would consider it odd for a young Asian woman to be playing the music of old black men. "There's wisdom there," she said. "The people who wrote those blues had to deal with the kind of problems that matter." She picked a couple of notes. "I don't think you can understand this music without playing it. The playing drives you below the lyrics to a place where you can begin to feel what they were singing about." At the time, Joe thought of that as artist's affectation. Now, listening, he believed.

He hadn't moved the guitar from the corner. He touched it, thinking he was at that crossroad, too. He couldn't see a way forward. The reliable "plan the work and work the plan" mentality didn't cut it. Really, what did it all matter? Florida Consolidated had done something terrible. He can't pin it on any one person or motive, but he couldn't go back to work and kowtow to the bastards who killed Cynthia. He had to do something, but who was going to believe him?

SEVEN

JOE STARED AT HIS monitor. Columns of cash receipts from different offices, a job he had done almost every business day for nine years. The numbers made no sense. He kept coming back to the insurance cost estimate and two sets of numbers from BlueLight.

Some days he was grateful for the routine of work. Structure made the pain recede for hours at a time. He almost enjoyed it when Milt dropped his "Joe is in a difficult period" persona and reverted to being a prick with a capital P. But then he would feel guilty for chuckling at Milt or laughing with an accounting clerk in the break room or noticing Maggie's décolletage when he dropped the daily report in her in-basket.

He shook off his reverie and focused on the cash forecast.

Central Florida collections up a bit; South Central down. He clicked to another window of bills to be paid, adjusted for known investment clearings. He was figuring amounts to be invested when Maggie rounded the corner of his cube. "Joe, I know it's a hard time for you, but I have make the transfers by 1:40. Should I use the usual formula?" Joe hesitated, then said, "Sure."

Milt would notice if the transfers were in even percentages. Approximation was fine when Milt did it. He said he was a big-picture guy, which as often as not an excuse for misunderstanding the problem while cruising through the conceptual stratosphere. The dumb mistakes that resulted were always someone else's fault. As "conceptual" as Milt was, he demanded precision from his employees; enough so people in Treasury routinely added a digit or two after the decimal point to give their estimates credibility. Of course, Milt couldn't do the calculations, so he was none the wiser. But if Joe gave him round numbers he would say, "I noticed the mix on yesterday's investments." He'd look over the top of the half glasses. "Of course, I know it's a hard time for you, but we need to pull together here. Rule-of-thumb doesn't cut it in Treasury."

Joe had heard it a hundred times these last weeks. Were they secretly rehearsing? Did they understand it was draining the small reserve of sanity he had left? Instead of all those management training workshops, they ought to let him give a very short, very real seminar on death and dying: If you're talking to a person who has lost the better part of his soul, don't say a goddamn thing unless you mean it because you don't know how hard it is. End of seminar.

Hard not to wallow in self-pity. But why let that self-righteous, anal-retentive brown-noser have an opportunity to gloat? Not a great way to feel better.

He concentrated on the numbers, spun the formulas.

"Maggie?" he said. "I've got some corrected numbers for you."

Maggie appeared again. "You told me to go ahead. I already put them in."

"Damn, it's only 1:15. I thought we had time. It should be 28/29/43. Plus or minus a couple of tenths, of course."

Maggie smiled. "Let me try something," she said and turned to go back to her desk. Joe, curious, followed her.

She logged in to BancSoutheast through IAC, identified herself, and canceled the earlier transactions out of the holding file. She logged out and back in as "Marcella Sampson." She opened the investment accounts, transferred 28.1% to several Florida Consolidated cash accounts, 29.2% to the overnight investments and 42.7% to the longer-term account. She startled, realizing Joe was standing behind her, and blanched.

"You asked me to do this, right?"

"Well, sure Maggie, but who the hell is Marcella Sampson?"

Maggie flushed. "Can we talk in your office?"

"Sure."

They went to Joe's cubicle, a corner office that had a "privacy" partition higher than the shoulder-lever partitions reputed to insure quicker, more efficient communication but always assigned to lower-ranked employees.

Joe repeated, "Who is Marcella Sampson?"

Maggie lowered herself into a side chair, folded her hands in her lap and looked down at them.

"Joe, if I followed protocol, we wouldn't get investments done most days." Her mouth set. "I have to get the numbers into the system by 1:40, accurate to the nearest tenth of a percent. Twenty-eight field units are supposed to report receipts by 10 a.m., but sometimes I don't have them all by noon." Joe nodded. "BancSoutheast gives me results from maturing investments and the overnight cash by 11:30. That is, if they remember. If Alessandra is not having a fight with her alcoholic boyfriend. If he doesn't hit her. And so on. Then you do your magic and give me your numbers, and I have to do the final investments. Forty separate entries."

She shrugged. "But most of the investment deposits don't change daily or even weekly, so I know most of the entries when I come in at 8:30."

She frowned and continued.

"A couple of years ago, BancSoutheast was late on investment results *and* South Beach results came in at 12:30. Milt called me into his office. The cute young relationship manager from the bank was perched in Milt's visitor chair. He gave me a tongue-lashing about FCE's standards and 'being on time means being on *time*.' "

Maggie looked as if she'd tasted something bitter.

"I decided that wasn't going to happen again. I had been over at the bank and watched Alessandra use a second IAC ID to correct information she plumb neglected to get right the first time. I did some research and found there are a lot of avatars out on the IAC.

If even only half a percent of people have some good reason to be using the Yak, that's a couple of million. The Yak can't keep them straight, much less figure out where the real ones are at every moment, like the TV shows like to make you think. Now, Alessandra is not the sharpest knife in the drawer, but her boyfriend is very clever. He told me how to make Marcella Sampson. I can only move money once a day as myself. That's a failsafe the bank monitors. But FCE, with all of that focus on quality systems, has designed the system to make me fail if I operate by the book."

Joe nodded, remembering the high-flown "Statement of Purpose" and the abject lack of execution.

Maggie shrugged. "Anyway, if results are slow coming in, my Marcella person goes in mid-morning and sets up the entries I can make by then, and I go in as myself and put in the last twenty percent when the rest of the world finally gets its act together. Today, we were lucky. The data came in earlier than usual, so I didn't need to use Marcella...until now. So, you are happy. Milt is as satisfied as his ego allows him to be. All is right with the world. Except, if FCE finds out, I'll be fired, probably worse."

She drew a ragged breath and seemed ready to cry.

EIGHT

HENRY BARBER WAS READING over the Monday morning dump from IAC security. Mostly boring, desk-duty stuff. The ATF got the interesting leads. Barber's business crimes unit got everything else. People trying to do things they shouldn't and getting hooked and reeled in by some computer program running up in Bethesda. Reading the report made him feel like a pilot fish depending for its sustenance on the sloppy eating habits of large sharks. Henry was more comfortable in the field, talking to people, sensing their motives, weighing the always-imperfect memories of witnesses. But now most investigation was in the hands—well, the microchips—of the data evaluators. You had to live with it.

He scrolled to the bottom where the IAC summarized and suggested action. There, the geeks and freaks in Bethesda gave him direction disguised as suggestions. To add to the irritation, Henry had to respond to each suggestion. He had tried blowing off a ludicrous request when the report first came out a couple of years ago and had immediately gotten ***INADEQUATE RESPONSE***, which he ignored. At the end of the year, the tally of inadequate responses appeared in the new data-rich profile on his annual review. His boss, looking embarrassed, had to ask him to explain each inadequate response. Henry had learned to give serious-sounding but meaningless responses to items he didn't want to deal with, even though the tactic only delayed the inevitable.

On this day, one of the suggestions was to investigate an irregular cash transfer from Florida Consolidated Energy. This smallish transfer, apparently for some kind of bank charge, kept recurring. Henry's degree in accounting was the original reason for his assignment to the Business Crime Task Force. He understood the normal process for moving money, and this set of transactions seemed odd, but not spectacularly so. Might have been a lot of perfectly good reasons for it. But, it had appeared in his data dump several times, and he knew the "investigation pending more complete information" excuse was unlikely to work another time, so he queried the system.

The more he dug into them, the more the transactions seemed suspicious. He checked his contact list, which listed Tosheka Jackson as head of security. Henry remembered her name from the meeting he'd spoken to a few months earlier. Probably should have sent her an e-note, but he picked up the phone. Personal touch.

A video feed appeared on Henry's monitor. "Jackson, here." A beautiful black woman. Now he placed her. No man at the conference would forget the spectacular body and the assured stride when she entered the room.

"Ms. Jackson, this is Henry Barber. We met at the security officers' meeting back in September."

"Oh, yes, of course. What can I do for you?"

"Well, you may remember that I work on the Business Crimes Task Force. I've been following an issue on the IAC network that may be a problem. Not a big deal, and probably nothing illegal. But not ordinary, so I thought I'd check it out. I'm sure you have access to more information than our scan sees, so you may be able to clear this up quickly."

"Okay. Shoot."

Henry sketched out the problem, describing the transactions and why they seemed unusual. He finished, "Another thing that's odd is most transactions out of your financial section are handled by one person with Level 1 IAC clearance for wire-type financial transactions, Maggie McTillis. The odd ones are all handled by a Marcella Sampson."

"Well, thanks for the heads-up, Henry," Tosheka said. "I'll see what I can see in our system and get back to you."

He put a telltale on any IAC entries by Jackson. Just to satisfy his curiosity. Besides, now he wouldn't get pinged with ***INADEQUATE RESPONSE***.

***

Tosheka disconnected from Henry Barber, letting her collegial smile fade, and said, "Find Marcella Sampson." The pleasant, synthesized voice of the system answered, "Employee 10467." A file popped up. Theoretically, Marcella worked in Treasury, but there were no performance reviews, which she was certain Milt James would not overlook. If it was a female employee, Milt would not ignore much. At least not if his uncomfortably familiar "conference" with her about an imagined "security issue" over a manager wanting to see health records was any indication.

Interesting, though. This Marcella had IAC access. Not many employees needed it. Tosheka had it. Laura Raskin had it for personnel and medical issues. Maggie McTillis had limited access to move money. Given the legal and career liabilities associated with it, most senior management people stayed away from it like the plague.

"All entries for Florida Consolidated Treasury, fourth quarter." Marcella came up, along with Maggie McTillis and a Joe Mayfield.

She used her security clearance on IAC to put telltales on Milt James, Maggie McTillis, and Marcella Sampson.

Mayfield. Tosheka exhaled. She remembered, now. Milt had said Mayfield's wife was sick and had a theory that her health profile had been changed. She put a telltale on him, too.

Too close for comfort.

***

Milt liked to come in early but never stayed late. He said the quiet of the early morning allowed him to get things done without interruption. A good, acceptable justification. Of course, he was never specific about what he needed to get done or that it was outright theft.

It was Monday morning, and there were a couple of go-getters over in accounting buried in their monitors and spreadsheets. No one in Treasury yet.

He signed into the system using Marcella Sampson, the alias Maggie had set up to cover her ass when she couldn't get her work done in a reasonable amount of time.

Two years ago, he had discovered the avatar as part of a routine review of personnel records. He saw this "Marcella" had IAC access, whereas only Maggie McTillis needed access to transfer funds. After all was said and done about security, every system had to trust some human being to get certain jobs done.

Maggie fit the model of trustworthy person perfectly. She started her career in a large regional accounting firm. Say what you like about equality, if you're a single mother who has to go home to the kids during tax time, you're never going to make partner. So Maggie came to work at Florida Consolidated. Not going to be competing for higher-level management (Milt liked that) because she was paid well, and her life centered on her son and daughter.

Milt understood the demands of getting the daily cash tied down were unreasonable. He didn't care, but he wasn't particularly surprised that Maggie had to cut a corner or two to get the work done each day. Lucky for him, she was too honest to take a little extra and put her kids in a good school, or maybe buy some nicer clothes to show off her figure.

Watching Marcella's activity, Milt came to understand that straight-arrow Joe probably had no knowledge of the avatar's existence. He trusted Maggie, dope that he was.

Milt considered all of this in light of his own pressing needs.

After all, you take what you've got and do the best you can with it. Right? Right. So, here was an upstanding person breaking the rules. Maggie would never cheat, but Marcella might easily be skimming off the top, shipping it off to another account, right? What would you expect her to do? And if Marcella ever got found out? Well, Maggie would be responsible for whatever she did, right? Or maybe Joe Mayfield. He's a smart guy. It'd be pretty easy to convince the cops that he'd have figured out how to do it.

The more he thought about it, the more Milt realized he had found a gold nugget right in his backyard. The opportunity to move a little of that cash the big milch cow didn't really need to more productive uses...*his* uses. And, best of all, close to perfect deniability.

That was two and a half years ago. It took him a month to piece together the password Maggie used for Marcella. Fortunately, because Maggie's job was a single-purpose, repetitive task, the IAC didn't require the thumbprint/retina scan of higher-level access.

After that, once a week, always early in the morning, "Marcella" paid a direct bill from a firm called Resolution Enterprises. Milt made it appear to be a banking fee. Usually only $10,000 or $15,000. Small for a big utility like Florida Consolidated, so it would never show up in an audit.

Milt wasn't greedy.

NINE

MOST HACKER STORIES BEGIN with visuals of geeky dudes crouched at arrays of panels, sending their ingenious code over the Internet. There are millions of those stereotypical hackers. Weezy would tell you they're pretty easy to pick off, at least for her. She'd explain the best way to hack into a system is the physical approach: break in and plug in.

Florida Consolidated's sales training room had been on the 6th floor, unused after a shuffle of departments. Joe took the stairs rather than elevators during the day, noticing security cameras on the odd-floor mezzanines. He paid cash for a personal e-pad—cheap, plenty powerful for his needs and not registered in the corporate system.

By 6:30 p.m., most people had left for the day. Joe followed a circuitous path from his office to the sixth floor, avoiding cameras. He had decided to be out by 9:00 to avoid the security staff and cleaning crew. His late hours would be recorded, but he had set himself a major project and a false deadline as a reason for working late. People shook their heads and assumed he was burying his grief in work. Still, he was sweating. He had no excuse to be in the training room.

Maggie's avatar was a remake of a terminated employee from Florida Consolidated who did not have clearance to use the IAC. With over two million IAC users, new names were being added every day for perfectly valid reasons, so an application that did not seek national security clearance usually got access.

There was a counter along one wall with fifteen access ports for e-pads. In the opposite corner, the trainer's desk nestled in a carrel. It had a desk, an access port and a window that allowed Joe to keep an eye on the hall. He plugged in his e-pad, hands shaking.

The FCE header came up. Still connected.

He entered as John Maxwell. John had recently left the firm for other employment. The system should have deleted a lot of the information on Maxwell, but enough remained to enter the system as a trainee, and nobody had bothered to change the general password TRNG that Joe used in his last class a year and a half earlier.

Joe tried several times to get into his own record and Cynthia's insurance file. He was not successful, but he did acquire the personal information of several employees no longer with Florida Consolidated before shutting down and retracing his path to his office. He moved some files on his workstation to establish a pretext for staying late, then left the building.

At home, Joe was too wired to fall asleep, so he began building his avatars from the information he had collected. By 5 a.m., he had filled in most of the information he needed for the IAC applications. He couldn't allow himself to sleep, so he showered and went to the office.

Milt James peered out of his office as Joe walked by carrying coffee and his satchel and said with his signature insensitivity, "You sure as hell look drug out."

***

Joe spent a couple of days waiting for someone from IT to come and ask him what he had been doing online in the training room.

Nothing.

He went back, same time, same path, and uploaded the avatars from his e-pad to the IAC. Each was accepted...at least, he got to the screen that allowed him to hit the "done" button.

He held his breath, waiting

InterAgency Channel

Portal 5992

Name?

"Nicolas Sarcosy"

Identification code: 3e44981

<<enter>>

A delay. Two...three...four...five ....

-------------- Logged in as ---------

Nicolas Sarcosy

He whispered, "Yes!"

***

The anti-hacking software Weezy designed, called Revelator with suitable reverence by everyone in the National Operations Center of the InterAgency Channel in Bethesda, noted the four entries to the name list from Florida Consolidated Energy. A group of four names was somewhat unusual for an 8,300-person company. Thus, Revelator tagged each with the hexadecimal equivalent of a question mark and put it on Weezy's low-priority list.

The next morning, Weezy arrived at her workstation at N-Ops and scanned the entries but passed over them quickly. No actions from any of these new people yet. She asked Revelator to monitor the four, pushed the report to her Backburner file and turned to the more pressing matter of a hacker who really, really wanted classified information on shoulder-fired missiles. She tracked the hack attempt back through several servers to a survivalist cult in Texas and sent her file off to Enforcement.

She pushed back in her five-caster, body-conforming chair, shook her head and said, "Dumbass."

"Weezy's a pistol," was the throwaway line members of her tracker team informally known as the OddBalls used to salve egos she shredded. She certainly didn't look intimidating. Her face was angular, beautiful in some perspectives, plain in others. In junior high, a growth spurt stretched her to five-foot-eight, and she grew into her nose. "Weezy" came along with her younger brother's first words and stuck because "Louise Napolitani" was too long and too formal to fit her. She was slender to the point that Adam Ambrosio, the rookie member of the OddBalls, said with a grin, "Look at her sideways, all's you get is T&A."

Her Aunt Tonia, speaking in a stage whisper to Weezy's mother, had said, "Beautiful. She would be byootiful if she'd only take care of herself." 'Taking care of herself' would mean styling her hair, wearing lipstick to highlight her full lips and amending her already lush eyelashes. Instead, Weezy wore whatever was on top of the clothes pile in the morning, and details like combing her chestnut mop usually didn't make her priority list.

Fresh out of MIT at twenty with a Masters in Computer Science and Operations Research and glowing recommendations from her instructors, Weezy was snapped up by a Silicon Valley software firm. A year later she was back in her parents' noisy, happy Boston home. She had, after all, said the CEO's Big Freakin' Idea would never work. She had added she didn't give a rat's ass that he was one of Inc. Magazine's *30 Under 30*. The fact that she was correct about the BFI sealed her fate.

That year, repeated cyber-attacks from China, Russia and a series of Internet entrepreneurs in several other countries exploded into what the press called CyberWar I. In the wake of fires, floods, power-grid failures and a small nuclear episode, the United States rushed to develop the most secure, most expensive data vault in history. They named it the InterAgency Channel, and the acronym became "Yak" in popular speech. Weezy's advisor at MIT, one of the system's architects, mentioned Weezy to IAC's Director. "You have to have her," he said, adding with a smile, "Lord help you."

In a world normally ruled by protocols and algorithms, Weezy put a layer of intuition over her fine mathematical mind. As a result, and to the frequent frustration of her peers and superiors, she was N-Ops' best tracker.

***

Joe made two more after-hours trips to the training room. The first was to research Cynthia's MedRecord. That trip was a frustrating dead end, but he did figure out how to query FCE's employee database for some kinds of information. On the last trip, he used "John Maxwell" to search for records changes. He had thirty-four instances that seemed to have changed HealthScores for metastasizing ovarian cancer. He knew Cynthia's score changed from 84 to 62, so he queried the system:

HealthScore from 84 to 62. Date range from 29 Nov to 29 Nov

Almost instantly, the system responded with Cynthia's name and two others. So, Cynthia's score *was* changed. Others, too.

Joe leaned toward the screen, light-headed. Was it some terrible mistake? Did they kill her on purpose? Why?

Joe knew from his comparison of the two strings of numbers he had from Tom Shenko that thirty-three other scores were changed along with Cynthia's. But he had only numbers to work with, no names. By nine o'clock, using the same slow, frustrating search method he'd used to find Cynthia's change, he had identified six other employees whose scores were changed. Security would come through soon, and Joe's shoulders and neck were building a Class 1 tension headache. He had to leave, and he decided not to come back. He had plenty of evidence that Cynthia's score was not a glitch.

Revelator, noting Maxwell's query into personnel records, bumped up its priority a notch.

***

"Milt, do you have a minute?"

Milt turned from his monitor, irritated. "What do you need, Joe?"

"I need to set up a meeting with you and Laura Raskin."

"On what subject?" Milt's eyes narrowed, and Joe knew the answer was going to be No.

"I need to talk to both of you together about the insurance cost projection."

"Aw, for Crissake, Joe. We're done with that. Human Resource Services can screw with it all they want, but we're done."

"Milt, you know I made that projection. You probably also remember that Cynthia's HealthScore was changed—"

"Joe, I don't know that it was changed. I know it was different from what you wanted it to be. I don't know more than that."

Trying to stay patient, Joe said again, "Cynthia's HealthScore was changed." Milt was silent, but his expression said I-can't-believe-this-stupid-shit.

"I have pretty strong evidence some other scores were changed as well," Joe said. "If someone in the company is making changes like that, there's going to be plenty of liability to spread around."

Joe knew Milt saw the threat and was calculating the likely impact of such a catastrophe on himself. Milt studied his desktop, tapping his fingers, nostrils flaring.

Finally, he said, "I'll set up the meeting."

***

Laura Raskin led Joe and Milt into her conference room. She took the power position, back to the window, facing the door and outer office. Milt slid in beside her, making the discussion Joe vs. Florida Consolidated.

Milt half-turned to Laura. "Joe is concerned that there are irregularities with the MedRecords for some of our employees," he said, letting his disapproval shine through. "I'll let Joe tell you the story."

Joe explained his shock at the change in Cynthia's score and his subsequent analysis of the original and adjusted scores. Without mentioning his meeting with Tom, he showed the table of thirty-four scores that changed in the MOC category. Laura remained passive, a half-smile on her face.

Finishing, Joe said, "I don't know how this was done. I know our insurance cost came in lower as a result. This has to be investigated carefully and honestly."

Laura drew a slow breath and raised her eyes from the table of data. "I don't know what to say, Joe. The MedRecords are protected by the IAC. We can't see them. You know that. Only the HealthScore rating agency can make changes. BlueLight Insurance integrates them into our system."

Joe tried to push his anger down, control it, use it.

"Laura, Milt, do me a favor. Assume for a moment that I am not a grief-stricken man who has just lost his wife and who tried to change her HealthScore to get her better treatment." He leaned forward, focusing on Laura. "Ask Tom Shenko to check the data we used to make the insurance cost estimate. Tell him to concentrate on MOC. I think you will find thirty-four HealthScores go down between two lists that were made only a few hours apart." He tried to not let the words spill out too fast. "Not the five or six points a big medical discovery would lead to, but more. The average of the original scores that got changed was 78, and the average for them after the 'adjustment' was 54. Twenty-four points. No way is that some sort of regular update."

A pause. Joe ignored Milt's angry stare, waiting for an answer from Laura. She exhaled and said, "Yes, I'd like to review this. I can't believe your analysis is right, but I'll check it out." She hesitated. "I'd also remind you, Joe, all personnel data is privileged and you may not, cannot, divulge or disseminate it."

Milt's lips were set in an angry line and his eyes narrowed. He hated "problems."

"Let's keep this close to our chests," he said.

Joe and Milt took the stairs down to Treasury. On the first landing, Milt cornered Joe. "I *do not* want this to become a problem."

Joe tried to keep an honest-but-determined tone. "Milt, this *is* a problem. Not of your making or mine, but it's a problem. Someone in this company is not telling the truth, and I believe it cost Cynthia her life." His anger gained momentum, and Milt took a half-step back. "Like you often say, data talks and bullshit walks. Well, the data is speaking pretty clearly here. The only question is the source of the data, and why it was manipulated. I will get to the bottom of this, and I hope I can count on your support."

Milt stared for a long second at the set of Joe's mouth and said, "Well, Joe, you're treading on pretty thin ice here. Sounds to me like Laura has decided you're lying and is working hard to cover her rather generous ass. I don't want this all landing in my lap. I think you'd better think through how ridiculous your accusations sound and come in tomorrow morning ready to get quietly back into the saddle."

Milt turned abruptly and continued down the stairs. After a few steps, he said over his shoulder. "Think about it."

***

Joe stood still, listening to Milt's steps echoing up the stairwell.

So Milt was going to try to sweep this problem under someone else's rug. Great. Joe would have no allies. Laura Raskin was circling her wagons. Tom, Maggie, and anyone else Joe tapped would end up getting hurt.

Joe returned to his office and stood, indecisive, tempted to do more research. Maybe he should go back to the training room and get more evidence. He had identified thirty-plus people ... surely there were many more if other diseases were adjusted along with ovarian cancer.

Lucky Monkey caught Joe's eye, and he heard Cynthia say, "Thinking like an accountant again, Mayfield."

She's right, he thought. The analysis would take hours and

hours in the training room. Something would go wrong. If Joe got caught, he'd be a common criminal, and the whole disaster would disappear.

Joe packed up and took the elevator to the ground floor of FlorCon Tower, the problem swirling in his mind.

If he let the issue ride, nothing would happen. Didn't he owe someone a good fight? Cynthia? Himself? What did the song say? *I'm standing at the crossroad, and I believe I'm sinking down.*

One side of the lobby had a public area full of interactive displays where schoolchildren came to see the wonders energy performed and the improvements being made every day to make the planet cleaner and energy cheaper and more plentiful.

On a whim, he turned into the exhibit. He passed slowly by the displays, an idea forming. Sure enough, several open ports were waiting for new displays. Surely part of the FCE system. Cynthia's voice hummed that song about the crossroad in his ear. For an instant, he thought she was there with him.

The security guy in the lobby was reading a magazine. There was a camera at the entrance to the exhibit, but none Joe could see inside. He pretended to be absorbed in the "Tiny Solar Generators Make Safe Power for Your Neighborhood" display, then reached to connect his e-pad to the port. There was no network security, probably an accommodation to make it easier to move display monitors in a place no one would think to jump into the system. He tapped out a message to the first person he'd identified:

To: Susan Rodriguez

Susan, check your HealthScore. Do not plug your HealthCube into any system...just read the score on something not connected to the system. Unless you have had a physician visit in the last 3 months, your cube will say your HealthScore for code 14, metastasizing ovarian cancer, is 82 (excellent...you are at low risk). If you plug into the system today, you will find it has been changed to 58 (poor risk). Someone has scammed you and me. It was someone at FCE or BlueLight. I can't tell you what to do, but be warned!

He hesitated. Signing it "A Friend" was trite. "A fellow employee?" Risky. He thought of cutting to the core of this sad obscenity and signed,

RazorBlue

He realized he was sweating. This could be the start of something bad, he thought, but what choice do I have? He saw himself stepping out of the crossroad and pressed Send.

TEN

AFTER MAYFIELD AND MILT James left Laura, she fished her personal e-pad out of her bag and said, "Frank Hoskins, private."

The video opened, and Frank said, "Yes?"

"Frank, that situation I described over coffee has matured. The employee in question understands more than I thought."

Frank cocked his head, not fully disengaging from the papers scattered on his desk. "So, what's your solution?"

"Well, Frank, I think it's best to bite the bullet. What we did was wrong and it had horrible consequences, but there was no criminal intent. Honesty from us might defuse the situation. There's nothing we can do about his wife, but it was an administrative foul-up on BlueLight's part that was really at the center of it. I believe we could keep this whole thing quiet with a settlement ..."

"A settlement?" Frank was all attention. "You mean pay him off?"

"I'm just saying that he wants to know the truth. He'll be furious when he gets confirmation, but he already knows most of the story. I think I can direct his anger to BlueLight."

Frank had started shaking his head at "furious."

"I don't like it. If it doesn't work, we look bad. And the settlement would have to be pretty big, enough that it might have to go to the board. And be disclosed. Then the media would get ahold of it, and you know how terrified the board is of bad press."

Laura shrugged and said, "Well, Frank, I don't think he's going to drop it. I guess the question is, do you want to let him go public and deal with the shit storm that surely will result, or do you want a smaller shit storm that you control?"

"Okay, Laura." Frank considered for a long ten seconds. "You make a lot of sense. I'll have to give this some thought. I'll get back to you." He turned back to the papers on his desk.

Laura felt some of the weight lifting from her shoulders. "I'll wait to hear. I'll be down in Tampa tomorrow at an org development conference, but I'll have this personal phone with me at all times. Sorry to bring an uncomfortable issue to you, but this is the kind of thing that might blow up quickly."

Frank cracked the grin that always reminded Laura her boss was human. "Yeah, yeah. But that's what I get the big bucks for, right?"

"Thanks, Frank."

**

The monitor in Tosheka Jackson's console popped to life. A preternaturally calm, synthesized voice said, "Urgent message from Frank Hoskins." The message on the screen was simple: "My office."

She took the stairs to 14 quickly, knocked on Frank's door and entered.

"Sit, please." Frank paused for a moment, seeming to size her up.

"I've got a problem and need your help."

She nodded.

"We have an, ahh, employee situation. A Treasury manager, Joe Mayfield, is convinced we somehow altered his wife's medical records. She was given limited treatment and died. He's on a tear about it. Not-so-veiled threats to his boss and Laura. You have let me know Mayfield tried to access confidential personnel records."

Tosheka nodded, wondering where this was going.

"I think we have grounds for dismissal," Frank said. "But I also think that, based on Mayfield's behavior so far, he's likely to make a big stink if we go through the normal warning-counseling-dismissal protocol. I want him out of here, and I want to convince him not to discuss this in public. I want to cut this malignancy out of Florida Consolidated. Can you do that for me?"

Tosheka saw worry and a touch of fear behind the steel in his glance.

"Frank, I can do it, but I'd have to go around Human Resources."

"The less they know the better. If you do it tomorrow, Laura will be away at a seminar. I'm sure she'll be relieved to have the problem gone."

He had never gone around Laura before. Was this an opportunity to get out from under her problem? "Okay," She said. "We can do it tomorrow, based on the breach in the system. But if this blows up, we'd better be ready to settle before he sues us and we have to haul out the really big checkbook."

***

"What the hell's the plan?" Joe realized he'd asked it out loud. He was alone at his dining room table, drinking morning coffee the day after his meeting with Laura and Milt. He imagined his father leaning across the table, ready to pounce on any syllable of doubt. "You always have a plan, right, son? Always know what you're going to do a half step before that dummy next to you, right? Or the lion eats you instead of him, right?" He would have concluded, "Plan your work and work your plan, son." Dad had said a lot of things that drove Joe away, but this one stuck.

Joe mulled his options, finally deciding it was maybe best to lie low and observe. He couldn't plan with no data, after all. He imagined his father's disapproving stare.

At FlorCon tower, he joined the river of people passing through the revolving doors. The security guard at the information kiosk gave him a nod of recognition, but not his usual cheery, "Mornin', Mr. Mayfield."

As Joe angled toward the Florida Consolidated elevator bank, he realized there was a man on his left, closer than the normal jostle of the morning rush. Then one on his right.

Joe was beginning to be annoyed.

The first guy took a step ahead of him and turned to block his passage. At 6"1' and broad-shouldered, Joe was rarely intimidated by other men, but this man was couple of inches taller than Joe and broader, with a black, skin-tight T-shirt showcasing the upper body of a weightlifter. A tattoo circled his left bicep, emphasizing its size. He wore his dark hair short and had a military bearing. He was handsome except for acne-scarred cheeks.

"Mr. Mayfield?"

"Yes. Joe Mayfield."

"Come with us."

The second guy's hand hooked Joe's right arm, pulling him out of the flow of people moving toward the elevators.

"What's going on?"

Joe glanced at the guy holding his arm. An inch or two shorter than Joe. Bald, with a round head, gimlet eyes, nose squashed into a lump and a bow mouth that made him look like a malevolent Pillsbury doughboy.

The taller man was at Joe's side again and put a salad-plate sized hand in the small of his back, directing him toward the information kiosk.

"Who the hell are you?"

"Mind your manners, buddy. You have been terminated for violating the rules and policies of Florida Consolidated Energy," said the tall guy, obviously in charge. "Read this and indicate that you understand it." He produced a single page on Florida Consolidated letterhead.

Joe jerked his arm away from the shorter man and said to the guard, "Call upstairs to Florida Consolidated Human Services." The guard's eyes slid away, and he gave a small shake of his head. Joe turned to the tall man and said, "Identify yourself and your partner. *Now*. My friend here—" nodding toward the guard, "has witnessed your assault and will call the police if—"

Tall guy patted the pocket of his black jeans.

"I seem to have left my card back at the office." He gave a snort of a laugh. Then he turned his forearm so Joe saw his tattoo was a snake, the tail circling the bicep, body undulating down the inside of his forearm and ending in an evil-looking head with adamantine eyes and a red tongue flicking between its fangs.

"You can call me Snake. This here's Big Louie," he chuckled, nodding to the bald guy. "He left his card in the office, too." The doughboy looked at Snake wide-eyed. Apparently Snake's nickname was news to him.

Snake put a finger on the letter and said, "Read it."

The letter was signed by an assistant counsel whose name Joe didn't recognize. It said Joe was terminated for cause, effective immediately. It warned that his discharge in no way affected his responsibility in the "ongoing investigation of employee malfeasance" or his liability, both criminal and civil, in the matter.

Joe read the text again, playing for time. Of course he understood it. If the letter was to be believed, a big rock had been dropped on him. It seemed as if the rock had been carefully crafted to say nothing explicit (which would be embarrassing and costly if proved wrong) and imply everything (to cover the legal waterfront).

"Do you understand it?" Snake's expression made it clear that he didn't care one way or another.

"No. I don't understand it. Why don't we go upstairs and have my boss or someone from Human Services explain it to me? Or maybe we should dispense with this bullshit and I'll call my lawyer."

Joe pulled his folded e-pad out of his briefcase.

"How about you follow me out the door without making a fuss?" A half smile, not intended to be friendly.

Joe stared him down. Of course, he had no lawyer to call. He was halfway through dialing Milt James' number when Snake ripped the e-pad out of his hands.

"No. This is not right. I won't—"

Snake moved quickly, jerking Joe's hand down into a come-along hold.

Joe gasped at the pain. Righteous indignation melted into fear. "Let's go."

Snake dragged Joe toward the back exit, seeming to lean toward him in friendly conversation. Big Louie pressed close on Joe's right side.

No one seemed to notice them leave.

***

Snake shoved Joe into the back seat of a black SUV parked in the loading zone. Big Louie followed him in. Joe slid across the seat to the driver's side and fumbled for the door handle. Locked. Louie grabbed his arm, and Snake appeared outside the door and waved a finger, naughty-boy style, then got into the driver's seat. He looked at Joe in the rear-view mirror and said, "We understand you have material belonging to Florida Consolidated. We're going to take you to your home, and you're going to give us that material."

"So, you're adding kidnapping to simple assault?" Joe said. "Have I got that right?"

Snake's eyes flicked toward Big Louie, who turned toward Joe, his bow mouth working into a nasty grin.

The gut punch came like a sledgehammer, doubling Joe over, forehead to knees, making his heart pound in his ears. Big Louie grabbed his hair, jerking him upright, forcing him to look at Snake in the rearview.

Snake seemed to find humor in the situation.

"You were saying?"

Joe said nothing, gasping, gagging.

Big Louie gave an almost girlish giggle, "Sounds like he's gonna come, boss."

Snake looked mildly irritated. "We're simply giving you and the personal items from your office a lift home. You're going to turn over Florida Consolidated material you have in your possession."

Joe's mind raced over the last few days. There was a problem or they wouldn't be taking him...where were they taking him? He fought to get his breath back, panic rising.

But they drove to his apartment. When they arrived, Snake said, "Stay where you are." He got out of the driver's seat, opened the back door and motioned Joe out. Big Louie got out and picked up a cardboard box from the front seat. Joe stepped out, stooped over from Big Louie's punch. Snake grabbed Joe's arm and marched him to his door. Big Louie followed with the box Joe recognized as his personal things from work.

Inside, Big Louie put the box on the dining room table. Snake spun Joe around, clamped one big hand on each shoulder and focused a "don't even bother to lie to me" stare on him. "All right. Where's the data you took?"

"Pardon me?"

The slap came so quickly that it couldn't have been as hard as it felt. Just a tap of the right hand. "You can't do this to—" The second slap made everything go black while his brain rebooted. Then the searing pain. "Where is it?"

"Where is what? I don't know ..." Another slap, this time more like a punch, on the left side. Joe reeled toward unconsciousness, feeling strong hands lowering him into a chair. He was left to drift. Noise of things being moved around, objects dropping to the floor. He fought his way up toward awareness, seeing vague shapes coalesce. Louie and Snake were tearing the place apart. Joe's shirt was wet, and his mouth tasted of iron. He pulled at his shirt and realized he must be bleeding. "Guys! Guys!" Louie stopped pulling books out of the bookcase, turned to Joe. Snake was nowhere to be seen.

"Guys! I don't know what you want. I can give you what I have, but I don't know what could be worth risking going to jail for." That got Big Louie's attention. A slow process of cogitation seemed to begin, the effort of which furrowed his brow. Snake appeared from the bedroom, picked up a dish towel as he passed the kitchen and threw it at Joe. "Wipe your face. I didn't even break your nose." His tone implied, "You wimp."

"You have a list of employees you stole from Florida Consolidated Energy and instructions as to how to break into the Florida Consolidated system. You need to give us those things."

So Raskin and Milt knew he had actual names of people affected.

Joe pressed the towel to his face, fury at the whole mess rising.

"Look, I work in finance. I did an analysis that raised a red flag about one of the projects I worked on. I mentioned the problem to the Director of Human Services and my boss. I never made a secret of it, and the data I used is easily available in several places at headquarters. There's nothing here unless there's a green cube holder in that box you brought from work."

He realized he was babbling, watching Snake, waiting for the next slap.

Snake nodded to Louie, who went over to the box of Joe's things and turned it on its side, spilling out pens, books, pictures, and finally Lucky Monkey. The statuette rolled head over heels, lost a bright blue paperclip that had been his left foot, and came to rest face down near the edge of the table. *Bad luck!*

Snake exhaled irritation and strode to the table. He sorted through the pile, held up a lime-green cube holder.

"This it?"

"Yes. Some of the cubes are Florida Consolidated's. There are also some personal things. Like pictures of my wife, who died of cancer two months ago. I want those pictures."

"Okay, let's see those cubes," Snake said. "You can keep the personal stuff."

Joe's e-pad was on the table next to his empty coffee cup. Snake pushed it across the table to him. "Here."

Joe opened the green cube holder and pointed to four buff-colored cubes. "These are all FCE. The one marked 'SL' has the project I told you about. You're going to take them, so we don't need to look at them."

Snake nodded agreement.

The last cube was magenta in contrast to its dull cousins. Joe inserted it into the e-pad. A smiling Cynthia filled the screen, and Joe's breath caught.

Snake leaned closer to the e-pad, bringing the scent of aftershave mixed with peppermint gum. Big Louie watched over Joe's shoulder. Snake said, "Show me the index and the files."

Joe paged through the files...pictures, videos, holos, accounting for Cynthia's art, and inventory of her work. Snake was finally satisfied. "Pretty woman."

"Yes," Joe said. "And a beautiful person. She died February the eleventh."

Snake seemed like a bright guy, maybe reasonable behind the macho posturing and the tattoo. Gaining confidence, Joe said, "And you surely know following me into my home is a crime you can be arrested for, not to mention the assault and battery."

Snake contemplated this new information. He smiled to himself, a private joke perhaps. Joe's confidence drained away. Snake picked up the antique wooden pencil Cynthia had given Joe along with a green eyeshade when he got his accounting degree.

"Listen, and listen carefully. As far as I know, you're a criminal. We're going to be keeping track of you, making sure you don't step out of line. And we decide what 'out of line' means, so it would be a good idea for you to be a very careful, very quiet former employee."

Snake leaned close to Joe, holding the pencil in his fist and tapping his index finger on the eraser.

"Know what this is?"

Joe pulled back. "An eraser."

"Think of this and picture my partner and me."

He smirked and snapped the eraser off the pencil.

"Very careful, very quiet. Got it?"

The fear returned, redoubled.

"Yes."

Snake turned to Big Louie. "Put the books back." Louie's wide-eyed surprise showed that he probably wasn't much of a poker player. But he nodded, collected books and replaced them on the bookshelves. When he finished, Snake gave Joe another hard stare. Big Louie followed up with a scarier one because it held nothing but meanness. Snake said, "Have a nice day" with no apparent hint of sarcasm. They left Joe to put Lucky Monkey back together and sort out his life.

ELEVEN

JOE SAT IN THE dining nook with his box of possessions and empty coffee cup. His head and neck throbbed from Snake's love taps, blood stiffening his shirt as it dried.

Had it really been an hour? He imagined Cynthia sitting across the table from him, saying, "Joe, you have to take care of yourself. Take a shower. Eat. Maybe a walk in the sand. You know, *'mens sana'* and all that." One of those quotes she used to finish for him, not quite making fun of his fascination with aphorisms. He had always liked the thought, "A sound mind in a healthy body," but Juvenal's second line, *fortem posce animum mortis terrore carentem,* slapped him like Snake, only harder. "Ask for a brave soul that fears not death." He smiled. Not a happy smile. He didn't feel like a brave soul.

He gathered his scattered possessions and put them back in the box. He picked up Lucky Monkey and the paper clip that had been its foot. He got some glue, squeezed a drop on the paper clip and pressed it to the monkey's leg, carefully setting it on the table to dry. The line from Juvenal repeated, now in Cynthia's voice. Was he going crazy? Was she watching over him?

He set the monkey on the table, reached for his e-pad and called Laura Raskin.

The nicely modulated, synthetic operator's voice explained, "Ms. Raskin is away from the office today. She will return on Monday." Joe hesitated. Maybe wait until Monday and go see her. No, he needed to get a marker down.

"Laura, this is Joe Mayfield. As you may know, I was fired this morning. I'm not surprised that you're away today because I suspect the firing would have been handled more...uhh, legally...if you had been involved."

He recounted the beating and accusations, finishing with, "I'll be sending this information to you in written form. I'll attach the picture of me you're seeing right now, before I change clothes and wash off the blood. The two goons warned me that they were watching me and threatened my life. I'd like an explanation of what's going on. Give me a call today or Monday. Tuesday, I'll pass this along to my lawyer and the police."

***

After composing and sending the e-note to Laura Raskin, Joe took a shower. His face was tender, but the water washed away everything but the rising bruises. He lingered in the warmth, the water beating white noise on his head, wanting to sort things out. Should he call the police? Would they do anything? Or would they write him off as a crazy guy who got fired? Snake and Big Louie said they'd be watching. Would he get another visit if he tried anything?

Finished with the shower, he made a sandwich he didn't eat. He paced the apartment, not sure what to do next but needing to do something. Finally, he put on running clothes and went out to the shaded path that snaked over toward Rollins College, walking half a mile, then picking up the pace, working the kinks out, surrendering to the rhythm of the run.

Returning to his apartment, he checked cars around his building. All familiar. The "we'll be watching" was probably like a quarterback's faked throw that pins the defense, a threat to keep him from complaining about being roughed up.

Still, he eased the door open. Nothing. He looked out the window. Nothing. Rechecked the living room. Everything was as he had left it. Except.

Lucky Monkey sat on the floor, foot intact. He would have remembered if he had swept it off the table. Did they break in to show they're watching? Must be a warning. Did they search the place again?

Infocube!

Joe had stored a cube with his own study of MedRecord data in a bottle of bouillon cubes in the kitchen, where he also kept the cube with his financial information. A cheap trick he saw on television, but it made sense. The standard infocube was the size of a bouillon cube. Could be a lot smaller to hold three terabytes of data, but people lost them often enough as it was. Of course, Joe's always smelled like chicken.

Joe was halfway to the kitchen cupboard when he realized that the simplest way for them to find the infocube would be to let him know they can get into his place at will, put a camera somewhere, sit back and let him lead them to it. He stopped, reached into the cupboard, took down a mug and made a cup of tea.

Later, at the counter making dinner, he glanced across the dining alcove at the bookcase and felt a surge of irritation at the disordered titles. He remembered Louie jamming the books back in. Now, everything was haphazard, mysteries mixed with biographies, science with thrillers. As he chopped a pepper, he noticed a thin volume he didn't remember, the word "self-actualizing" in red on the spine. Joe knew his library, and neither he nor Cynthia read self-help books.

***

Milt James popped an antacid tablet as he worked through the calculations Joe had done for several years. "Damn spreadsheet!" He thought Maggie could just plug in numbers. It couldn't have been this complicated. But it was.

He never liked Mayfield. Too smart. Too nice. Made everyone dislike Milt. But the firing that morning was meaner and messier than Milt had bargained for. He had arranged a meeting at the bank so he could be away when it happened. When he returned, Maggie and two other women were sniffling and he felt barely disguised contempt from several people in the break room when he got coffee.

He made the obligatory announcement to his staff, concentrating on sternness nuanced with humanity. Finishing with "Our primary concern is that Florida Consolidated's assets are preserved and protected for the good of FCE's shareholders."

After the presentation, he felt good enough to reward himself with a large, greasy, delicious burrito for lunch. The combination of the burrito and the realization that Joe's balancing out of the daily cash receipts was considerably harder than he had expected required a second antacid tablet.

He sat back, waiting for the antacid to work and saw Tosheka Jackson striding purposefully toward his office. Beautiful legs, sculpted by the triathlons she did regularly. Short hair that would look butch on a lesser woman. Cafe au lait complexion. Strong features. A body no business attire could camouflage. He briefly pondered how it would be to undress her slowly while she begged him to stop. Handcuffs, maybe. Ropes.

Tosheka stepped into his office, took a seat unbidden, and shattered his dream.

"Milt, I want to know more about this business with Joe Mayfield."

No hint of friendly, director-to-director banter. No recognition she might consider him anything other than Assistant Treasurer Milt James.

"Specifically, I'd like you to go over the meeting between you, Mayfield and Laura Raskin." Milt felt himself beginning to sweat. Did she know about the Sampson avatar?

"Well, Tosheka, Mayfield thinks someone changed a bunch of HealthScores in the system. He said his wife's score was changed, and he thinks she got less treatment because of the change. That's pretty much what we talked about."

Milt swallowed. His throat was dry.

"And how did Laura respond?"

He saw opportunity. Deflect the focus to Laura.

"She said she'd look at it again. I think this was a discussion they'd had before. Mayfield thinks he discovered the problem when he was working with Personnel on an estimate of medical insurance cost he's done for the last couple of years. Anyway, she was pretty conciliatory."

Milt began to relax. Tosheka was interested in Laura and Mayfield.

"Uh huh. And what about this rogue account where all the money went?"

Milt tried to control his breathing. He watched Tosheka observe a drop of sweat run from his temple down his cheek.

"All I know is there is some sort of imaginary person who has access to IAC," Milt said. "The only real person with that kind of access is Maggie McTillis. I never suspected she might be cheating. I'm guessing it's some sort of collusion between Maggie and Joe. Maybe Joe just figured out how to peel a copy off of Maggie's IAC registration. Do you think that can be done?"

"Well, Milt, I don't know, but we're looking into it."

He didn't like the sound of 'we'.

Tosheka put four infocubes on Milt's desk. "Meanwhile, Mayfield gave us these when he was discharged. Will you figure out whether there are any clues there?"

Milt, now thinking maybe the "we" meant he and Tosheka might become partners, said, "Sure. No problem. I'll have 'em looked at right away."

"No, Milt." Her eyes bored into him. "There are already too many people involved. Work on them yourself."

"Sure, Tosheka. I'll do that."

"And then, Milt, you can explain Resolution Enterprises.

The accusation hovered over his desk, fixing to fall squarely in his lap. Internal alarms shrieked in his ears. He took a couple of quick breaths, trying to bring himself back in balance. "Resolution what?"

"Milt, you should see your face right now." She half smiled. "Let me jog your memory. It's the company out in Ocoee that has only one customer, Florida Consolidated. The same company that transfers cash to a...let me see...a Barbados bank account. But then, you know about that, don't you?"

Milt drew himself up and put on what he hoped was a steely glare.

"No, Tosheka, I do not know about Resolution Enterprises. I take it that has something to do with the missing money. I'm as shocked as you are, and I intend to get to the bottom of it. And I think...no, I'm quite sure...that the 'bottom' is going to be Mayfield or Maggie McTillis. Furthermore, I'm concerned about your implication—"

"Milt, spare me." Tosheka wasn't smiling any more. Fear layered over the righteous indignation Milt had been working up.

"Let me give you some data," she said. "Most of the transactions by this zombie person are to BancSoutheast, and most are in the midmorning or early afternoon. They never result in any loss of funds, so no real harm done. Then there are the semi-regular transfers to Resolution. They are cash out the door."

Milt stared at her, trying to control his breathing. A memory from earlier in the day grabbed his attention. The break room. Hushed talk about those big goons that grabbed Mayfield. Tosheka continued, "Going back three years, over a million dollars. All of these transactions were initiated in the morning between 6:45 and 7:20."

"Yes, well, you know Joe kept pretty long hours, and—"

"Milt, do you think I'm stupid?"

Tosheka continued after a short pause to let Milt reflect on the likelihood that a hard-working, hard-eyed, hard-bodied woman was as dumb as he had hoped. "Mayfield usually doesn't come in early," she said. "Stays late a lot, but rarely comes in early. And when he is early, it's really early, so I have a card swipe. They happen during budget and tax time, and Resolution doesn't get a transfer."

She paused, gave Milt a smile that wasn't quite a sneer. "McTillis never comes in early. Her coworkers say she delivers a child to school. She arrives punctually at 8:30. You, however, do come in early. Not so early as to have to swipe your card, but according to various people in Accounting, often before the others in your department."

Milt's pulse pounded in his ears.

"There's a small chance," she said, "that you're going to help me tie up some loose ends. If you can help me, maybe you're not going to be sharing a medium-security cell with a guy named Bubba for the next several years. I can't say for sure, but I don't like loose ends, and you may be able to help me keep one of them...the one named Joe Mayfield...on ice." Tosheka underscored the threat with a tight smile.

Milt nodded.

Tosheka squared her shoulders, the soft cashmere of her sweater turning the simple action into an advertisement for riches Milt could only imagine, turned and left the office. Milt popped a third antacid tablet.

TWELVE

ON MONDAY, LAURA RASKIN was in early. Her Friday seminar in Tampa had lasted late enough so that she could relax on the Intercity, have a glass of wine and not return to the office. She spent the weekend with her children and husband without checking her messages. She arrived at FlorCon Tower energized from her early-morning swim and excited to start implementing some of the ideas she had heard at the seminar.

Her computer produced the daily calendar and several messages. A note from Frank Hoskins in the IMMEDIATE category said, "Terminated Joe Mayfield Friday. See me."

Laura exhaled. So much for ideas from the seminar. *Damn!* She hated Frank's tendency to freelance in her area of expertise. She hated it even more that he often justified his behavior by painting her as a hidebound bureaucrat when she was usually trying to protect his gun-totin', cowboy-swaggering, "You're either part of the problem or part of the solution" butt.

She called before she cooled down. His voicemail answered. Probably not in yet. She said, "Frank, this is Laura. I got your message. I hope Mayfield tried to shoot someone. Otherwise, you shouldn't have fired him without my help. Call me back, please, and bring me up to speed."

She went out to Tom Shenko's workstation. "Tom, have you heard anything about Joe Mayfield being terminated on Friday?"

"Officially, no. As far as I know, nobody contacted Personnel. Unofficially, it's been the subject of quite a bit of conversation. He must have done something pretty bad. Two security guys nobody's ever seen before grabbed him down in the lobby and took him out of the building. And by 'grab' I mean *grab*. No exit interview. The information desk attendant saw it all but won't talk. Some office wag coined the term 'ejection interview' for what they did. But, no, nobody here has seen any paperwork."

Laura heard her phone and sprinted back into the office. She tapped her console to answer, and Hoskins' image appeared, his back to her. "Frank, what's going on?"

Frank continued to take papers out of his briefcase, lining them up along his credenza. "Well, Laura, seems like this Mayfield is a bad actor. He's the guy whose wife died, right?" Frank closed his case and turned to Laura. "You were right to be suspicious. Seems like he's been trying to break into the data system through some sort of false IAC identity. Also, there's financial funny business going on, most likely associated with Mayfield. So I had...well, Tosheka had...Mayfield removed from the premises on Friday morning. You were enjoying a relaxing time down in Tampa. So you better get on with the paperwork."

"You fired him for cause without a review?"

"It seems like he's a criminal, Laura." Defensive tone, and something in his eyes she had never seen before. Indecision? Fear?

Laura saw it coming. Hoskins was going to call her a bureaucrat. Obliquely, with a smile, but the meaning would be clear. She usually swallowed the insult, but this time her indignation moved her past diplomacy. "I hate to tell you, Frank, but 'seems like' coupled with no negative reviews is a recipe for a big-ass lawsuit. What's the situation now? Has his access to the system been shut off?" She sensed Frank's anger building but continued, "Has his accrued vacation been calculated and paid? Has his retirement plan been figured out and cut off?"

Frank said, a little louder than necessary, "I expect your group to do that kind of stuff. In your absence, I couldn't be acquainting your staff with a security matter, so I trust that you will now get the paperwork done right. Except, don't pay his money out. He's probably been stealing from the system for some time."

"Frank, let's pay him what we owe him and worry about the

'seems like' problem later." Seeing Frank working up a response, she hurried on, "I intend to arrange for that. You'll be happy we did, believe me."

"Okay, Laura, I don't like it, but go ahead. And let Tosheka know what you're doing."

"Got it." Laura signed off and sighed. What a colossal mess, mostly of Florida Consolidated's making. Well, honestly, of her own making. She wished she had been clear with Frank when she began to understand what might have happened. And she shouldn't have met him at Lequ Coffee. If she'd gone through the system, there'd be a record. Now she was on the Titanic, riding it down.

She keyed Tosheka's contact.

"Jackson, here." Tosheka's ID photo appeared.

"Tosheka, tell me about Joe Mayfield." She heard anger in her voice.

A live feed replaced the photo.

"Well, Laura, not much to say. We had to let him go on Friday." Tosheka's expression gave away no emotion. "I'm still trying to figure out what he's been up to."

Laura said, "Can you fill me in?"

"Sure. I became aware that some irregular transactions have been going on for quite a while. Cash transfers to a service company. The transfers went through an IAC client that seems bogus to me. Milt James accused Mayfield." Tosheka inspected notes on her desk. "Nothing clear on the cash, but Mayfield tried several times to get into his wife's medical file through our system. I think she died a couple of months ago, and he was upset about the treatment she got? Anyway, several weeks later, another entity, one with IAC authority, started hitting the same records. It was different from the one I was already watching, but it seems likely to be bogus, too. I reported all of this to Frank. He talked with James, and because people in Treasury can control corporate funds, we decided we had to move quickly. In your absence, we terminated him on Friday."

Tosheka looked up from her notes, her expression saying she wanted to be done with the conversation.

Laura said, "Tosheka, we should have played by our rules. Mayfield's been an exemplary employee for more than a decade. If he was stealing, we lose nothing but a day or so by setting this up right. On the other hand, if he wasn't...or if we can't prove he was...we have set ourselves up for a lot of trouble by dumping him the way we did."

Tosheka bristled. "Laura, I had my boss and the assistant treasurer on my ass, and I had considerable evidence that some bad things were going on. He's certainly not lily white in this, so we cut him off. He's not going to be making a big stink. Humor us and fill out the paperwork. Meanwhile, I have to prepare for a meeting."

Tosheka signed off, leaving Laura staring at a blank screen. She couldn't believe Joe Mayfield was stealing. She remembered the conversation when he'd said, almost in tears, "you'll never, never hear 'dishonest.'"

Absently, she scrolled through messages and saw one from Mayfield. She clicked it open. Joe stared out at her, face bruised, shirt bloodied. His voice was deliberate, if not calm. She sighed. Not too hard to figure how that video would play on the web. She cradled her head in her hands, headache forming.

I made a mistake, she thought. A big one. I yielded to pressure and watched something I should never have allowed to happen go tragically wrong. I should have owned up to it right away.

She turned to her e-pad and wrote an e-note to Frank Hoskins. Normally, she dictated, but this one required more care.

***

Tosheka signed off from talking with Laura. She stared at her desktop without seeing, said softly, "Damn." She was watching the situation unravel. Too many people involved, too many loose ends. Mayfield was not as big a problem as Laura feared. In theory, they might have violated some rights, sure. In practice, the poor slob was probably cowering in his boots, fearful of Florida Consolidated's wrath and wondering where he could get a job. But he did meet with Milt James and Laura Raskin about his wife's MedRecord. No idea what was said, but it was a loose end. Then the bozos she hired. What did those meatheads mean by "we convinced him pretty good"? Still, Mayfield was probably not a problem. But Laura was a loose end. She always stuck to the straight and narrow. Rules and procedures work fine for honest, uncreative people. But the rest of the world...

.

***

At mid-morning, two stories above Tosheka on the floor colloquially known as "Hallowed Ground," Frank Hoskins returned to his office from the CEO's staff meeting and glanced at the calendar on his e-pad. A couple of reminders, several meetings. A list of messages, including two new ones that made him cringe. The first was from Laura Raskin titled "Termination of J. E. Mayfield." He hoped for a one-liner recognizing the requisite paperwork had been completed. Instead, it was a carefully reasoned case for investigation of the Mayfield incident. It was entered into the secure personnel system and thus indelible. Laura concluded the note,

If we are culpable in any way, we need to go public with our findings sooner rather than later. I will contact Mayfield and assess the situation.

He swore under his breath and moved to the message from Tosheka Jackson.

Hoskins, F.J. from Jackson, T.T. // Security issue re: Mayfield

Frank,

Laura Raskin called me this morning about Mayfield. She's concerned that regular termination protocol was not followed.

I explained the criminal investigation and the exposure of
corporate cash.
There are a lot of loose ends here. I will put together a plan
and talk with you later today.
T. Jackson

At least someone has a plan, he thought. We have a problem
with HealthScores, and a rogue employee may know about it.
Laura's the only other person who knows, and she's armoring over
her ass in case anything bad happens. So, pretty simple. Mayfield
has been fired and is unlikely to cause much trouble. Laura, on the
other hand, is a problem.

He reached for his phone.

***

Tosheka Jackson strolled through a shaded mall fronted by
upscale shops in Winter Park. She bought a coffee and used the
creaming and sugaring of it to scan the area. Satisfied that no one
was following, she crossed to the park to the old South Florida Rail
line that had become LRT North. No tails, as far as she could see.

"Alpha from Lion." She hated the code name crap. "We have
exposure in Florida. A Florida Consolidated employee may have at
least partial understanding of Phoenix."

After a short delay, video opened. The handsome man on the
other end said, "Explain."

"My boss, the VP-Operations, gave me correspondence from
the director of personnel. It's clear that she understands that
MedRecord scores were changed. Also, an employee's wife died.
Her husband, the employee, has suspicions, maybe some evidence.
We have terminated him, but the director is investigating. I've
asked her to hold off contacting the employee, but that will only
work for a day or so. When she talks to the employee, she will
most likely make a statement to the press or law enforcement.
Advise."

The answer was almost immediate.

"Eliminate the threat." His expression admitted no emotion.

She said, "I cannot do that without broken glass. Expensive broken glass."

The man grimaced, gave a slight shrug.

"Eliminate the threat."

Tosheka said, "Understood." She closed out her connection and sighed.

Laura was the problem. Even if she was only suspicious about the scores, she could figure out the problem. Maybe Mayfield was suspicious, but Laura could look at the data. And she would follow up, tight-ass straight arrow that she was. That would be a disaster for Phoenix and for Tosheka. Mayfield was easier. They could paint him as a garden-variety thief.

She dug into her purse and pulled out a disposable phone. Simple number pad entry, no video. She keyed a number.

The phone clicked twice, then "Zimmerman, here." There was loud conversation in the background.

"Paul, I have another job for you. Can you talk?"

"Nope. But I can take a message." Code for "I'll call back shortly."

A few minutes later, the disposable announced an incoming call.

Zimmerman said, "Sorry for the delay. I was helping convince a couple of small time drug dealers that their rights are fragile and tenuous. Anyway, you called?"

He always had to drop some macho bullshit on her, she thought, picturing the serpent tattoo.

"What's the status on Mayfield?"

"As far as I know, no change. I talked with Louie a couple of hours ago. Mayfield was in his apartment working on his résumé."

"Keep track of him. I want daily updates. But no reports...just be ready to talk to me when I call. It'll always be right around 6 p.m., and I'll call on your personal phone. Understood?"

"Understood."

She paused, then said, "Paul, I have another job for you."

THIRTEEN

TOSHEKA JACKSON'S VOICE HAD been cool and calm, but serious.

Exposure in Florida. It was bound to happen eventually.

Jason Squitieri pushed back from his desk, leaned back and stared at the sagging ceiling tiles in the former warehouse that was now the headquarters of US Health Audits. If he quit now, Phoenix would come crashing down, just as it was starting to pay off. He knew he had to make it work, at least until he could withdraw quietly.

Five years before Tosheka's call, a client meeting in a Washington watering hole had produced the straw Jason Squitieri grasped to save his struggling company. At the time, US Health Audits was one of what his venture capital backers called The Walking Dead— a failing business model, cash almost gone, going through terminal maneuvers. Jason had promised insurance companies substantial recoveries from the "errors in the massive, imprecise" federal medical reimbursement program using his "sophisticated algorithms." The software cost the insurers nothing, but USHA kept thirty percent of the savings it discovered. Unfortunately, the savings had been far smaller than Jason's optimistic projections.

There's an old story that a frog, put in cool water, will tolerate increases in temperature until he is cooked, just so long as the change is gradual. It's not true. The frog always jumps out of the water well before he is parboiled. But in some ways, the story is proof that frogs are smarter than Jason Squitieri.

As Jason tried to figure out whether the company credit card would support another expensive dinner, the potential client, made loquacious by several bourbons, leaned over to Jason and said,

"The real money in the insurance industry is with the policies. See, the rest of it, the claims processing and all the other stuff...is pretty transparent. The client can see what you're doing, so the competition is cutthroat. But there's big money in the insurance itself, courtesy of the rating companies that generate HealthScores and, of course, their bought-and-paid-for affiliates in Congress."

The client paused, his attention momentarily sidetracked by a pretty girl passing their table, then leaned back toward Jason. "See, the way they calculate those HealthScores is proprietary and secret. They blow a bunch of smoke about DNA profiling and genetic research, sure. But nobody knows how those scores are calculated. Magic. Sooo ..." he paused to gain Jason's attention, "sixty or seventy percent margins. I wouldn't say there's collusion. No, no." He combined a hiccup with a laugh. "But big profits."

A frog would have jumped out of the hot water, but Jason saw opportunity.

What if he could change some scores...just temporarily...and give the buyers an advantage? He'd reverse the changes after the buyers had firm quotes, and no one would know better. He'd keep a piece of the savings. It would be a logical extension of his existing business model. His financial backers would like that.

Jason went home that night buzzed from the booze and the prospect of rescuing USHA.

After the headache cleared the next morning, he realized it would be hard to sell something that was flatly illegal as well as morally repugnant. Then he had a flash of insight. If he turned his existing software on its head—use it to create plausible billing for high-level treatment while paying for low-level treatment—he'd solve his financial problems.

Jason had the USHA programs rewritten into two pieces of software called REDIRECTR and SLAudit. Under the cover of a scoring "update" from one of the companies that calculated HealthScores, SLAudit would change some high scores to lower ones and notify REDIRECTR of the changes. REDIRECTR had to be installed in the IAC to do its work. Jason didn't worry too much about that. His connections in the insurance companies and the funds he had helped flow to Washington campaign coffers meant he had friends in high places.

Jason named the project Phoenix. The software was ready and, since Jason had spent his small cash reserve, he had to go. The frog had hopped off long ago; the water was boiling.

***

Rakesh Thakur's office manager smiled at Jason and waved him in to the senator's inner office. Several millions directed to a campaign fund had that effect.

"Ricky" Thakur was on the phone, leaning back in his chair, feet on his desk, eyes closed. The person on the other end of the line was excited, or angry, or maybe a lobbyist making an upbeat sales pitch. Sen. Thakur punctuated the flow of words with variations on "uh-huh" at appropriate pauses.

Spotting Jason, Thakur removed his feet from the desk, squared himself in the chair, turned on video and said, "Sam, I hate to interrupt, but I'm late for a meeting. Can you send some background? I promise we'll give it full consideration." Jason took a seat and waited for the senator to finish the obligatory inquiry about the wife, the kids and the grandchildren. Finished, Thakur disconnected with a flourish.

"So, Squitty, what's up?"

Jason didn't like being called "Squitty." He knew it referred his distant relative, Arnold, once underboss of the Gambino crime family. But Ricky Thakur gave mildly insulting pet names to everyone around him. One of the perks that came with controlling expenditure of hundreds of millions of government dollars.

Jason handed Thakur a two-page brief titled, Medical Equity Project: Extending Horizons. He summarized it in a few words, concluding, "I don't have to remind you that you're by far the strongest supporter MEP has on the Committee." MEP had, of course, given money to the Thakur campaign. Unspoken but understood by both Thakur and Jason was the reality that Jason's contacts within the insurance industry had given far, far more.

Ricky Thakur flexed his shoulders, ran a hand over his telegenic hair, and said, "Okay, Squitty, let's get that request on the agenda. Anything else?"

"Yes, as a matter of fact, there is."

"Shoot."

"I want to get a friend placed in the IAC. This person was high up in Siemens information organization. Great résumé. There's always an opening if Ricky Thakur asks, I bet."

The senator smiled expansively. The give and take of favors. Just another snout in the trough of government largesse, after all.

"Send me a résumé."

"Got it right here," Jason said, covering his elation with a bland smile.

The plan was in place, now the game was afoot. Time to start selling the program to insurance companies.

***

Five years after Ricky Thakur had helped place Jason's handpicked analyst in the IAC medical records administration office, Jason was enjoying a martini in a frequent traveler lounge at the San Francisco airport. He reached for another handful of wasabi peanuts. His appreciation of the bite of the wasabi over the cool flowing of the gin was interrupted by a discrete buzz on his e-pad: SLAudit injected into BlueLight-Florida's system.

Chalk up another set of potential participants.

Easier to think of them as "participants," as if they were somehow volunteers. Jason sipped the martini, enjoying the moment and the potential upside of landing BlueLight Florida, USHA's biggest account yet.

So far, only four cases from earlier installations in

Pennsylvania and California had gotten sick and died—"cashed out" in Jason's casuistic lexicon—but the long-term potential was huge. Normally, there would be a bank loan or some eager angel investors, given the promise of millions, maybe billions as the participants "matured" and cashed out. But this was an opportunity Jason couldn't pitch in a business plan, since it depended on causing the unnecessary deaths of hundreds or even thousands of people.

A chime announced his flight to Washington was ready to board. Time to relax. Maybe another martini.

FOURTEEN

JOE SPENT SATURDAY AND Sunday after his firing in stasis. On Sunday afternoon, stir crazy, he took a run to burn off the building frustration. As he crossed the street on the trail toward Rollins, a black SUV slowed and kept pace with him for a block.

Maybe it was a coincidence.

At home, he wrote a detailed description of what happened. Sunday evening, he composed several cover letters, passing through anger to sarcasm to stoicism. He deleted all of them.

Monday wound Joe tighter. He couldn't believe Laura Raskin hadn't called. She must have listened to the message. But maybe she knew the plan to fire him all along. Or maybe she was embarrassed, or maybe...

Finally, at noon, Joe made his decision. He rode the Intercity Rail to a coffee shop near Associated BancShares, where he'd deposited the life insurance check that came several weeks after Cynthia died. He'd opened the Cynthia Chin Mayfield Memorial Fund with the check, remembering her tweaking him for being a softy when his college buddy sold him the policy.

He bought a coffee, took an outside table, and pretended to check job openings on his e-pad. When he was sure he had not been followed, he crossed the street and drew $9,000 in hundred-dollar bills. He said, "Fundraiser" to the teller's quizzical look.

Outside the bank, he found a bus going south toward the Disney complex. It got him to within a half mile of the train station. He walked the rest of the way. The station was a beautiful building, something out of the old, genteel South. Pleasantly out of place in a mishmash of distribution businesses, bars, strip clubs and fast food joints.

Inside, he inspected the schedules. He used his cash card to buy a ticket to Chicago leaving in two days. Then he stood in a different line and paid cash for a ticket to New Orleans, leaving shortly after the Chicago train.

Across from the station, he found a convenience store wedged between Your Dreams Gentlemen's Club and El Taco Loco and bought two disposable phones. The clerk gave him a half smirk, and Joe realized the preppy clothes, if not the bruises on his face, set him apart in this neighborhood. He wondered what kind of no good the clerk thought he was up to. Suddenly worried, Joe realized he had not carried more than pocket change for years. He crossed the street back to the station and took a cab back home.

***

To Laura Raskin, morning was the best part of the Florida day. Coolest in the summer, never colder than bracing for most of the winter. She and her husband bought the house in Maitland when the kids were young. A selling point was its proximity to the club, with its heated outdoor pool. She could drop in early and swim, almost always alone. On Tuesday morning, the sun was not quite up, and Laura saw a sky full of stars. Fog rose where the heated water met the morning chill. Brisk now, but it would be hot and humid later.

She lowered herself into the water. She was cold for several laps, swimming fast, then relaxing into a slow crawl. Thirty laps, down-back-breather at the shallow end. It was good exercise, and she cherished the feeling of well-being as the endorphins kicked in. She wished it would help a little more with the weight that had crept on to her thighs, but she welcomed the energy it gave her to start the day.

In the pool, Laura was in a world of her own. A glance at the depth markers every other breath, a turn at the end of the lane, a remembered song that ran in time with her strokes.

Turning, her eye caught a movement in the shadows at the far end. Maybe water on her goggles. She swam back to the shallow end and stopped for a breather. Then, a swift movement from the shadows. Something had her arm! The adrenaline hit before the fear.

"What?!"

A large, bald man had her in a vise grip. She twisted, straining to wrench her arm away. There was a sting in her deltoid.

"What the hell are you doing? Let go of me!" She took in breath to scream, but nothing came out. The man let her go. He smiled. Ugly, gimlet eyes. Then, a curtain of darkness dropped down, and Laura observed herself, disinterestedly, as she slipped beneath the surface.

***

Tuesday morning. Still no call from Laura. About noon, Joe's phone buzzed. *Finally*.

He answered. No video. A muffled voice, one he knew he should recognize. "Joe?" A pause. Sounded like the person was crying.

"Yes?"

"Joe, it's Maggie."

"Maggie, I didn't recognize your voice. What's the matter?"

"Oh, Joe, I don't know how to say this, but Laura Raskin died this morning. Drowned. They say she went swimming every morning at a pool near where she lives, and she was...she was fine as far as anyone knew, but she didn't come into work, and her husband...Oh my God, Joe. She has two kids."

His mind told him this must be coincidence; his body chemistry disagreed.

Maggie paused, then said, "Joe, are you okay?"

Joe heard fear and doubt in her voice.

"Yes, Maggie I'm okay. How are you doing?

"Not very well." She drew a long, ragged breath.

"They confronted me on Friday afternoon, after you...after they took you away. They took me to the small conference room, and there was an FBI agent there. Milt, too, and Tosheka Jackson. First, they talked about avatars, but not only Marcella. Did you make avatars?"

"I did, Maggie. Only to find out what was going on with Cynthia's—"

"They didn't seem to care about the medical files, but they wanted me to admit I stole money from the company. I told them why I made Marcella. You should've seen Milt. Getting redder and redder and swelling up like a great gasbag. The FBI agent was actually pretty nice, and Jackson, well she's just plain scary."

Tosheka Jackson again? Maybe not surprising. But the FBI?

Maggie continued, "Milt has been plain nasty today, and I'm afraid I'm going to be fired. I can't afford to be out of a job. Anyway, I went up to Human Resources right before I left on Friday and asked to see Laura Raskin privately, but she was gone for the day. She never got back to me on Monday, and then today …" Maggie's voice trailed off.

"I don't know what to do. It seems that nobody at Florida Consolidated is going to go to bat for me now that you're gone. What should I do?"

Was she setting him up? No, not Maggie.

"If there's an FBI agent involved, they're probably focusing on the theft," Joe said, sounding more confident than he felt. "I think you should document the creation of Marcella, including when you did it and why, and explain how I found out about it. Send it to Human Resources, probably to whoever is named as director. You might ask Tom Shenko how to proceed. He's the analyst I worked with on the insurance cost estimate, and I think he'd give you good advice."

"Thanks, Joe. I really miss you already. What are you going to do?"

"I think I'm going to visit my parents up in Illinois and take some time to...heal."

"Okay, Joe. You know, a lot of people at Florida Consolidated care about you. Stay in touch with us. Let us know what happens in your life."

Heartfelt, and Joe knew it.

After he disconnected, Joe tapped away at the résumé to buy time. He began planning the trip Cynthia had always wanted them to take. "Drink some whiskey, eat some étouffée...Take off up Highway 61...my old soul looking down." They were together again, she in the hospice bed. "Find another lucky woman and have kids..."

He stared at Lucky Monkey, who seemed to be saying, "Go!"

***

Tosheka keyed a disposable phone.

"Zimmerman."

"Jackson here. Do you have a report?"

"I do. The first objective was accomplished early this morning by Louie."

"I know. Were there any problems?"

"No. Clean as far as I can tell."

She paused to digest the fact that she was guilty of murder.

Paul Zimmerman continued, "The second objective was to cover Mayfield. Over the weekend, he basically worked the résumé, went out a couple of times to exercise. In other words, not much activity. I have been in the precinct today, so Louie covered Mayfield. When he checked this morning, Mayfield had gone out. He returned in the afternoon and dropped some documents on his table. I checked his credit card account, and there's a charge for a train ticket to Chicago. He told a friend who called a couple of days ago that he might take a trip to 'sort things out,' so maybe that explains the ticket."

"Paul, 'maybe' is not an acceptable answer! We have to find out what he's up to. Look at that ticket...see where he's going. If he's going."

"Alright. I don't mind doing research and providing you with information, but let's not get ahead of ourselves. When this whole thing started, Louie and I were supposed to impress on what you called a 'rogue employee' the wisdom of keeping quiet after you fired him. A little muscle, that's all. Maybe keep an eye on him for a while." He sighed audibly. "I hired Louie because he's been reliable in the past, and he can cover Mayfield while I'm on duty. Then this 'project' of yours gets, uhh, pretty complex. Now we're in the business of eliminating one of your problems. And it has to be quick. I have to use Louie. He is not good at complex problems. Muscle, okay. Stakeouts, okay. Problem elimination, risky as hell. The beat cop in me can smell another of those rush jobs coming, and we need to rethink our relationship before that happens."

Tosheka frowned. "I didn't expect this to get as...complex...as it has. It kind of blew up in my face and I was directed to move quickly to control the problem."

"Well, Tosheka, this kind of work is a lot more expensive than you originally thought. Whoever is directing you to do these things needs to be paying a larger retainer."

"Seems to me that you're arguing after the horse is out of the barn."

There was a short pause, then a change in his voice.

"I don't think so. You'd be in a difficult position if someone learned that the security director of Florida Consolidated solves the company's PR problems by offing the source."

"So would you, Paul. So would you. But I understand. I'll be back to you tomorrow."

"One hundred K, Tosheka, beyond the original agreement."

"Okay. As I said, I'll be back to you. Now, can you tell me what Mayfield's up to?"

"I'll do my best. I'm on duty tonight, and I'll get on the system and see what I can see."

"Okay. I'll call tomorrow, same time."

Tosheka signed off and grimaced. How had they gotten to this?

FIFTEEN

ON WEDNESDAY MORNING, HENRY Barber still wondered about the odd meeting at Florida Consolidated on Monday. Strange that they should wait for, what, three months since he and Jackson talked, then suddenly, the Monday meeting. Both Jackson and Milton James were leaning pretty hard on Maggie McTillis, though the "evidence" they presented seemed to Henry to exonerate her. Her boss, Joe Mayfield, had been fired, but they weren't eager to contact him...pretty stupid, considering that he could be a suspect. Finally, there was no representative from Personnel in the room. Very strange, given the "great place to work" image Florida Consolidated strove to maintain. But no real course of action for the FBI other than to follow up on the money trail. Henry had assigned that task to Jennifer Rowland, who had joined the office the previous year.

He looked through the morning data dump from the wizards in Bethesda without much enthusiasm. Another window on the monitor held his aggregator, an idea Jennifer had suggested.

She had been in the office for two weeks when she had appeared over the top margin of the *Orlando Sentinel* as he read it at his desk, lower drawer out, feet propped, comfortable. "Henry, it really isn't necessary to read the newspaper to get the news, you know. You can build an aggregator and let the software deliver the relevant stories."

Henry had sighed inwardly and put the paper down. "Then I'd only get the stories I had the foresight to ask for. I get the stuff I didn't think of looking for when I scan the paper."

"Like the ..." Jennifer leaned over and looked at the paper. " 'SWF looking for 40-ish SWM for walking on the beach, good conversation and Christian fellowship'? Bet that'll be a nonstarter."

She smiled. The young pup nipping at the ears of the old dog. "But seriously, Henry, you can set the software up to pull the stories that might interest you. Over time, the aggregator learns to scan for you."

He couldn't disagree that the aggregator was valuable, but the whole exercise made him feel like rounding error in the great FBI scheme of things. It was the era of young agents, data mining, analysis. Then along came the case of the president of a construction company behaving strangely. Henry wanted to take the case, just to get out of the office, kick some tires. But Jennifer needed the experience, so he gave it to her. After days of data analysis and exegesis of the FBI manual, Jennifer came to Henry for advice. Henry asked for all sorts of information that Jennifer provided without rolling her eyes...quite. He saw the human solution...a greedy mistress, no less. He told Jennifer how he thought the sordid affair would play out...and was right. She got the credit, and Henry gained guru status in the eyes of incoming agents.

Henry had added Florida Consolidated to the aggregator after talking with Tosheka Jackson in January. He usually got at least one hit on the name a week. Mostly boring stuff. Self-congratulatory press releases. Promotion announcements. Citizens' groups upset over this and that.

This morning, there was an item about the head of Human Resources, Laura Raskin, who drowned while taking her morning swim. Henry opened the item. Tragic accident. Two small children. Swam almost every day, in excellent health. Shocking. Neighbors horrified. A sad situation. Probably not connected to the interrogation on Friday, but odd just the same.

Henry saw spider web lines beginning to connect apparently unrelated things. It was a feeling he trusted and the Bethesda computer geeks didn't get at all.

He beeped Ashley Parry in the Orange County coroner's office. "Ashley, this is Henry Barber over at the FBI. Give me a call please. Confidentially. I need to discuss the case of Laura Raskin, who drowned yesterday in a club swimming pool up in Maitland. I want to be sure you do an autopsy."

Ashley called back quickly. Freckles and a smile. Looked about twenty, Henry thought, but she was the best technician at the Orange County morgue. "Henry, we're moving quickly on this one. Pretty clear that she drowned, and there's no reason to suspect foul play or suicide."

"Is there any indication as to why a young person in perfectly good health who swam every day just up and drowned?" Henry asked.

Ashley thought for a moment, flipping papers, shuffling, lines of concentration on her forehead.

"Nope. You're right, Henry. There should have been at least a contusion. A bump on the head or something like that. Maybe a cramp if the water was really cold and she was inexperienced or out of condition, but none of those things were true. But it's only the initial report. I haven't seen her yet. We're under pressure to move this along. She was important and well loved. The family is Jewish. Custom dictates a quick burial. That said, they want the autopsy, too, because it's not clear what happened. Now that I've talked with you, I'll be extra careful."

***

Ashley's message came the next day.

"There's nothing immediately obvious about the Laura Raskin case. Nothing I can hang my hat on, anyway, but the autopsy also didn't explain how she died. The tox screen showed nothing unusual. No illegal drugs, a trace of Valium. I'm doing a couple of extra screens because it's not clear she drowned. She may have had a heart attack. I'll be back to you soon."

"Soon" turned out to be early afternoon.

"Henry, I have some disturbing results from the Raskin autopsy. Your concern raised a hint of suspicion. So I looked beyond the routine tox screen. The blood chemistry was normal except potassium levels were a little high. She aspirated some water, but it seems like her heart stopped. I'm no expert in the top-secret spy stuff, but there are some chemicals that cause death quickly and then disappear without a trace. They generally work by interrupting the rhythm of the heart, and the only telltale is elevated potassium, but even that disappears after an hour or so under normal conditions. In this case, though, she sank to the bottom of the pool, and cooling from conduction might have kept the potassium from dissipating."

"So, you're saying that somebody killed her?"

"Well, the potassium is...I should say, was...speculation. But it did make me suspicious, so I went back over the body again. I found a small bruise on her deltoid muscle and, under close inspection, a tiny puncture mark and a scratch on the bone. It might be hard to prove in court, but I think someone gave her a shot, not too expertly. Yes, I think somebody probably killed her."

"I don't know where that leaves us," Henry said. "You'll have to let Orange County know. I'll continue to be involved because of the money transfer issue. And Ashley, great work."

Ashley blushed. "Thanks, Henry. Your intuition started the ball rolling."

SIXTEEN

ON THURSDAY MORNING, JOE rose early. His train was leaving at six. He packed a few things in a small bag, an old-fashioned Dopp kit and a selection of cubes into a carrypack. Dawn was showing gray as he left the apartment by the side entrance. He hoped nobody was watching, feeling foolish even as he thought it. Probably nobody cared.

The day before, he had managed another two draws of $9,000 from the Cynthia Chin Mayfield fund. He had bought a box of tissues at a drugstore near his apartment, gone to the men's room in the bank, removed the tissues and packed the money tightly into the box.

At home, he'd taken down the jar of bouillon cubes, spilled them, said, "Damn!" and managed to palm the infocube with the insurance data on it, later transferring it to the Dopp kit.

He walked through the quiet predawn streets over to the light rail on the I-4 corridor. The few cars that cruised by seemed innocent enough. The light rail took him to the Amtrak station. He entered through a smaller side entrance and scanned the people waiting, reading, napping on the benches. Nothing suspicious.

The train to Chicago was scheduled to leave a few minutes before the train to New Orleans, two tracks over. Joe waited on a bench until the Chicago train was announced and strolled toward the gate. Not many people boarding. He stopped at a newsstand, bought an *Orlando Sentinel* and opened it.

The Chicago train pulled from its berth, big motors straining to build momentum. Joe heaved a sigh of relief and glanced over the paper at the train. In one of the last cars he saw the blur of a face turning to stare at him...shock registering...shaved head, ugly...*Big Louie*.

***

Crap! The bastard is standing on the platform. How'd he get there?

Louie grabbed his phone. Forgetting the phone protocol he had rehearsed with Paul Zimmerman, he shouted "Zimmerman!"

An older woman on the other side of the aisle jumped, then glared at him.

A pleasant synthesized voice informed him that Officer Zimmerman was away from his desk but would return his call as soon as possible.

Shit!

"Paul, this is Louie. Need to talk to you about our project."

He disconnected and began figuring out his situation. By the time Zimmerman called him back ten minutes later, Big Louie's blood pressure had returned to the high end of normal and he had figured out that he could get back to Orlando by 7 p.m.

"Louie, where the hell are you?"

"Where I'm supposed to be, goddammit. On the train. One problem, though. Mayfield's not."

"How?"

"Dunno. He came to the station. Went out to the train. But I'm pretty sure I saw him standing on the platform as the train...with me on it...pulled out of the station."

"Oh, man, Louie. He's a freakin' businessman. How the hell did he lose you? Don't answer that. When can you get back here?"

"I'll be able to get off in Waldo in an hour. No train back to Orlando. No way to rent a car in Waldo, but Amtrak does run a bus through there three times a day, going to or coming from Jacksonville or Gainesville. I can get a car either place. Fastest I can get back is tonight, no matter how I do it."

"Well, I guess that has to be okay, Louie. I can check our video feed, but I bet I won't find him at home."

***

The train to New Orleans took Joe to Tallahassee, Pensacola, Mobile, Biloxi, and the Big Easy. Seven hours of anxiety mixed with boredom. Nobody could know which train he was on, or could they? But he was pretty sure he had seen Big Louie, so somebody must know he's not Chicago-bound. He plugged in earphones, hoping Cynthia's music cube would help him relax.

Dozing. Drifting...remembering. Images flipping, moving. Riding the Intercity train with Cynthia to Jacksonville. Cynthia messing with her soundcube. Snippets of her favorite songs appeared, disappeared, collided. Scratchy old voices from another time, then a hurdy-gurdy, of all things. Must be dreaming. The Mississippi Sheiks sang,

> *You don't like my peaches, don't you shake my tree*
> *Get out of my orchard, let my peaches be*
> *And now she's gone but I don't worry*
> *'Cause I'm sitting on top of the world.*

She smiled that oblique, suggestive smile he loved, full of promise.

Milt James sitting across the aisle from him, reading the *Wall Street Journal* on his e-pad, upside down. Pointing to graphs, trying to explain something to Big Louie, who fingered a handgun. Gimlet eyes found Joe, and Louie smiled, revealing several missing teeth. Milt said, "It's like insurance ..." Louie raised the gun.

The Sheiks again, looping over and over, merging with the rhythm of the train.

Idontworryldontworryldontworrydontworrydontworrydontworry

Cyn tried to say something he couldn't make out. Crying. She held a plastic bag of liquid with a tube winding across her lap into her arm.

'Cause I'm sitting on top of the world

There was a "pop" from across the aisle.

Joe woke as the train rattled over a trestle and slowed on its approach to New Orleans.

***

"What?!"

Tosheka bolted out of her chair.

"Tosheka...Ms. Jackson...we have temporarily lost Mayfield."

"What do you mean, lost?"

"Well, he had a train ticket to Chicago that he purchased a couple of days ago, and he said to a friend he was going up there to visit his family. He got up this morning and packed a bag. I had Louie down at the station. Mayfield arrived, went out to the train, Louie got on, and...Mayfield isn't on that train."

"Where the hell is he?"

***

On the Internet, L'home Joli looked just right for Joe's purpose. Nine rooms, near the French Quarter, but not so near as to be too expensive. Hard up beside the Storyville district, where so much of the music Cynthia loved came from. Pretty picture of gables, wrought iron, bougainvillea. However, the Internet had not captured its chief asset, the owner, Francine Bilodeau.

"Everyone calls me Billie," she said as Joe signed the register. "Y'all stayin' a while?"

Joe smiled. "A week, at least. Depends on the music."

"Y'all goin' to be stayin' the summer or more if you're usin' that measure."

Billie was big, amply supplied with the external aspects that bespeak womanhood. Some would say oversupplied, but Joe understood from Billie's confident stance that she would not put much value in such opinions. She was quite possibly on the far side of fifty, hard to tell. The precise but rarely discussed racial accountancy of New Orleans would likely make her an octoroon. That first day, she wore a shift with splashes of bright color that almost seemed as if they were laughing at you. Cynthia would have loved it.

Joe signed the old register book with his real name. He had no identification for any of the avatars. Besides, honesty was simpler than lying.

"Now, all I need is a card swipe."

"I'd prefer to pay cash," Joe said.

"Hmmm. You hidin' from someone? 'Cause if you are, I don't want no po-lice comin' in here, bustin' up the place, scarin' my honest customers!"

"No, I just like my privacy. I won't be causing trouble here. I'm trying to stay off the radar while I enjoy the city."

Billie cast a skeptical, appraising eye on Joe, then inspected the register. "Well, Mr. Joe Mayfield, we got no radar here in the Big Easy. We got jazz music, got blues music. We got the best food you'll ever eat, got anything a man could want and some things no proper man would dream of." She put a hand on her hip. "But we got no radar." She rewarded him with a broad smile. "You know, this here place o' mine has a French name. Means 'the beautiful home'. I try to make it exactly that. But you know what else?" She raised her eyebrows. "You drop the -e off 'home,' and you get Lou'siana French for 'the nice man'. You be a nice man, you pay a week in advance, then you can pay cash, and this will be a beautiful home for you."

She must have said that to a thousand men. But he admired the artistry of the line of patter and paid seven $100 bills, which Billie made disappear into the folds of her shift.

Joe's room was up a narrow staircase to the second floor. It had a bed with an ornate brass frame, a small bureau, an upholstered chair that had surely seen many decades of use, and a tiny bathroom with a pull-chain toilet and a shower that allowed for only the most carefully planned movement. The brass bed brought back Cynthia's urging to take this trip, and the bittersweet memory of rolling in her arms.

That night, Joe found a simple restaurant where he ate a delicious étouffée. Afterwards, he returned to L'Home Joli, and slept without dreams for the first time in weeks.

SEVENTEEN

WELL INTO THE SECOND week of his stay, Billie and Joe sat on the porch of L'Home Joli sipping sweet iced tea and contemplating the goings on in the street in the comfortable silence of a developing friendship. Dusk was gathering, and the heat receded from a day that said summer was at hand.

Billie turned to Joe, "I think somebody's trying to find you."

Joe tried to hide his surprise. Billie raised her eyebrows.

"Fortune-tellin' lady in me says you know what I'm talkin' about."

"What makes the fortune-tellin' lady think this?" Joe asked, trying to appear nonchalant.

"Fortune-tellin' lady has her crystal ball workin' and her finger on the pulse of the information highway. The real information highway, I mean."

"And what," asked Joe, "does this information highway tell you, anyway?"

"It tells me, Joe Mayfield, that somebody is in town lookin' for a man of your general physical description, and the somebody is a private party. Puttin' out a description, laying down some cash for information."

Joe hesitated. Billie waited not too patiently. A band struck up *Eh, La Bas* somewhere over toward Rampart.

Finally, Joe said, "I don't want to tell you the whole story, but I discovered some bad things where I used to work. That's probably why there are people after me. You don't need the burden of knowing enough that they'd think you are a threat to them. I appreciate the warning, and I should leave."

"So, where you goin' to, Joe?"

"I don't know for sure. North. Maybe Illinois, where my

family is. Maybe back home to Orlando. Less you know, the better."

"Uh-huh. Well, one thing's sure," Billie said. "If you don't want to be noticed, you won't be travelin' on a plane or train. You might get on a bus without registering, but I doubt it."

Joe knew she was right. Snake and Big Louie would be all over the train trick if he tried it again. Planes and busses no longer accepted cash for tickets.

"If you could raise some cash, you might want to take that trip you were tellin' me about," Billie said. "You know, up the Blues Highway. Hafta do it by car. You go up into Mississippi, you'll be driving back a hundred years. Those folks are mostly off the grid. You could disappear for quite some time."

Joe shook his head. "Great idea, Billie, but if I buy a car, it will set off all sorts of alarm bells. Registration, money transfer, you name it."

Billie inspected Joe over her half glasses. "Well, Mr. Joe Mayfield, fortune-tellin' lady has friends. Friends who will help her out. If you were to go up to Rampart, past all those fancy used car places, you'd find Big Al's Automobile Emporium. Now, Big Al is a friend of mine." She smiled. "A real good friend. If you have some cash money, I believe he will be able to help you out."

The next morning, Joe followed Billie's directions down Esplanade to Rampart and turned east. He passed a national dealer, a large used car lot and, finally, a smaller one: **BIG Al's**. Smaller letters scrolled around the oval sign: *Everyone rides at Big Al's Automobile Emporium.* Must be the place, but it didn't look open. He passed by slowly, checking out the cars.

At the edge of the lot, he turned back to find a large black man leaning on the hood of an old Honda Element and sizing Joe up. Big Al — and no doubt that this was indeed Big Al — carried what must have been 270 pounds easily on a six-foot-four frame. Large features, big hands. Smile punctuated by a toothpick. One of those rare human beings who can look friendly and terrifying at the same time.

"Y'all in the market for a fine automobile, son?"

Nobody had called him "son" in twenty years.

"Well, yes. I need something inexpensive."

Big Al cast a knowing glance at Joe and said, "Well, we have something for almost every budget. Depends what you call inexpensive."

Joe ran his eyes over the cars in the lot. "I'm looking for something under $3,000. A cash deal." The big man gave a skeptical chuckle, so Joe added, "I've been staying at L'Home Joli, and Billie Bilodeau said you are the man to talk to."

Big Al smiled a big smile and said, "Yes, yes. Billie and I go way back." He rubbed his chin as he contemplated his lot. "Hmmm. When you say 'inexpensive' you mean close to downright cheap. But lemme see here, what I got in that price range."

He ticked off several models, pointing them out, then dismissing them. He ended with the faded metallic green Honda Element he leaned on. "This here's a classic. It's twenty years old but runs just fine. Retrofitted with the second-generation autopilot, GPS o'course, standard electronics and phone uplink, and it's big enough so you can sleep in it on a road trip. Al opened the clamshell doors, flipped a couple of levers, and pushed the seat back effortlessly into a horizontal approximation of a bed. "Just drop the seat ..."

Joe wondered how hard that would be for a normal human being to do.

Al stopped as if struck by inspiration and turned to Joe.

"You say you want a cash deal?"

"Yes, I just sold some stuff for cash, and I was hoping ..."

"Okay, I believe I can meet your needs. Now, we both know that any cash deal above $5,000 needs to be reported. I, being a law-abidin' citizen would, of course, comply with that regulation." He gave Joe a look closer to the terrifying end of the spectrum than the friendly one. "What you know and I don't is why in the hell a nice white man dressed oh, so proper is comin' into my neighborhood mentionin' he knows Billie Bilodeau, which may or may not be the case, fixin' to offer me cash to buy an automobile." The toothpick shifted. "One reason might be that he just sold his maiden auntie's heirloom and for some unknown reason got paid cash. Another possibility might be that this honest-looking gentleman has got an arrangement with one of the dozen or so bad people who are probably watching us intently right now, and those bad people figure they can get that money back just as soon as you drive off with the car." The toothpick moved again. "Now, tell me, mister, are you a nautical man?"

Joe was puzzled. "A what?"

"A nautical man. You know, a sailor."

"No. Canoe. Not a sailor, though."

"Well, then, you maybe won't understand that when they tried that trick on me last time, the guy that showed up here to take the money back wasn't a nautical man either. He was not familiar with the useful figure-of-eight knot I learned during my Navy career until I tied him into one. Am I making myself clear?"

Now the look was terrifying.

"Absolutely. That wouldn't happen. I just need a car my wife won't know about. But, speaking of cash money and those bad people you mentioned, if we can cut a deal on a car, how should I get the cash to you?"

The toothpick shifted again as Al considered. "I surely would not come down here with a bag fulla money, pilgrim."

"Okay. Let's say I buy the Element from you," Joe said. "I can give you a few hundred as a deposit. I'll be back tomorrow to pick it up, with the balance, and you'll have it in tip-top shape. Will that work for you?"

Al smiled another big smile and said, "Pilgrim, that Element ain't never gonna make 'tip-top' again, and it goes for six thousand, rock bottom. However, it does ..." Al cast an appraising glance at the car "...require some work, which I believe I can have completed by tomorrow noon. I can sell this Element to you for $4,500. I estimate the minor repair work will run, oh, $1,500. On a separate bill, of course. Cash."

$6,000 seemed like a fair price. He gave Big Al the $500 he had with him as a deposit. Al shifted his toothpick one more time and disappeared into his office. No paperwork. Had he been taken for five hundred dollars? He looked again at Al. Not likely. Besides, the Element appealed to him.

***

The next morning, Big Al was waiting in his office when Joe arrived, this time by cab. The Element looked pretty much the same as it did when Joe left the day before. The transaction was quickly done, since Al's sales process required little data entry.

Al produced a pair of reading glasses and a battered e-pad.

"Name?"

Joe wished he could use an avatar, but the only real ID he had was his own.

"Joe Mayfield."

Al punched at the keyboard as if it was at fault for his two-finger style. Amazing the e-pad had lasted long enough to look worn.

Joe gave a false address near his parents' old home. Close enough to be explainable as a minor clerical error if the police stopped him, he hoped.

How many laws had he broken by now? A dozen?

Big Al's state-mandated identity check consisted of peering over his glasses at Joe and saying, "Now you sure all this information you gave me is right?"

"It's all okay. And thanks for turning the repairs around so quickly." Joe couldn't keep in a grin. Al pulled a serious face that disintegrated into a smile and then a bellow of a laugh.

"Like the sign says, pilgrim, Everyone Rides at Big Al's."

Al repositioned the toothpick. "Now, you might want to set yourself up in your new vehicle. All the settings are at factory, right now. That's state mandated. That baby's got an old GPS, installed before the privacy laws, so it's assuming it's going to transmit your position continuously to tell your lady friend where you are accurately within five meters at all times. If I'd done that with my first wife, I woulda been shot at least three times. But, read the manual. With that older system, you can turn the GPS off."

Joe knew Al saw relief on his face.

"Also, autodrive is set to 'on.' You should turn it off unless you're on an interstate. The Gen2 autopilot is dicey on the back roads."

Joe nodded and took the obligatory circuit around the car to check it out.

The Element was a small version of the SUVs that were all the rage a couple of decades ago. Boxy, with a lot of space in the back and an efficient gas engine. Like Al said, retrofitted electronics. Tires were in good shape. The rear license plate came with the car. In the front holder, a glossy black plate with a hot pink lettering announced that the former owner was a Devil's Child.

"Gonna hate to see this baby go," Big Al said. "One of the last of the old timers. Not many people are willing to put up with a guzzler anymore. That's why you got such a good deal."

Joe slipped behind the wheel of the Element, and the old thrill of having a car...freedom!...washed over him. The floor mats needed replacing, the upholstery was worn and witness to the prior owner's fast-food consumption habits, but the engine sounded fine. He opened the glove box. The well-thumbed owner's manual said somebody had cared about this car.

Big Al leaned down to the driver's side window, patted the

roof lightly and said, "So's we understand each other, this being a cash deal means this car is sold 'as is' and I do mean 'as is.' " The friendly smile appeared and the toothpick moved again. Joe mumbled his thanks, turned off the autopilot, and drove out of the lot in search of Highway 61.

The automated voice of the car's nav system was pure Louisiana, pure girl. The Devil's Child that owned it before must have synthesized herself. So much for "factory settings."

North of Metairie, Joe pulled into Saint John the Baptist Parish Airport. Several small airplanes and a couple of cars in the parking lot. Nobody seemed interested in him, so he settled down to make some changes to the Element. The Devil's Child plate came off. He shook out the floor mats. He paged through the owner's manual and found out how to shut off the GPS send. Another manual explained how to reset the nav system's voice. The current setting was *BeeBee/CajunUS*. Devil Child must be BeeBee. Joe hesitated. The GPS window offered American English, Spanish, Mandarin and Other vocabularies in standard male and female voices. Downloads were available (ten bucks for a "genuine Elvis" voice).

Over the last two weeks, he'd grown fond of the vocal style of New Orleans, so he left BeeBee alone.

He said to the nav system, "Memphis, Tennessee, via US 61."

"Straight 400 feet," BeeBee said. "Then hang a right, goin' west, then north."

The autopilot wanted to kick in, but Joe kept his hands on the steering wheel, enjoying the feeling of being in control of at least this aspect of his life.

***

A few days after Joe left L'Home Joli, Billie was at her desk, checking off her calendar for the next week. The front door bell jingled. She smiled and stood to greet the visitor. "Welcome to L'Home—"

"Seen this guy before?" The man was round-headed, bald, with small eyes. Billie recognized in his lack of expression the facial scar tissue of a boxer, like her second husband.

Billie's smile faded, and she studied the picture of Joe. "I don't believe I have."

The registration book faced the man, with the last week's guests showing. He reached down to turn the page back. Billie put her hand on the book. "My guest book is not public information." Big Louie's slap came quick and hard, forcing Billie back against the wall. Her eyes hardened even as an involuntary tear ran down her cheek. He flipped the pages and saw Joe Mayfield's entry, put a stubby finger on the name. "Where'd he go?"

Billie curled her lip. "No idea. Just another guest."

He came around the end of the desk, repeated the question, shoulder muscles bunching.

The beaded curtain separating the reception area from Billie's private rooms clicked softly, a barely noticeable susurration. Big Al was there, making the room seem smaller.

"Billie? What's the matter here?"

Louie's lower brain was running way out ahead of his cognitive faculties. As a result, he began to sweat profusely even as his upper brain ticked slowly through the possible outcomes of having just slapped a 6-4, 270-pound man's special friend, who was herself substantial of frame, serious of purpose and reaching into the well of the desk for a heavy blackthorn walking stick.

Big Al smiled and said, "Tell me, pilgrim, are you a nautical man?"

EIGHTEEN

JOE TOOK A COUPLE of days to get from New Orleans to Baton Rouge. He stopped first in a musty but friendly motel in Vacherie. The next night, he stayed in a trailer park near Prairieville and concluded that very young and/or very small people would probably find sleeping in the Element quite comfortable.

On the third day, Joe parked the car under a spreading magnolia tree at a branch of the Baton Rouge library. Thank the lord for the library, he thought. A lot of countries wouldn't let their citizens have free access to books, much less communication tools. Joe ran his hand over the beginnings of a beard. There must be cameras, but do libraries upload their info? Probably so.

He explained to a friendly media technician that he was traveling and realized he had to file tax information for his business. Could he use a terminal with secure access? The tech glanced at his ID. No pass through the scanner. Thank the lord for all those touchy folks that sued everybody in sight over information privacy when the Yak came up to speed.

He signed in as John Maxwell and sent the same note he'd sent Susan Rodriguez, this time to Courtney Gresky. Her score for MOC went from 76 to 52. Signed it RazorBlue.

Smiled his thanks on the way out, trying not to appear furtive. Back in the car.

Drove a couple of blocks before his hands stopped shaking.

In the IAC system, the Revelator noted the hit and bumped up Maxwell's significance.

***

From Baton Rouge, Joe took Highway 61 up to Natchez. He decided to drive along the Natchez Trace, used for millennia by prehistoric peoples, Choctaws, Spanish and French, and finally

Europeans coming down from the Ohio River following the hypotenuse to the Mississippi. Rolling not too fast, struck by the quiet beauty of the Trace. Cynthia's music playing on the Element's sound system. A group from years ago called Canned Heat sang older words from Sippie Wallace:

I'm going up the country, baby don't you wanna go
I'm going up the country, baby don't you wanna go
I'm going to some place where I've never been before.

Pines gave way to hardwoods as he drove north and east toward Jackson to find another safe library. So many species of trees, so many shades of green. Cynthia would have loved the interplay of light and shadow and the varied colors.

Suddenly, he was crying, a hard knot rising in his chest. He turned off the music. Too much Cynthia, too many memories. Sometimes good memories are harder to bear than bad ones.

Jackson was genteel and, as if worried that we might all forget the War Between the States, punctuated with statuary celebrating the fallen heroes of that conflict. There were several nice libraries. Joe picked a smaller branch, signed in as Chester Burnell and sent another warning,

***

The Revelator, interested in the Chester Burnell message — if software can be said to be interested — mapped it to the file holding the four names Joe had added, flagged the odd signature *RazorBlue*, and raised the file's significance two steps.

Weezy had written the original Revelator in her first year at MIT and called it Anomalies R Us. It started as a simple idea: isolate outliers. Most programs searched for events that correlated to each other. But the outliers, the events that most statistical rules jettisoned, were often the most valuable to a tracker. Over time, Weezy amended ARU, and it began to learn on its own. By version ARU.49, its processes had grown so complex they were hard even for Weezy to trace back. Explaining the software to a group of

Senate staffers who had appeared on a facility tour, the IAC's perky press relations person said. "It's like peeling back the layers of an onion." Adam Ambrosio, the newest member of Weezy's team, smirked and said a little too loudly, "Yeah, an onion the size of freakin' Utah."

In recognition that ARU.49 was IAC's most powerful tracking program, the N-Ops crew named it The Revelator after Son House's song *John the Revelator*. For hackers, it was often as apocalyptic as the book of Revelations.

***

Joe made a slow progress through the Delta, where so much of Cynthia's music originated. He found a small motel in Cleveland, Mississippi, near Clarksdale. The proprietor, Mase Jarvis ("like the jar"), had the soft diction and slow cadence of his birthplace, and had honed both over the years to draw listeners like Joe into the thread of his stories. Over the next few days, Joe heard about the Delta, the sharecroppers, the juke joints, the exodus to jobs up North, and the real story of Bessie Smith's tragic accident not far from Cleveland.

"They say Bessie died because the white hospital in Clarksdale wouldn't take her, but that's not right at all. Perfec'ly good black hospital in Clarksdale. But it took a while to get in touch with the funeral parlor, get the hearse to come out." Mase paused, assembling his words, "See, they didn't send no ambulance to get a colored person in those days. Just a hearse so they wouldn't have to make two trips if the person happened to die on the way to the hospital."

Joe followed directions to Robert Johnson's third and final grave, over near Greenwood, and to Mississippi John Hurt's family graveyard, in a silent grotto where the hills began to rise toward the Piedmont. In the evenings, he went into Clarksdale where the blues music Cynthia loved was still played.

***

There's a certain point when relaxation becomes evasion. Joe began to feel like a man who ordered one drink too many and belatedly realized it. He'd have been only too happy to listen to Mase painting the story of times past for a lot longer but realized he had to play out his own story.

He packed up his kit, said goodbye, and drove up through Clarksdale. Another stop, another library, another warning. Not nearly as nervous that time.

Then toward Tunica. A century or more ago, the town had been an important cotton port on the Mississippi and therefore a place where many of the bluesmen congregated. When the channel silted up, the economy went bad and people left for the North. By the 1960s Tunica was the poorest county in the United States. The solution of the local powers was to encourage casino gambling. Tunica became the third largest gaming location in the country.

"Great big jook joint in the honky-tonk of life," was how Mase described it. Joe still wasn't prepared for the colossus of pink, orange, aquamarine and neon that rose like a malignant growth from the verdant green of the winter wheat and young cotton plants sprouting from the black Delta soil. It was easy to get a room without any ID. Apparently, a lot of people liked to gamble without identifying themselves.

In a small but fully equipped library, no doubt purchased with gambling revenue, Joe sent his last notes from RazorBlue to Rachel Phillips and Jonas Stritch.

In Orlando, Jonas saw the note, glanced around his work area in the repair bay, and keyed his e-pad.

I have contact with RazorBlue.

In Bethesda, Revelator associated RazorBlue with the avatars, conducted a discriminant analysis. It followed up with a Markov process and dumped the file into the "likely" bucket, one step below a full analysis.

***

Nearer Memphis, catfish ponds that had taken over cotton fields a generation ago were being converted to fields of solar energy cells that rose a few feet above the ground like leafless crops.

Finished. No more names, Joe thought, and pretty near finished with the Delta, too. What next? Not much I can do, except go back to being normal. Get a job.

He passed around Memphis. He would have liked to go into the city, but it was too risky, too connected. Instead, he found a motel perched on the fringe of New Madrid, Missouri, where he spent a couple of days watching TV and feeling depressed.

He had gotten used to bad beds, tired furniture, musty linens. Down-and-out places barely getting by, manned by down-and-out people. Drive on to another nameless place, or sit on the broken chair in the cheerless room and think? Listen to Cynthia's music until it hurt too much? Constant boredom punctuated by the crossroads question. Like one of those old records that got stuck in a groove and would repeat, repeat, repeat. Same question, "What should I do? What should I do? What should I do?"

Joe's practical side said he should trade what he had for a clean bill of corporate health. His résumé listed only one employer, who wouldn't say anything good about him. A call to Milt...no, Frank Hoskins...laying out the fraud, attaching the picture of Joe in his bloody shirt? Followed by an agreement to let the matter drop in exchange for a glowing recommendation when and if some prospective employer called? Maybe he should be realistic. Get what he could. He wrote the note a dozen times in his mind, then mentally crumpled it up and threw it away. Backing down would pollute every memory of Cynthia. She would understand, and he imagined the "love you no matter what" look in her eyes. His sanity couldn't afford that.

Joe thought through his options. The "whistleblower to the

FBI" option would have made most sense before Snake and Big Louie, but that option might lead to arrest and a dead end, particularly if they think he stole from the company. The "more research" option was appealing. Get Sarcosy back into the FCE system, find more names, make the case stronger. In the end, he realized the idea was an accountant's excuse for inaction. The option he finally chose had been running through his head for quite a while: the public Internet. There's a whole world out there. Set up a website and put the warning out there, like bait. See if anyone bites. Who knows? If a lot of other people were affected, he might build a case that way.

He drove into New Madrid. Near the historic riverfront, he found Zap-O Technology Services and Supplies. He inspected several e-pads before choosing one. The woman who sold it to him wore three carefully delineated colors of eye makeup and had a tattoo of a dancing lady on her wrist. She eyeballed the cash Joe offered, exhaled, and popped her gum. "Hold on," she said, and turned toward the back of the store. "Jerome, can you do a cash transaction for me? This guy needs change." The woman looked Joe up and down as if to assess whether he might be an alien. A door slammed in the back, and Jerome (must be Jerome) shuffled toward the counter. "Whatcha need?"

"Uhh. Change. Twenty-three dollars and fifty cents."

Jerome dug into a bank deposit bag. "Nope, only twenties."

"Why don't you give me a twenty," Joe said. "Maybe you can answer a couple of questions for me." Eyeliner controlled her eye-roll nicely. She was ten years or so younger than Joe, but she clearly considered him a geezer. Jerome handed him the twenty and looked at Joe expectantly. "Questions?"

"I'm replacing an old e-pad. If I go on the Internet, will the new e-pad show up as different from the old one?" Eyeliner smirked. She apparently had a pretty good idea what Joe planned to do on the Net when his old lady was away.

Jerome took the question head-on. "Probably not. You're really much more identifiable by where you go...what Net addresses...than what machine you use. The only issue is practically all shopping websites want to put small trackers on your machine. Used to call 'em cookies, now they're often crackers, which grab a lot more personal information than the original cookie. Crackers are technically illegal, but there are a lot of 'em out there. You can prevent those bits of code from entering, but you have to know what you're doing."

It was absolutely clear to Jerome and Eyeliner that Joe had no idea what he was doing. As a result, Joe ended up with a piece of software (an additional $100) that purported to prevent such crackers and cookies from ending up in his data.

He retreated to his motel, found its Wi-Fi link, began researching how to make an old-fashioned website, and reserved *RazorBlue.net*

NINETEEN

AFTER NEW MADRID, JOE passed up through Iowa and into Minnesota. He spent the evenings building a website, enjoying the challenge and the busy work. When he finished, he activated the site. After a couple of days, there had been a dozen hits, all promotions for services he might need as a webmaster. On the third day, he decided to prod his Florida Consolidated names, hoping to bring eyes to the site. In the library at Fergus Falls, he entered the Yak with Sarcosy and sent a brief message to each:

Check out RazorBlue.net.

One of them saw the note four minutes after Joe sent it and forwarded it to Tom Shenko. The note produced a soft chime in three other places: Tosheka Jackson's office, Henry Barber's computer, and the Backburner file at Weezy's workstation.

Weezy was busy with a rash of hits from the Far East. She saw the reference from Revelator and put the file on her e-pad for later. This Mayfield wasn't trying to do anything destructive as far as she could tell, but *RazorBlue.net* concerned her. Wingnuts often jump on the web when they can no longer contain the truth and beauty they have concocted. At home, she took her e-pad and a cup of tea to her overstuffed chair, sat, and began to read the website.

***

The next morning was muggy and warm in Bethesda, not unusual for June, and Weezy was still sweating from the ride into work.

Adam Ambrosio passed by her station and said, "Did you see Revelator's latest catch? It'll only —"

Weezy held up a finger. "Hold on." She was concentrating on a hapless dude trying to penetrate the Yak through a backdoor called California Occult Science Institute, which she had discovered a while ago and left open. In her weekly report, she called it a "dumbass weir," getting a chuckle from her boss, P.E. Smith, and a surreptitious dictionary search for "weir" from the N-Ops' director.

Finished with the dude on monitor four, she sat back and stretched. The powerful voice of Son House, singing the first line of his song "John the Revelator" issued from monitor three, a reminder. Adam was still waiting on the other side of her monitors.

"Yeah?"

"Revelator? It'll only talk to you."

She tapped monitor three.

From: Revelator to L. Napolitani

Subject: Repeating intrusion to medical records of Florida Consolidated Energy (FCE); RazorBlue.

I am tracking five persons; entry attempts from multiple places, similar targets at Florida Consolidated Energy. Only one, Joe Embry Mayfield, is certified. The others may be avatars. They are: Nicolas Sarcosy, John Maxwell, Chester Burnell and Stevie Ray Morse. Over the last six weeks, the potential avatars have hit FCE personnel records in the sequence Sarcosy, Maxwell, Burnell, Morse. There is a connection to the term RazorBlue. The calls originate over a route beginning in New Orleans, proceeding regularly up US Hwy 61. Last contact June 12, Fergus Falls, MN. There is no apparent significance to the choice of route, except that three of the names may be loosely related to 20th C. blues musicians, and the route they are following northward on US Hwy 61 is called the Blues Highway.

"Anything interesting?" Adam was hovering. As the newest member of the OddBalls, he was always looking for opportunities to impress Weezy.

"Strange, probably an artifact," Weezy said.

The Revelator's report continued, giving statistical backing for its conclusions. Weezy scanned the data, recognizing the misspelling of Sarcosy as a common cloaking trick. Somebody had been to basic hacker school.

"I'll check this out." Adam looked disappointed but said "Okay. If you need help …"

After Adam had gone off toward the break room, she said to the monitor, "Pull Florida Consolidated Energy."

The public web page came up. "Energy of Today, Building for Tomorrow." Offshore windmills. Solar panels. Hot springs in Hungary.

She tapped a finger on the desktop, thinking. "Personnel Yak, Florida Consolidated Energy."

Warnings appeared: *individual records are private, protected by federal law.* Weezy put her thumb on a panel next to her display and spoke the daily code.

FCE's system came up on monitor two. She began crawling through the data. Looking for bots and traps, pretty much like playing the video games she loved as a kid. Down corridors and alleyways, but no ogres with scimitars at the end. Good security around the personnel records area. She searched on the five names. Two came up, Mayfield and John Maxwell, who had left the company and was working in Atlanta.

"Pull Mayfield...umm, Joseph." Mayfield, Joseph Embry popped up on the screen, listed as terminated and with his Network ID blocked. Weezy knocked around FCE's system and found that they were using commercial software designed to provide "gold standard" security. She said, "Download Screwdriver." Just like a screwdriver pops the lid on a can of paint, Weezy's application opened the software protecting the personnel system.

MAYFIELD, Joseph Embry

Born in northern Illinois. Family moved near Tallahassee when he was a teen. Excellent test scores, academic honors in high school. Florida Northeastern University. Academic honors again. Accountant. Hired as trainee out of college. Good to excellent reviews. Promotion to Treasury. Work plan for upcoming review cycle filed December 11 last year. Terminated.

Curious, she did a background search. Apartment in Winter Park, Florida. Link to Cynthia Chin Mayfield...enthusiastic review of Cynthia's work at an Orlando art show. Advertisements for galleries in Key West, Santa Monica and Provincetown. Cynthia recently deceased.

A series of pictures showed Mayfield smiling for his ID photo. Serious in a group picture. Relaxed and happy at an art show, smiling at a beautiful Asian woman. Cynthia? Probably, given the look in his eyes. Finishing a 10k. Posing in a football uniform in high school. A big man, not scary big. Probably six feet. Strong features, leaning toward handsome. Dark hair. Looked fit, but not aggressively so.

Intrigued, she sent the Revelator material and the entries in Backburner to a project file she labeled "MedRecord."

She flipped back to Mayfield's personnel record. A bright man with what appeared to be a flawless work record lost his wife so young, then they fired him? Suspicious, she switched to detail view and saw a string of code lying in wait for Nicolas Sarcosy. A trapping function. So there is a connection, she thought. Somebody's up to something, and somebody at FCE knows it. Bet they don't know what, though. That's why they're trying to ambush Nicolas.

Then, right below the trapping function, an innocuous housekeeping code attaching a file designed to collect certain documents — office equipment return forms and such. The file was locked. It took Weezy three minutes to break the simple code. Sure enough, a portal with a hexadecimal identifier. She punched on it, and the system reported, "This series is reserved by Federal Bureau of Investigation."

So somebody was up to something, somebody at Florida Consolidated knew it, and the FBI wondered why.

***

"P.E., have you got a minute?" Weezy leaned against the doorjamb of her boss's office. P.E. looked up from her monitor. She seemed irritated at being disturbed, but said, "Sure, but I have a meeting with the Director in fifteen minutes, so you'll have to be quick."

P.E. was tall and substantial, gray hairs appearing in her black curls over the past couple of years. She wore purple that day and, as always, pearls. She had worked in the Social Security Administration before it was downsized, and before that she was with the FBI for a decade. She was the first black woman to become a director at IAC. She didn't understand the technology of the Yak in depth, but she knew the internal and external pressures of the big bureaucracy, and she managed to insulate her employees from them much of the time. Everyone respected that and valued her leadership, so much so that nobody, but nobody, called her by her given name, Priscilla.

"P.E., I'm following an interesting intrusion. I'm not sure what it is. There's not much danger of it causing a problem for us, but it's possible this hacker is after someone who has already breeched the system. I can see what he's doing, and I can speculate why, but the whole thing is...strange." P.E. nodded for Weezy to continue. "He's not trying to do anything obvious, like stealing money or military secrets. I've been tracking him for over a week. Then, yesterday Revelator suggested a strong association with a website that went live not long ago. I think the author of the website is the same person who's been hacking us."

"Good. Send his info off to Enforcement." P.E turned back toward her monitor.

"But, if we grab him," Weezy said, "we may miss the real problem. When I saw that a website had gone up, I thought 'Oh, good, another wingnut.' I was expecting the standard riff...you know, innuendo and a few mutilated facts blossoming into a conspiracy theory. But his story is straightforward and might mean there's something bad going on in our MedRecords database. I'll send you his web site, but I don't want to pull the trigger on Enforcement yet."

***

Over the next two days, Weezy waited. Revelator added nothing on RazorBlue. On the third day, she was again at P.E's door, fidgeting.

"I need a chit to go find this MedRecord hacker and figure out whether there's a real threat or not."

"Louise, you've surely heard of the dog who chases the car until he catches it." Weezy nodded, steeling herself for a lecture. P.E. continued, "What will you do when you find him? Are you going to put your teeth into his tire and get spun around? What if he's violent? Are you going to bring him to justice, all hundred pounds of you? Why not identify the threat and let law enforcement take over?"

"Well, actually I'm 114, and I don't think he's breaking any law, except hacking IAC. And we know how ugly it sometimes gets when we prosecute and the press gets ahold of a sympathetic story. I have a feeling he's trying ineffectively to right a wrong rather than do something nasty." She paused, then added, "If anything, he's violating some corporate laws or agreements he has with his former employer."

"So, let the company know and let them solve it."

"That would be okay normally, but it's at least possible that the real damage to the IAC is being perpetrated by the company itself."

"And you are so persuasive, so empathetic...Don't worry, I've heard the 'dumbass' comments...You're going to get this man to sit down and spill his guts. Have I got that right?"

Weezy flashed P.E. a toothy grin and said, "Yeah, boss."

TWENTY

JOE LEFT FERGUS FALLS feeling lighter. Be it ever so insubstantial, RazorBlue.net was out there, carrying his story. He skirted Fargo and turned west, moving toward the Missouri River and Lewis and Clark country.

A couple of days later, he approached Underhill, North Dakota. It had been a long day, keeping an eye on the rearview, wondering if he was registering on the grid as he passed through each little farming town, watching for a black SUV.

A weathered billboard five miles out proudly announced "Near Lake Morain and the Missouri River, great hunting and fishing. A small community with a big heart." The sign at the edge of town said Population 840 and was buckshot-riddled, as if to reinforce the claim of good hunting.

The old motel clung to the small business district, across from gas pumps at the SuperShop. The person who rose grudgingly from the chair behind the counter didn't bat an eye when Joe paid cash. The town's diner, two blocks down, closed at 7 p.m., so he went back to the SuperShop and bought a bottle of beer and what aspired to be a sandwich.

Back in his room, he slanted the blinds upward to shut out the view from the parking lot. He opened Lucky Monkey's box and set him on the bedside table with his e-pad. It had become a ritual, one he reminded himself was foolish superstition. But still, Lucky Monkey was a little bit of Cynthia keeping him company. Who knew, maybe protecting him.

The old bed groaned as he sat down. He unwrapped the sandwich, twisted the cap off the beer. Another night of boredom overlaid with fear and the gnawing grief of having lost Cynthia.

He took a bite of the sandwich, staring at the monkey. He had done what he could to warn the people who might be hurt by this thing. He took a long pull on the beer. Really, nothing left to do...but what? Oregon? California? He couldn't go back to Orlando, with Snake and Big Louie waiting to finish him. He couldn't keep driving aimlessly for the rest of his life. Couldn't start a new life without crawling back on the grid with the other 99.9 percent of the world.

The beer released some of the day's tension, and Joe leaned back on the headboard, tracing the brown watermarks on the ceiling tile.

Several hours later, he woke, stiff and shaking off the shards of a bittersweet dream, remembering where he was. Small town. Old motel. North Dakota. Moisture puddled around the warm, half-full beer bottle on the bedside table next to the unfinished sandwich.

Yawning, he undressed and lay down on the lumpy bed. The pink wash of the SuperShop's neon sign, refracted through the sagging venetian blind, flashed *Open Open Open,* even though it hadn't been open since 9:30. He tried to go to sleep, but Cynthia's favorite songs kept playing in his mind, blues of pain and suffering, lost love. His blues.

In the halfway state between sleep and awareness, he reached out to touch her and startled awake. She wasn't there, wouldn't be there, ever. He tried to go to sleep again, but she was too much with him. When you lose someone you love, it's little things that come wandering. Remembered habits. Gestures. The way the corners of her mouth curled up right at the beginning of a smile. The texture of the soft skin on the inside of her thigh. The smell of her hair.

The sign asked *What if? What if? What if?*

***

Joe startled awake from a dream that had him moving toward a goal that was never quite clear. Dishwater light filtered in through the blinds. It was still early.

He showered, then shaved, feeling strange staring at himself. The man in the mirror looked the same as he always had. But the person riding around in this body was smaller now, drier and sad.

Joe packed his gear, bent down a slat of the blind to check outside. Nothing. He walked quickly to the old Element, got in, and turned out of the parking lot toward the town center. It was nearly empty, sucked dry by the pull on its young people of big cities, bright lights, good jobs. The town surely remembered the days of wagons jammed up on Saturday, bringing vegetables to market and crops to the elevator, the farmers buying hardware and shots of whiskey and bolt cloth for the missus. The weathered boards of the storefronts bore witness to long service. Now there were only faded ads in the windows and handwritten signs offering poultry feed and antifreeze. Across the street from the motel, there had probably been a stable and a blacksmith, which would have been the site of a substantial part of the political discourse in the county. Now the space was occupied by the bright, plastic façade of the SuperShop camouflaging a cinder block box filled with fast food, stale coffee and impersonal good cheer.

As he passed down Main Street, Joe saw a waitress in the window of the diner and had a sharp pang of wanting to talk with her, with someone, anyone.

Joe wheeled into a slant parking space. You can't be careful all the time or you go insane, right?

The diner door complained about its years of use as he pushed it. He stepped into warmth, the smell of bacon and coffee, people talking weather and crop prices. This place took breakfast seriously. An older man stood and hitched the galluses of his bib overalls and said, "Gettin' late." Joe glanced at his watch. 7:30.

The waitress smiled a welcome, a lock of hair loose from its clip. He picked a booth on the window side, in the sun. She followed him and said, "What can I get you?" Friendly but efficient.

He considered the menu. "Umm. The American breakfast, eggs over medium, toast, hold the potatoes, please. Coffee." He ordered slowly, wanting to prolong the contact, but knowing that he shouldn't become easy to remember.

The waitress smiled in a way that could almost be an invitation. "Comin' right up."

An old couple in the booth across from him were having a quiet conversation. The woman was telling a story, touched the man's arm across the table, gently. They both chuckled, and Joe saw the recognition of bygone passion in their glance. What would Cynthia have looked like at that woman's age? Where would the wrinkles have creased her skin? Would she reach to touch him, too?

The waitress brought breakfast. "More coffee, hon?"

Joe smiled at her, seeing the soft contours, the subtle promise of pleasure.

"Yes. Sure. Great."

She poured. A half-smile.

The older couple left, the man holding the door for a young woman in baggy shorts, a T-shirt with an MIT logo, a tangle of chestnut hair.

MIT? In Underhill?

***

Mayfield had been pretty easy to find. Burger Heaven's data stream put him near Fargo day before yesterday. Then the SuperShop in Underhill picked up a dark-colored Element with a Louisiana plate last night. Small town, one main drag, Louisiana license might as well have been flashing neon.

Weezy plopped into the booth.

"So you're the dumbass."

He gaped at her. She got a frisson of pleasure from the way he put down his fork and said, "Pardon me?"

She picked up a menu and pretended to concentrate. Let him stew in his juices. Then back to him and said, "Joe, I've been tracking you since New Orleans."

That shocked him. Good.

"You should have stayed away from Burger Heaven. It's a national chain, you know. Streaming data."

It was kind of fun watching him try to control his expression.

"Then this RazorBlue thing you're doing on the Net. Really! Besides, driving an old guzzler with a Louisiana plate in North Dakota? I suppose you might have been easier to spot if you had a tractor with wings, but not much."

She told him part of what she knew, trying to put a layer of intimidation under a friendly, feisty surface. Shake him loose. Get him to tell his story.

It didn't work.

He leaned forward, eyes hard and angry. "My wife's dead." There was a hitch in his throat. "My life's gone to hell." She saw pain and loneliness in his eyes. "Ever wondered what to do with the rest of your life when most of what you care about is taken away?"

He shoved up from the booth.

"I will leave you now to enjoy your breakfast."

Suddenly, she was on the defensive. "Well, you did hack the Yak," she said to his back. His shoulders flexed, and she said more softly, "Sorry about your wife."

He turned back toward her, looking furious. He leaned down, face close to hers and said through clenched teeth, "You're sorry about my wife? My wife! Listen, you tell Florida Consolidated—" She shook her head No. "— They can think whatever they want, but you bastards killed my beautiful Cynthia." His tears began to flow, changing the calculus of the situation.

He drew a breath.

She tried to stop him, wanting to apologize. But Mayfield was on his way out, tossing money on the counter.

He got into the Element and drove off. She had a sinking feeling that maybe this project was a mistake. This was not some self-absorbed hacker. This was a man in pain, maybe dangerous, maybe in danger.

The waitress brought breakfast, setting it in front of her too firmly.

"The guy paid," she said, not waiting for a response.

Weezy ate, not enjoying the breakfast she had looked forward to. Finally, she pulled out an e-pad, inspected a map of the area, then tapped out a message. One more try.

TWENTY-ONE

IN ORLANDO, MILT JAMES paced the fifteen feet from window to office door, door to window, window to door. All that money...his money...locked up in an offshore bank with Tosheka Jackson watching it.

He shouldn't have left it all in the account in Barbados. Seemed sensible at the time. Dump Rosalyn for Gloria, keep the cash off the personal balance sheet, away from Rosalyn's lawyer.

How did he know Gloria expected cash and the high life but was not ready for eternal devotion? Or Rosalyn would find out about Gloria and extract a complete makeover of the kitchen, as well as of a couple of her body parts?

Milt gnawed a thumbnail. He turned back to the view of I-4 out his window, staring but not seeing, thinking.

Slow down. Jackson isn't holding all the cards. She had been pretty intimidating a couple of months ago, but she's got problems, too. Otherwise, she would have turned the avatar thing over to that FBI agent, Barber. She could have turned me over, for that matter. But she didn't. Then Raskin drowned. Might be an accident, or...maybe?

He said to his console, "Tosheka Jackson. Give me voice message." A pause. The friendly synthesized voice intimated that Ms. Jackson might be available for a voice conference. Did Mr. James wish to connect? "No. Voice message."

After the pip, he said, "Tosheka, I may have some new information about the Mayfield issue."

That ought to pique her interest.

***

Tosheka tapped a pencil on her desk, thinking.

No call from Zimmerman, no report from Big Louie, who was

somewhere in the Deep South on her ticket. Henry Barber evasive about the Raskin case, which they should have tied up by now. Sarcosy just tried to enter the system. Loose ends all over the place. And now, this message from Milt James. What was that about?

The facts and events and loose ends wound tighter and tighter. She took a deep breath, held it, let it out, held it. Square breathing, a technique for centering, for relaxation.

It didn't work.

This was supposed to be a straightforward insertion. Two years at most, Squitieri said, then on to the next client. Watch over the process. "Tweak it if necessary," he said. It sounded so simple, like it had been for the first couple of companies. Nobody saw any problems, the program went in and did its business, and she moved on to the next assignment. And for that, $200k for each successful startup on top of a decent salary. Then, Florida Consolidated.

Well, this tweak was getting pretty involved. An accountant from Treasury managed to evade her high-priced team and was apparently not going away quietly. Half the team spent a week recovering from multiple contusions in New Orleans, and the other half was busy at his day job. The Director of Human Resource Services was...tweaked. Now, she got an imperious-sounding message from Milt James.

She keyed her e-pad. Milt answered, "James here." He switched to video but continued a conversation with someone out of view, giving instructions. Why didn't he let it roll? Ah, yes. He was reminding her that he was important.

"Milt, if you need to get back to me, I'll be in most of the afternoon."

"No, no. Almost finished here." He turned toward the person on the other side of the desk. "Maggie, go ahead and do 30/30/40." He waited until Maggie left, then turned back to talk to Tosheka and found her eyeing him coolly.

"I need an update on the Mayfield issue," Milt said. "Can we meet?"

***

Tosheka strode across the open area toward Milt's office. Milt watched her through the glass partition. Gorgeous, no other word for it. She entered, remained standing. Formal. No trace of camaraderie. No trace of respect. "You wanted to see me?"

"Ahh, yes. Close the door, will you?"

She wore the usual conservative skirt but a silk blouse, light and supple enough to outline perfect breasts.

"I wanted to discuss the issue of the transfers to Resolution Enterprises."

Tosheka half smiled and shook her head. "You mean, you're wondering why I didn't explain what I know to the FBI and let them work out the rest of the story?"

Milt put on a serious demeanor.

"No, Ms. Jackson—Tosheka. I want to offer what I believe will be a mutually beneficial solution to a problem I am quite sure you want to make go away. It seems to me you're facing far more serious issues than a relatively small amount of missing cash."

"Milt, a million and a half is not a small amount."

Now, she's negotiating, he thought.

"Uh-huh." He smiled and let his gaze move over her body. "Tosheka, I move $130 million through Treasury each day. We're talking rounding error, practically."

"Look, Milt, it's pretty obvious how the money got stolen, and it's pretty obvious who did it. I'm willing to let it lie for the moment, but don't think that it won't come roaring back to bite you if it you step out of line."

Milt half stood, leaned forward over his desk.

"Alright, Tosheka, I'd rather not to have to play hardball with you, but look at the facts. I have a rogue employee, possibly stealing using a fake IAC person pretty clearly created by a mousy but intelligent treasury clerk. You discover the rogue employee's trying to get into medical records in violation of company policy." He paused, waiting for a nod of agreement that never came. "Instead of going to Personnel to have Mayfield disciplined, or going to the police to track down the missing cash, you bring in some outside security force to manhandle Mayfield out of here. Subsequently, he disappears...to where, we don't know. Pretty suspicious, I'd say." A knowing grin. "The head of Personnel raises a stink...yes, practically everyone in the company knows about that meeting...and she conveniently drowns in the nice, warm water of a swimming pool she's been using for a decade. I think the person who has to worry is you."

Tosheka stared at Milt, lips tight together, her face a mask. Then she broke eye contact, seeming to deflate, to soften.

"Milt, I...I probably made some mistakes. This is a pretty unusual situation. I would do anything to tie up the loose ends in this case and move beyond it. I'm sure we can reach an agreement that would make the Resolution Enterprises issues go away. After all, what's done is done. I'm not anxious to pursue it."

Surprised at the sudden thaw, sensing victory, Milt pounced.

"So, Resolution is going to go away?"

She shrugged. "I can put the FBI off the scent by saying that we found out the Resolution payment is okay...I'm sure you can provide me with a robust, believable story."

She looked up at Milt with a soft half-smile. She had never smiled at him that way before.

"I can do that," Milt said, wondering why the sudden change of heart.

Businesslike again, Tosheka said, "This has to be entirely off the grid. No calls, no e-notes. Oh, and Milt?" A half smile. "Twenty percent."

"Twenty percent?"

Tosheka let the smile turn coquettish, something Milt had

never seen or imagined from her. "Twenty percent of the $1,563,289 in that Barbados account." She leaned across his desk, picked up his e-pad, and tapped a series of numbers. "I've given you transfer instructions. Assuming I see the wire go through tomorrow, I'll talk with the FBI. Then, why don't we meet to celebrate?"

What was she saying? Could it be?

"You reserve a room at the Bohemian and bring a bottle of Champagne, and I'll bring...well, I'll bring myself."

***

Tosheka sighed.

Milt leaned over his desk toward her, saying, "...I'd rather not to have to play hardball with you, but look at the facts."

His eyes flicked from her face, to her breasts, to her face, back to her breasts, diluting what he surely thought was a stern, businesslike manner.

She half listened. First it was Raskin, then Mayfield refused to go away, and now this buffoon. Loose ends.

Then he delivered the threat.

She fixed her eyes on the floor, relaxed her shoulders. Then raised her eyes to his.

"Milt, I...I probably made some mistakes."

He was surprised but not shocked by her apparent change in personality. Of course, she thought, he thinks he's intimidated me. She laid out the plan.

" Oh, and Milt? Twenty percent." Then he *was* shocked. Fortunately, he got the wrong impression. He thought she was a scheming, greedy woman. Good.

She gave him the wire instructions, then the offer. He was gaping like a fish out of water. Couldn't believe his good fortune. He actually thought she'd fuck him for $300 k. Of course, she would. Almost.

***

Tosheka found that she liked being a whore. Maybe it was because she was fulfilling her mother's worst fears.

Her father had been an Army staff sergeant. He ran his family like his platoon, with precision and discipline. By the time Tosheka was born, her father's rigidity had worn its way through her mother's personality and driven the poor woman to religion. Being born beautiful was a burden, making Tosheka's father suspicious and her mother critical. "Don't you be walkin' out this house lookin' like a whore," her mother would say whenever Tosheka wore anything nice.

As she entered the Bohemian to meet Milt, she knew she was a moving violation from her head down to her bright red toes. Her short hair was concealed under a cascading wig. The red button-front dress showcased her figure, its short skirt and the high heels conspiring to prove to the world that strong legs can be beautiful. Big dark glasses covered the high cheekbones, but really, there was so much to take in, what man was going to remember details? And the women, well the women were going to be blind jealous.

The lobby went stop-action as she passed through to the elevators carrying a bag from Neiman Marcus. No one had the temerity to stop her. On the way up to the 12th floor, she put the wig into the shopping bag, which held a small leather kit, the tiny lavender teddy she had purchased in the "sexy little things" section of NightTime Online a while ago and the bondage appurtenances overnighted from Foxy.com.

She knocked softly, and the door opened immediately. Milt managed to look both nervous and expectant.

He wore a linen shirt, slacks and expensive loafers. She said, "I see you brought the Champagne."

Milt closed the door. "And did you see the transfer?"

"Yes, I saw it. I had a conversation with Henry Barber. I'm pretty sure he will close out the case for the FBI. I wrote an e-note to my file that will close it as far as Florida Consolidated is concerned. You probably saw the copy."

Milt smiled. "Indeed I did. So there's good reason for celebration." He popped the cork and poured.

She smiled and began to unbutton her dress. The poor chump. Get this over with.

Milt was suddenly on her, caressing, poking, pinching, moaning.

She disengaged firmly, saying, "My, my, my. Just give this lady a couple of minutes to get ready, big boy."

Before he could answer, she stepped into the bathroom with her bag

Slipping into the teddy, she ran her hands down the silky material, seeing her reflection in the mirror, steeling herself. At least he'd be happy.

She prepared the needle, palmed it as she picked up the ropes and scarves.

"Milton James, I hear you have been a bad man." She cracked the door open.

Milt stood next to the bed, pants off, shorts and shirt still on, looking unsure of himself.

"Huh?"

"A very, very bad man."

To Tosheka's great relief, Milt had apparently been through this drill before.

"So, who's saying I've been a bad man?"

"I'm saying."

"And what're you going to do about it?"

The tent in his shorts said he had a pretty good idea.

"You need to be punished for being a bad man, Milton."

"Milt. Call me Milt, not Milton." He *had* been through this before.

She crossed the room, putting a hand to his chest.

"Down!"

She knelt, in one motion pushing him to the bed with one hand and putting the hypo on the floor with the other.

She brought his left hand to her breast while securing his wrist with a silken rope. He moaned.

When she had him undressed, spread-eagled, tied down four ways, she stepped back.

She brought the teddy over her head.

Milt's eyes widened. "My god. Beautiful. You are the most beautiful woman…"

"Do you want me?"

"Yes, oh Yes, oh Yes."

She went to the bed and knelt to kiss his midsection lingeringly while picking up the syringe.

Then she was on top of him, straddling a leg. She slowly ground on his hipbone and found her own breathing quickening. Moistness. Pleasure. *Yes*.

"Milton?"

"I said, call me Milt."

"Milton, do you know what we do with pricks like you?"

She leaned down and across him, her perfect breast cutting a sensual furrow across his cheek.

His voice rose half an octave. "No, what do we do?"

She plunged the needle into his shoulder.

"Ow."

"We eliminate them."

***

Jennifer Rowland trotted toward Henry Barber's desk.

"Henry, have you seen the news feed today?"

"Yes, I have. Not much interesting, except the possibility of a new soccer team."

"Didn't you see the clip about the guy from Florida Consolidated?"

"No. What guy?"

Jennifer came to his side of the desk, leaned over to view the screen. When she concentrated, she squinched up her face. Red headed. Delicate skin. She would have wrinkles by the time she was thirty if she kept on doing that. He wondered if there was a nice way to tell her.

"Your feed should be picking that up. We need to go over your keys later." Whatever that meant.

"Anyway, Milt James, the guy you talked with from Florida Consolidated Energy, was found dead in the Bohemian early this morning. The media are keeping a lid on it to some degree, but the news sharks are bound to blow it all over the Net soon. He was...uhh...naked, tied to the bed, apparently died of a heart attack. The desk clerk remembers a young woman going through the lobby last evening, probably not one of the registered guests."

"There's a lobby video. Here, I can show you."

Her fingers flew over the keys of his console. On his monitor, they watched a beautiful woman walk across the lobby of the hotel. Probably even better in the flesh, judging from the slack-jawed expressions on the faces of the bellhop and several of the clientele. Long hair...might be a wig...mocha complexion, large dark glasses, even though it was past sunset. High-class ladies of the evening probably don't want to be recognized.

Jennifer said, "Find similar."

The system searched briefly, then a new video came up. Same woman, passing through the lobby, half an hour after entering.

"James is the same man you were watching in that funds transfer case at Florida Consolidated. He is...was...Joe Mayfield's boss. You asked me to keep an eye on that account, the one in Barbados that was the final home of the money after it passed through the intermediate accounts. There was no in or out activity over the weeks since we set it up, so I wasn't watching it carefully. When I saw this clip, I checked the account. Yesterday, there was a wire to a bank on Nevis. We'll never get the name on the Nevis account, even with a court order, but I tagged it in case someone we can identify draws on it."

"Seems like a lot went on yesterday," Henry said. "I got a call from the director of security over at Florida Consolidated ..." Gorgeous legs, short hair but the same mocha complexion "... with what seemed like a good explanation for the Resolution Enterprises charges. A miscoded vendor account. Plausible, except it's odd that a small business from Ocoee would be transferring its money offshore through dummy accounts. Somebody who knows the banking system pretty well set it up. Maybe they thought or hoped we wouldn't catch that odd twist."

Henry thought back to the strange meeting in April. James was there, the treasury analyst and Tosheka Jackson. He remembered sensing that the analyst was innocent and wondering at James' bluster, always a telltale for misdirection. And Jackson's formal, closed demeanor. But there was something...

"Jennifer, I need your opinion. I'm going to call this Tosheka Jackson. I'd like you to watch the conversation from your monitor. But first, rerun the lobby tape a couple of times. Also, I need to get in touch with Ashley Parry. I'd like her to look at Mr. James' body."

TWENTY-TWO

WEEZY SPENT MOST OF the trip from North Dakota to Bethesda running the Mayfield story through her mental algorithms. Seventy percent likely there's something to his story, she concluded as the plane touched down.

Getting off the plane injected her back into the Metroplex, people hurrying, pushing. An autocab took her home.

Her apartment—rooms, really—used to be the carriage house for a lovely old home three miles from the sprawling NIH complex. The IAC offices were tucked in a corner of the campus, if five hundred people can be said to be tucked away. She was grateful to have found such a perfect location and such a perfect landlady, although she would never dare call Vivienne Beaumont Janssen "landlady" to her face.

Weezy let herself in, tossed her bag on the couch and let out Sappho the cat, who stalked off into the underbrush on an urgent feline errand. She started up Joe's e-pad and said to it, "Open Net, Olegarten Fabricating."

There was a knock at the door, which opened before any response from Weezy.

"Louise, dear, you're back! How was your trip? You must tell me all about it."

Weezy sighed. She wanted to be alone, but there was no putting off Bo's combination of life force and inquisitiveness. She was tall, slender and silver-haired, always beautifully dressed for the part she played so well, that of aristocratic intellectual.

"Where did you go? Was it exciting? Who did you meet? Any eligible men your age? Any eligible men *my* age?"

"IAC business. To North Dakota, no less. Flat, quiet and without social amenities. I did meet a man, but he's not eligible right now for anything but arrest under federal hacking statutes. Had a great piece of apple pie at a diner that must have been transported out of the last century. That's pretty much it."

Bo brought Weezy up to date, in detail, about the happenings around Bethesda for the last three days and her husband Clive's apparent attempt to reopen communication channels after having decamped with an Egyptian undersecretary he met through his work at the State Department. "He called and said in a jaunty tone, 'Vivienne, I think it's time we began negotiations.' He thinks he can treat me like those Middle Eastern protectorates he used to deal with." She painted insouciance over her pain. "The pompous bourgeois ass!" she said, lips trembling. "I'll negotiate when Hell freezes over!"

After Bo left, Weezy again raised the Olegarten website. On the lower right corner of the home page was a small white, spiky flower, a memory of Olegarten's Norwegian heritage. Weezy punched the Bakkekløver and an innocuous screen with what appeared to be old-fashioned HTML code opened. She clicked on a segment buried in the middle of the sequence, and a chat room opened. She selected the thread Hotcakes. There, she wrote some code to scan the ordering page for the phrase "Neapolitan steel" and to open the Hotcakes thread. As she finished, a chime sounded.

Hotcakes, where the hell you been? Jake

"Traveling for the day job, Weezy said. "How they hangin'?" Jake was a grandmother from somewhere in Wisconsin.

High and tight. Nihow, greetings, salutations. But mainly, What's up?

Another chime. Hey, Hotcakes, wanna boogie low & slo?

Weezy sighed. It was HoHum, actually a guy. Adolescent fantasies projected quickly on the Net.

"Not with you, dumbass!"

Ah, there's the Hotcakes we all adore! Pardon me while I

take care of a little personal problem that just popped up.

"You said 'little,' not me."

Ohhhh. Slay me, please. But, hwRU?

A chime, and a message from luckymonkey appeared.

Weezy said, "Gotta go" to Jake and HoHum and clicked on the link to luckymonkey.

"Joe, how are you doing?"

Okay, but I got a scare yesterday. The guy that's been following me appeared in Underhill right after you left. I think I sent him off in the wrong direction. Modifying our plan to include a long loop to get away from him. Can people see me when I'm on the Internet?

"Press video," Weezy said.

Several seconds later, Joe appeared. He was sitting in a Naugahyde-upholstered armchair next to a crooked standing lamp.

"First, to answer your question, yes," she said. "Theoretically, anything you do is visible on the Internet. But the way I have you set up, probably not as long as you don't go onto RazorBlue.net. You're visible in Olegarten now, but only as a salesman entering orders. What happened in Underhill?"

"Big Louie showed up in the diner. I caught a glimpse of him as I drove back through town."

Joe told Weezy about the SuperShop and the phone.

"Clever, Joe. Quick thinking."

"I'm going to put a marker down to try to mislead him," Joe said. "But he's out there somewhere."

Weezy hesitated. "Yeah. And you need to stay off the grid as much as you can. I know you must want to see what's going on with RazorBlue, but let's be safe. I'll go in with a made-up name, see what's going on and report to you here. Check in at 10 p.m. Eastern tomorrow."

Joe nodded. He seemed more relaxed, more like those happy pictures in the dossier.

As Weezy closed out Olegarten, she heard Sappho announcing that she was, again, on the wrong side of the door. When Weezy rectified the situation, Sappho bounded in, sleek and satiated. She deigned to give Weezy a head-butt, ending the aloofness that always followed any time Weezy was away.

Weezy made a cup of tea and found RazorBlue.net. The site had grown since she first picked it up only a few days earlier. Membership was 4,039. She saw comments from the very odd or thumping mad people she often saw in her work. But there were seemingly sensible people, too, saying things that made Joe's story sound sickeningly common.

***

Morning. Bethesda was warm, and Weezy's ride to work was invigorating. She was still not sure what to make of her North Dakota encounter with Mayfield. It was good to be back at the familiar console, the desk chair that practically wrapped itself around her, even the jibes of the other programmer-geeks in the bullpen.

She activated her monitor and checked her integrator.

International news (*skip*)/ National News (*skip*)/ IAC News & updates (*skip*)/ Pukka (*skip*)/ Operations (*open*).

The Operations folder had several status reports from the bullpen and some of the several contractors working on Weezy-supervised projects. At the bottom, she saw:

01:07Z: Burnell, C: Working on the L1389 anomaly. Believe I have worked out the problem I mentioned.

She spent most of the rest of the day clearing out issues that cropped up during her three-day absence, but the message from Joe Mayfield stayed in the back of her mind.

Finally, toward the end of the day, she wrote a report that

suggested continuing to track Joe and asked to analyze MedRecords. She kept it brief, concentrating on the possible risk to the IAC. No outright lies, she thought as she read over the text. Evasions, but no lies. She would talk to P.E. tomorrow.

***

Weezy slipped into her boss's office and perched on the edge of a chair, fidgeting. P.E. Smith finished a sentence, frowned at it, shrugged, and shifted her attention to Weezy.

"I saw on my calendar that you got in yesterday and filed a trip report that probably tells me part of the story." Weezy stopped fidgeting and pulled a serious face. "That's true. As I wrote in the report, I'd like to follow up on the situation. There's a chance I am being scammed...not a very good chance ..."

The ghost of a smile on P.E.'s face let Weezy know P.E. was enjoying the sales pitch.

Weezy continued, "But a chance. The guy I met...Mayfield...pried up a big rock, and I think there may be some pretty bad stuff underneath it.

"Give me a rundown," P.E. said. "Why should we spend precious resources on this project?"

"It may not be a big deal, but if it is...Wow. Might kill a lot of people. The company where Mayfield worked employs 8,000. From his small sample, I think 150 or more are affected. If this *is* real, there had to be collusion with either the private companies that do the ratings or the insurance company. That means there could be other companies, maybe millions of people and...who knows?...thousands of lives."

Weezy briefed P.E. on Joe's suspicions and some of his activities, not mentioning the arrangement she'd made to communicate with him.

Finishing up, she said, "I think it's safe to say Mayfield's committed a minor system violation, the kind that might get major negative publicity if we were to prosecute him. However, I...we...

need to follow up on the issue he's raised. The hacking doesn't worry me...I can keep track of that." Weezy paused to let P.E. digest her suggestion, then continued, "We don't want Mayfield out there as a loose cannon. I need to get to the bottom of this without the cannon going off."

P.E. pursed her lips. After a moment, she said, "Louise, if you're sure this Mayfield can't penetrate us, why don't we let one of the patient advocacy groups—HealthAid or MEP—and run this down? They're pretty good at investigation. Let them expose the problem."

"But P.E., if Mayfield is right, it's not an issue of patient rights. It's a sophisticated attack on our database that happens to be running through medical records. The patient advocacy groups don't have access to the Yak, and they can't do the data analysis I can."

"So, what's your plan?"

"I need to understand the MedRecords side of the Yak. Maybe talk to someone in that division, because either Mayfield's good at lying or someone is getting into our files and changing them."

"Okay, Louise. Talk to Annika Dreher. She's the director over at MedRecords. But, fair warning...if this turns into a personal project involving one needy soul, it's going to have to stop. We can't do work based on a single case. It's not only a resource issue. It's the one-offs—the special cases—that blow up. So I want a regular report on where you're going with this. You have to understand that I, not you, decide how far we take it."

P.E. paused and exhaled, probably remembering the last time Weezy used her intuition on a project. That time, she crashed through the New Jersey portal leak like a cowboy bulldogging a Brahma. She had solved the problem in record time but had simultaneously flamed on several others working on the project.

"Talk to Annika but run your questions through me. Understood?"

Weezy hesitated, formulating a rebuttal. Finally she exhaled and said, "Yeah, boss."

***

Weezy called Annika Dreher, switching her monitor to video. A woman who looked to be Weezy's age appeared. "Dreher," she said, her expression saying she'd rather not be interrupted.

Weezy said, "Napolitani, here. P.E. Smith said to call you —"

Dreher's severity dissolved into a grin. "So you're the *enfant terrible* of the trackers. P.E. told me you would call. A MedRecord project, isn't it?"

Weezy was taken aback. "I didn't know anybody outside the bullpen knew me."

"New Jersey portal?" Annika said, her grin growing broader.

Weezy cringed inwardly. She wondered if Annika was one of the people she offended over that clusterfuck. "Oh, yes. I guess that one did get me some exposure. I hope I didn't...I mean, I hope you weren't ..."

Annika chuckled. "You mean, was I one of the people you accused of being a dumbass? No, and I don't suffer fools gladly, either."

Weezy heard a slight accent. Cultured, but hard to place.

"But Louise, P.E. didn't say what you're working on, other than it involves MedRecord files. Can you fill me in?" She sipped from a bottle of water. "In fact, if you don't mind a short walk, let's talk in the commons park in back of the main NIH building. It's beautiful out today."

***

The commons was ablaze with summer flowers. A light northeasterly breeze made being outdoors a pleasure. Weezy spotted Annika on a bench under a crabapple tree. As Weezy approached, Annika stood. At five-ten, she didn't tower over Weezy, but she was substantial enough to make it seem so. Dark hair pulled back. Professionally dressed.

Annika put out her hand. Weezy hesitated, then they shook and sat. Annika said, "I'm always tentative with the handshake here in the States, but old habits die hard. In Austria, you can have known a person for twenty years, and you still shake hands every morning when you get to work."

"I think it's a nice idea," Weezy said.

"So, what questions do you have about MedRecords?"

"I am working on a case that involves a man who believes his wife's MedRecord was illegally altered," Weezy said. Annika frowned. "Specifically, her HealthScore was changed, which resulted in limited treatment for her cancer. She died last winter."

"You mean, the HealthScore stored in her MedRecord file changed?"

"Exactly."

Annika drew a breath and said, "How much do you know about the HealthScore system?"

Weezy told Annika what she had learned.

Annika listened, finally nodding. "That's right." She paused for a moment. "The IAC protects the data but makes no changes. Only the HealthScore rating agency can change them. "

"What if I wanted to see the history of my own HealthScores? How would I do that?"

Annika shook her head. "You can't."

"Why not? Why would that information not be easily available?"

Annika said, "The official explanation is that the current HealthScore is the most up-to-date, most accurate summary of the best genetic information for that individual. That should be the truth."

Annika lowered her voice, "I think the real reason is that the rating agency wants to keep the process of setting HealthScores secret. A clever person like you, given a database of historical health scores, could probably figure out the formulas they're using." Annika stopped for a passerby enthralled with his e-pad to move out of earshot. "Every so often, there's an attempt to shed some light on the data, and it always gets quashed by the courts or the government. They say that they're protecting the sanctity of personal information, but it's really the HealthScore rating agency models."

"Back to the original question," Weezy said. "How do you fix a problem when you can't see history?"

"We have a program that checks individual changes as they happen and reports outliers," Annika said. "That's how I will check whether there's any record in your case. Tell me the details."

"The company is Florida Consolidated Energy, and the changes probably happened in late November last year."

Annika made a note, then said, "*Enfant Terrible* jokes aside, I'm glad to have met you. This is an interesting issue, and I'm happy to be able to work on it. Between you and me, I don't really trust the HealthScore rating agency. I can imagine a dozen ways that they can abuse their jealously guarded secrecy for profit. That's not the kind of thing I can say back at my desk."

So it wasn't only the summer weather that made Annika suggest meeting out of the building.

"Annika, I'm glad we had this meeting here, too. P.E. Smith knows what I'm doing, but I need to keep this confidential. If you need to get in touch with me off the grid, address me as Weezy through the system and I'll know that you need to talk."

Another handshake, and Weezy watched Annika stroll back toward IAC's West Annex.

***

Annika Dreher scanned the workstations as she entered the MedRecord control area.

"Tommy?"

A head popped up several cubicles away. "Annika? Over here, in the intake area."

"Can you come to my office?"

Tomasz Fischer followed Annika into her office. She motioned for him to sit.

"Tommy, I want you to do a search for me on outlier HealthScore changes for November...no, make it October through December...of last year. I'm talking with a person over in tracking trying to run down what are supposed to be some really big changes in HealthScores—20 or 30 points—for a few people at Florida Consolidated Energy at that time. I don't recollect seeing changes like that, but I wouldn't have to. That is, if they happened at all."

Tommy rubbed his brow, concentrating. "Nope, I can't remember anything, but I'll get right on it."

Annika watched Tommy return to his cubicle with an easy, confident stride. His curly, light-brown hair and athletic build had made him the object of the ruminations and daydreams of several women in the office, including Annika, as well as a couple of men. Annika and Tommy often slipped into German to joke about the job or the clueless Americans they worked with.

Later that day, Annika got a note from Tommy saying that there were no big changes in the IAC Master. She breathed a sigh of relief and wished for the calming rush of a cigarette, though she quit a year ago.

***

Jason Squitieri was making sales calls at the US HealthAudit office in Anacostia. He had given his upbeat rendering of the opportunities offered by the new program called SLAudit. Now, he was listening to his quarry bitch about the government, ignorant customers, and his wife. Jason's e-pad announced an incoming message from Tomasz Fischer, the analyst Jason had placed in the IAC with Thakur's help. As the potential customer droned on, Jason brought the message up in text.

A Yak tracker has asked some questions about the master files. I put a trace on her monitor and found she ordered an audit for one individual from the BlueLight operation. It's one with an altered HealthScore, and the person died several months ago.

It had to happen. The chance was always there. Small, but there. But so soon?

The message continued,

I directed queries to a dummy file controlled by REDIRECTR. The system will see the same score and information on the IAC master file.

Jason realized the guy on the phone had asked him a question, and put on a smile, "Say what, Sam?" He answered the question and ended the call. He let his smile fade along with his mood.

Florida. Of course.

TWENTY-THREE

WEEZY SPENT THE AFTERNOON rolling over the Mayfield possibilities in her mind, picturing the IAC data structure, trying to use facts to solve the difficult human question. Was Joe lying to her? She was pretty sure he was not. Was he lying to himself? That question was harder to answer.

At day's end, she checked the Mayfield file. He had checked in. The long Fourth of July weekend lay ahead, and everyone was anxious to pack it in.

Weezy's apartment was just under three miles from IAC headquarters down beautiful countrified roads winding through the understated, expensive homes owned by top-level NIH administrators, doctors and lawyers. The short bike ride was a pleasure except on the harshest winter days. Her bike was a Bianchi. She loved the simplicity and beauty of its physical design nearly as much as she loved a simple, elegant algorithm. She had been advised to get a cheaper model to ride to work but refused to give up the pleasure the bike gave her. She had a good lock and could complete the ballet of attaching the bike to the outdoor rack efficiently and quickly.

The day was warm, with the lush scent of summer in the air. Heavier traffic on Georgetown Road than usual, going to the beaches. A black SUV, a rarity these days, seemed anxious to follow her across Georgetown but continued on Battery as she branched off on Goddard. She was almost home when her peripheral vision caught something in her mirror. An SUV? When she looked in the bike's mirror, but saw only the road, fences, and foliage.

At home, she waved across the lawn to Bo, who was getting into her mono, no doubt to go to one of her soirees. The sight of the elegant woman dressed to the nines getting into the tiny car still seemed incongruous. Big cars were getting rarer, but most of Bo's wealthy neighbors drove guzzlers. They all cared about the planet, mind you, but in the theoretical way that excluded choices close to home. Loved fuel economy, except when it came to their own cars. Loved clean energy until someone wanted to put up a wind farm near their summer residence. Except Bo. It was important to Bo to make a statement.

In the apartment, Weezy dropped her bag, took care of Sappho's immediate needs, and prepared a light supper for both of them. Her small kitchen window looked out toward the road that ran in front of the house. As she pared a carrot, she noticed a black SUV drive slowly by the driveway. Strange.

Finished with dinner, she opened her personal e-pad and signed into Olegarten Fabricating. No message from Joe. Not surprising. She wrote a private message that would appear on his e-pad when he signed in:

Joe: Need to talk with Stevie Ray. Need to locate Cynthia's MedRecord.

Getting no reply, she chewed the rag with several Olegarten friends. Still no Joe, so she signed off.

She listened to some music, tried to enjoy a movie everyone said she *must* see. At 9, she called Derrick. When his phone rolled to message, she said, "Thought you might like to drop by." By mutual understanding, "drop by" meant conversation, some red wine and some scratch-where-it-itches, good friend with many benefits, sex.

They were a couple for a while, even considered living together. But each had lived alone for a decade, and neither wanted to submerge valued habits and quirks in an emotional democracy. They had stayed close and saw each other every couple of weeks.

Derrick was dark-haired, dark-eyed and slightly built. He had an infectious grin and a scathing wit that Weezy loved.

He arrived, a bottle of what he called "guinea red" under his arm and a long, involved, hilarious yarn about a clueless venture capitalist who wanted a piece of Derrick's small software firm. Laughter eventually gave way to passion, and Derrick is two-thirds of the way down to scratching Weezy's itch when her personal cell rang. The helpful feminine voice said, "Stevie Ray is calling you."

"No."

"I'm so sorry, I have to." (Heavy breathing.)

"Let it roll."

"I can't." (More heavy breathing.)

She answered, and Derrick rolled to the other side of the bed.

"Yes, Joe."

"Did I get you from something?"

"Yes, but it's important that I talk to you."

Derrick muttered, "Better be."

"Joe, can I see Cynthia's MedRecord?"

"Yes. Why?"

"A couple of curious things came up on this end."

Derrick got out of bed, picked up his clothes, left the room and quietly closed the door behind him.

Joe said, "What do you mean?"

"Sorry to be obscure," Weezy said. "I wasn't alone. I'm seeing the high score you mentioned, the 84, in some files here. I need to see the files that have the low score."

"Well, you have my e-pad…"

"The file doesn't jump out at me. Besides, it will be protected, and I need the password."

"I thought you were a code-breaking guru of some sort."

"Yup. I am, but it'll go a hell of a lot faster if you tell me the file name and password."

"Okay, go to the 'other projects' files, and you will find one I have renamed 'CCM Fund.' It has some financial records and a file called 'Med' that opens with the password 'gouache.' "

"Thanks, Joe. I'm seeing your log-ins as Chester. Where are you?...Strike that. Don't tell me. How's it going?"

"Okay, if living in off-the-grid motels and traveling aimlessly counts as okay. I need to get back to my place and get some stuff, but I think I'm going to move away. There are too many hints that bad things might happen if I try to go back permanently. But, how's your analysis going? Anything to report?"

"Not yet. Suspicions, but nothing concrete. I've got a long weekend ahead of me, and I should be able to sift through a raft of data I have here and give you some idea. Look for messages on Olegarten."

"Thanks, Louise. I really appreciate your help. Take care of yourself."

Weezy disconnected and realized Derrick had gone. She opened her e-pad and buzzed him.

"Derrick, you didn't have to leave. I'm so sorry, but I had to take that call."

With a half-smile, Derrick said, "Oh, baby. I know you did. You know, we'd have made a great couple if we could have gotten our priorities straight. Now you have to scratch that itch all by yourself."

***

Saturday morning. Weezy started up slowly, with Tai Chi and then coffee. Sappho finally condescended to sit on her lap, surrendering to a nap while Weezy dove into the data she brought from work.

Annika Dreher had delivered several data files to the project's folder. Weezy found the Cynthia Mayfield data and the Med file. Sure enough, Cynthia's score was 62. No amount of electronic nosing around yielded anything but the up-to-date file from November 29.

Weezy dislodged Sappho and stood to stretch. She went to the kitchen, made a second cup of coffee, returned to her chair, and tapped the e-pad's screen.

The IAC picture was consistent, but what she saw on Joe's cube was different. He must have updated the HealthCube normally. That ran through Florida Consolidated, to BlueLight, to IAC. So, either Joe managed to modify the record downward for some reason, or the chain of actions that updated the IAC went wrong.

Why wouldn't someone in Dreher's section have seen the problem and fixed the record? It seemed like Joe made the effort to get that done. He had talked bitterly about having "followed the process." There had been many attempts to open Cynthia's MedRecord from inside FCE. That must have been Joe. He had said as much, so his story held together.

How did the score get changed, and how did the change remain invisible to IAC?

It was the kind of problem Weezy usually liked, an interesting mental exercise, but the pictures of Cynthia, her artwork on Joe's e-pad, the hopeless pain in Joe's voice back in the diner made it hard to be dispassionate. She stood and paced, remembering P.E. warning her not to get sucked in emotionally.

There were only a few possibilities. If Joe wasn't lying, something went haywire in the sequence of transactions, whether by mistake or by design. That meant tracing how the updating data passed through IAC's files, which meant she needed to understand MedRecord file structure. Too big a job for the e-pad.

She rode back to N-ops, swiped her pass card, and went to her station. The place was mostly empty on the long weekend, so Weezy could relax with a big cup of coffee and use her access to the IAC supercomputers without prying eyes.

"Raise Structurepuppy."

A multi-colored flowchart appeared and she said, "MedRecord file structure," then, "Describe file update for an individual, all possible update actions." Structurepuppy's tortured flowchart confirmed that the MedRecords system was stitched together from earlier software, which led to many revisions and corrections.

Weezy was trying to get a sense of how HealthScores are updated when her private phone said, "Stevie Ray is calling you."

"Yes, Stevie Ray."

The phone showed Joe sitting on a park bench. "I wondered if you've found out anything."

Weezy said, "No...well yes, but it's confusing. The system says Cynthia always had a score of 84, and it seems as if she was treated appropriately, which means aggressively. I did find Cynthia's November 29 MedRecord on your cube, and I see the 62. The person who administers the MedRecord system for IAC said they saw no errors like the one that happened to Cynthia any time from October to December. So I'm trying to map the system to see where the problem might have been."

She realized that Structurepuppy had responded and was waiting for her next direction.

There are 369 files referenced in MedRecord updates.

"369 files!"

Joe said, "369 files in what?"

"I have to analyze 369 freakin' files! It's gonna take me..." she scrunched her eyebrows, "...46 eight-hour days, Joe, piled on top..."

"Weezy!"

"Yeah, Joe? What?"

"Follow the money."

"What?"

"Follow the money transactions associated with Cynthia's MedRecord. Won't that reduce the number of files?"

She stifled her irritation at the unwanted advice.

"It might. Let me think on it."

"Call me the minute you know anything.

***

Weezy inspected the tangled hierarchal charts Structurepuppy produced. The 369 files that made up the IAC's medical records and payment area were like a densely packed city. New York City Upper East Side or maybe Delhi. Like those cities, the software had grown without a master plan. A given individual's name appeared in thirty-nine separate files. A master program called IFIX0449.42 pushed changes in status around to the various files. There was a clear pattern of operations leading to a separate record for each person.

By the time she left N-Ops on Saturday evening, Weezy had a sketch of the structure of the MedRecord files, as well as the many opportunities for error in the system.

She intended to spend a quiet night at home, but the problem of Cynthia Mayfield wouldn't leave her alone. She went for a run to burn off her caffeine-fueled jitters, but she kept coming back to the problem. Clearly something was wrong. Two MedRecords disagreed, and the failsafes that were supposed to highlight the discrepancy were silent. Nothing — not cooking an elaborate (for her) meal, not watching television, not reading a book — let her ignore the problem for long. A hot shower and bed was good for an hour's sleep.

Waking with a start, she started churning through her hypotheses again. Maybe the failsafe failed. Where would she see that on the map? Maybe there's a giant conspiracy to co-opt the system. Maybe Joe changed the number somehow. He's a smart guy. But why would he change Cynthia's score downward? That would kill her. His grief seems real. The system thinks his wife was given top-notch treatment. Why wasn't she? We should go and talk to the doctors.

Finally, at 2 a.m., she threw off the covers, dressed, and

returned to N-Ops.

In the bullpen, lights were dimmed to energy-saving level. In the dusk, Weezy initialized her console and entered her IAC password. The management software everyone called Filbert asked, "Would you like the lights brighter?"

"No."

When Weezy was young, her dad sometimes let her tag along to the Boston docks, where he did his business. In the store next to her dad's stall, Vittorio Albigeri would reach into the great barrel of lobsters and expertly capture the exact size a customer wanted. Often, when Weezy opened her portal into the IAC, she felt as if she was plunging her arms into a great barrel of data.

She called up her sketch of the system and studied it. When she had a picture of how the system ought to work, she started backtracking Cynthia. Joe was right. Following the money was the easiest path. Final payment vouchers tracked back through IFIX0449.42 to Cynthia's personal record. The path wound through sixty-one separate files on its way to the record Florida Consolidated accessed. There was a change from 84 to 62 somewhere toward the end. No reason, no process defined. Just the change. Cynthia's ID number and full name remained unchanged, so it wasn't some system flub to mistake Cynthia for a nearly related name.

Cynthia's information seemed to be going down the data paths Weezy's sketch thought they would. None of Cynthia's other data changed across the system, yet there were the two different scores. Something must trigger the change, but what? Well, she thought, Sherlock Holmes knew that once you eliminate the impossible, whatever remains, no matter how improbable, must be the truth.

She wrote a program to do an exact compare of all thirty-nine times Cynthia's ID appeared in the system. The program produced eight copies that appeared to be identical to the other thirty-one IDs but were somehow different. After some tweaking and churning, Weezy found that the eight included a normally invisible hex code flag that forced the data attached to this form of the name to turn off the correct information highway into a digital alleyway that led to a program lurking unnoticed in the congested neighborhood of the IAC MedRecords. The same back alley held a stack of files, one of which was a mirror image of Cynthia's IAC MedRecord, but with a 62 for MOC. And the treatment of her illness was different: a whole series of entries go right up to when she died. Hospice, drugs, no high-level treatments.

Twelve hours after entering N-Ops, Weezy emerged bleary-eyed into the bright Bethesda sunlight. Happy, though—she had mapped the trail that led to the rogue program she now called Mirror. On her way home, she didn't notice the car tailing her.

***

Weezy slept for ten hours, woke feeling stiff and disoriented. The green glow of the digital clock announced 23:08. She got up, made a meal of popcorn and milk, and started up her e-pad.

Olegarten Manufacturing pulsated. Nighttime apparently was the right time for denizens of the Internet. She wondered how people managed to have day jobs and spend all night gossiping, gaming, or planning dubious Internet activities. As Hotcakes, she left a simple note for Chester Burnell. "Found a connection."

HoHum passed along some digital dirt. Weezy was preparing to sign off when, to her surprise, a response came from Chester Burnell. He was up late. She wondered where he was.

"Have Stevie Ray give me a call."

Joe called her private line. Weezy said, "Joe, we're onto something." *We're?* Weezy realized she had stepped over on to Joe's side of the fence.

"I can see both the 84 and the 62 scores you mentioned in Cynthia's record. I don't understand exactly how this was managed, but it's a sophisticated process, not just a system error that didn't get corrected. I have to look further, but we're definitely on to something."

Long silence. Then Joe said, "Thank you, Weezy."

Another long pause. "I want to find them...the people that did this."

"Joe, I'm going to figure this out. This is what I do for a living, and I'm damn good at it. I'll get back to you when I know more, but I think you can go home now."

"No, I can't. Not with people watching my apartment who must know they're facing a murder charge."

"You need to be careful, too," he said, and she saw friendship and concern in his eyes.

"Thanks. I'll be okay. But we better sign off."

At a nondescript office near the Anacostia River in a Washington industrial district, the trace on Weezy's phone also signed off and dumped its report to an e-pad in Winter Park, Florida.

TWENTY-FOUR

TOSHEKA SAT ON A bench in the park in the center of beautiful, upscale Winter Park. Most people were enjoying the beach or staying away from the heat. She called Zimmerman's private line for the daily check-in.

He answered immediately.

"Are you on duty?"

"Nope. Off for the day. You probably saw the trace on that woman up in Bethesda. She talked to Mayfield, so that confirms she's the right person to be monitoring. There was reference to a public website called Olegarten Manufacturing, and I've been able to get into it and check out what she's doing. She apparently gets reports from Mayfield on the site, but I can't find them. She uses the site mainly for gaming and cruising."

"Can you find Mayfield?"

"I think so. Easier to do following the phone he used, but I need police resources to do that."

Tosheka shook her head in frustration.

"Okay. Can you get in now?"

"That'd be really hard. I'm not on the roster, and I have the kids for the long weekend..."

So much for step by step. "Let me rephrase that," she said. "Get in now, find the phone, and let's find Mayfield. This is important, Paul. Mayfield's not going to stay put. We need to nail him now."

Zimmerman sighed audibly, but said, "I hear you. I'll pinpoint the phone and get Louie moving toward wherever we find Mayfield's signal."

They hung up. Tosheka glanced around, vaguely nervous, as always. She saw nothing.

A pretty redheaded woman sitting alone at a sidewalk cafe a block from the park said conversationally into her lapel, "Henry, did you get that?"

***

Big Louie Studt stood at the pick-up window of the Dari-Freeze close by the Missouri border when Zimmerman's message came. Back in the car, he put the Big Boy Shake in a cup holder and keyed voicemail.

"I got a hit from Mayfield's phone near Cleveland, Mississippi. Better get over there."

Louie acknowledged, pulled the door closed, picked up the shake, and tapped hard on the climate control button. Nothing worked right since the SUV went in the ditch back in North Dakota. Three days to get it fixed. Everybody in town seemed to know the story, if the smirks that greeted him at the diner were any indication. Worse, Zimmerman apparently thought the clusterfuck was somehow Louie's fault. Sitting in his air-conditioned office back in Orlando, of course. While Louie was in a car whose air conditioner wheezed and coughed, overpowered by Kansas heat.

Then Mr. Frickin' high-falutin' know-it-all Zimmerman told him to go to Colorado. "Looks like he's gone to ground," he said, whatever that meant. Now all of a sudden Mayfield was in Mississippi.

Louie took a long pull on the shake, relished the pain of the brain freeze.

A far as he could see, his bosses had no idea what they were doing. But, as long as the paycheck kept coming...

Louie shifted into drive. The undercarriage complained as he drove out of the parking lot.

Mississippi, for chrissake.

***

Joe was the single customer in the Launderette three blocks from the Cleveland Travel Inn. The heat of the Mississippi evening and the whirr and tick of the ancient dryer had him dozing, his mind rolling along with the dryer. Snake's warning. *Tick.* Cynthia. *Tick.* Lucky, the paper clip monkey. *Tick.* Dumbass. *Tick.* The line between Weezy's eyebrows when she concentrated. *Tick.*

He had spent the last week moving east and south from the east Colorado town where he left an electronic beacon. Snaking through Kansas and Missouri back roads, moving toward the Delta again. It was a long, slow slog, staying in places bypassed by the interstates, mostly manned by tired, sour souls. Keeping moving so he didn't have to sit on a broken chair in a cheerless room and think. Reporting to Weezy on the Chester Burnell phone. Listening to Cynthia's music until it hurt too much.

There was nothing to indicate Big Louie had picked up his trail, so he returned to Cleveland, Mississippi, where he had stayed in Mase Jarvis's motel on the way up the Blues Highway. Mase was glad to see him, and they spent a lazy Fourth of July holiday in friendly conversation.

The Launderette door opened, its bell startling Joe awake. A tall, handsome young man stood in the doorway, angry eyes on Joe, mouth tight. He was perhaps fifteen, slender calves and unlined face of a kid, chest and arms expanding toward manhood. "You Joe Mayfield?"

"Yes, I am."

"My Gramps said you better get out and get out fast. Don't go to Jackson."

"Mase?"

"Yessir. My Gramps."

"Why? What happened?"

"Some guy, white guy, came looking for you. Hit on my Gramps. I was bringin' in laundry. I think that scared him off." A flicker of pride.

"Crap! I've got to get back—"

The young man shook his head. "He said for you to go."

Run away again? It seemed like all the people Joe cared for got hurt because of him.

The dryer creaked to a stop. Joe pulled out his clothes in a ball, carried them toward the door. The young man held it open, looking uncertain.

"C'mon." Joe tilted his head toward the Element.

"He said for you to get outta here."

"I'm going back. You coming with me?"

The young man hesitated, then followed Joe and folded himself into the car.

"Don't know if this is a good idea. We see a black SUV, you better stay away."

They crawled down the side street. Seeing nothing, Joe parked at the far end of the Inn's lot.

"Wait here." Joe said, opening the car door.

"I'm coming, too."

They went down the long side of the building toward the office, staying in the shadow. The Open sign was off.

Mase sat in a chair in front of the desk, holding a handkerchief against his head. Joe cracked the screen door, and Mase turned toward them, chin jutting. His left eye was swollen nearly closed. His right eye held enough fury for both until he saw Joe. Then he glared at the young man. "Jayden, you were supposed tell him to get the hell outta here."

Jayden shrugged and spread his hands.

"He wouldn't listen."

Joe crossed to Mase.

"Mase, you have to see a doctor. I'm so sorry about—"

"—Don't you be worryin'. Man like that don't scare me none. I been through worse. But you gotta get yourself out of here."

Mase shook his head and chuckled through a split lip. "He called me granddad. Thought I was scared of him. I did my best house nigger...'ooooeee, Mista, ain't seen him since Sat'day evenin'.' Sent him down toward Jackson, so you want to go to the hill country, maybe Alabama. Or up to Chicago. Not Jackson."

"I'd feel a lot better if we got you to a doctor."

Mase shook his head. "I'd feel a lot better if you got outta here. 'Sides, I got me Jayden here to take care of me for a couple of days."

Jayden nodded.

"Mase, I owe you. A lot more than I can ever repay. When this is over—"

"—You come back and see me. I'll be right here."

"It may be quite a while, Mase."

Mase looked long at Joe and said, "Don't you worry none. I'll always hold you here," tapping his chest. "You keep me, too, same place, along with that wife a' yours, hear?"

The night was thick and warm as Joe left, heading east toward Grenada, then Birmingham. Cynthia's blues played on the sound system, a sweet heaviness lay on his heart.

TWENTY-FIVE

Weezy arrived at N-Ops on Tuesday morning after the long weekend. She had prepared a series of queries to reach into the system in search of whatever changed Cynthia Mayfield's score. She was deep into the system when P.E.'s image appeared in the lower corner of her monitor.

"Louise, can you join us in my office?"

Us?

P.E. was usually matter-of-fact when she called Weezy. Today, a laser-like stare put Weezy on edge.

"Sure, P.E. Want me to bring anything?"

"No, Louise, not necessary. We have some questions, that's all."

We?

A visitor rose from the guest chair as Weezy entered P.E.'s office, an expectant smile on his face. Tall, handsome. Impeccably dressed in a blue suit, white shirt, and red tie. Nobody dressed that way anymore except an inside-the-beltway Washingtonian.

He stood and extended a hand.

"Louise, this is Jason Squitieri," P.E. said. "He is a board member of the Medical Equity Project. MEP is working with Sen. Ricky Thakur to take a proposal to Thakur's committee. Mr. Squitieri needs to find answers to some questions that will surely come up. But I'll let him explain ..."

"Ms. Napolitani, P.E. has told me that you know the internal workings of the IAC better than anyone else. She has been kind enough to make you available to me." Smooth. Not slick, not slimy, but carefully polished.

She nodded, careful not to give into the temptation to look to P.E. for instruction.

His smile, too confident to be ingratiating, projected his assumption that Weezy would be eager to answer any questions he might ask. She tried to throw up her standard dumbass shield but found she could not help being intrigued by Squitieri's confidence.

"You see," he continued, "any senator who objects to registering what the website WolfPac.org calls 'overprotected indigents' is going to come up with questions about practicality. WolfPac has already said IAC is 'riddled with errors' and argued that 'hackers are running rampant' in the database. They amplify these unsubstantiated attacks by repetition and use them to imply that adding 'undesirables' to the medical rolls will expose honest folks to identity theft, digital pollution, unspecified rip-offs and so on." He gave Weezy and P.E. a smile that let them know he was on their side. "So we'll get questions about the security of IAC, with particular emphasis on MedRecords. I know of no major errors, but I don't work in the system. I want to be sure Thakur isn't ambushed by somebody producing an embarrassing error during the testimony and debate."

He finished and looked expectantly at Weezy.

"I may not be the right person to talk to," she said, "because I deal mainly with the hacker part of the equation."

Jason smiled. "I'm sure you could tell some pretty interesting stories ..."

The dumbass shield popped up with vigor. That was his idea of an effective fishing expedition?

But she smiled and said, "And, as I'm sure you know, I can't discuss them outside my group."

Another disarming smile from Jason managed to convey that bureaucratic procedures and rules did not apply at his level. "Yes, but if there's anything that might become public, I'd like to know it's out there. No details, just a heads-up."

Weezy put on her formal face. "Nothing I know of. I'm tracking several hundred hacking attempts, none of which have been successful so far. There has been one significant breech in three years, but we caught it. I understand that hacker is in a nasty jail in Romania. But you should talk with the MedRecords section of IAC. I believe the person in charge over there is ...” she looked at P.E. for confirmation, “Annika Dreher.”

Weezy realized Jason saw her tapping a nervous rhythm on the chair's arm. She hoped the interview was over. “But I do have a stack of hack attacks to go through,” she said, then cracked a grin. “Because hope springs eternal in these hacker dudes' minds, no matter how many times they fail.”

“Thanks. I'll call Ms. Dreher,” Jason said. “But I'd love to see a bit more about how you do your work. It would...uhh...help if I can sound knowledgeable when I'm questioned.”

Weezy turned to P.E., hoping for a reprieve. P.E. said, “Louise, why don't you give Jason a tour around the bullpen?” Then to Jason, “Louise can't discuss specific projects with you in any detail, but she can show you how the Tracker unit designs and develops the protections we have in place to ensure IAC systems stay secure.”

A perfect answer. Now she could blow this guy off, but nicely.

Weezy led Jason into the half football field-sized bullpen, thirty-odd consoles facing the wall-mounted status board. The room hummed—the sound of keys clicking underlying muted conversation. The status board dominated the room. Projects were listed using naming protocols that made the entries meaningless to all but the initiated. Weezy introduced Jason to the Oddballs, her four-person team. They repeated the OddBall motto (“We're all odd, and Maddie has balls”), which usually caused Maddie Hollingsworth to glow with pride. This time, she blushed under Jason's humorous smile and began to explain how the OddBalls do their work. (“Mad Dog was practically simpering over the hunk from DC,” Adam said later.)

The rest of the tour took fifteen minutes, and Jason was attentive to details and asked questions from time to time. He was, in particular, attentive to Weezy. Normally, a suit like Jason would take Weezy's apparent youth and her informal clothing to mean she's a low-level geek to be spoken down to. But not Jason. He focused his attention on her in a way that made her feel as if he was seeing under her skin. Uncomfortable, but not unpleasant.

Weezy finished the tour back at the status list, reiterating that there are no attacks that could cause embarrassment.

Jason smiled his relief, checked his watch and said, "Help me find some lunch. I'm sure there's a spot on this large campus where a couple of hard-working government employees can get a nice, quiet lunch. How about it? MEP's treat."

Weezy stifled her immediate reaction, which was to retreat into her work. Why did Squitieri want to take her to lunch? Inside information, of course. She'd have to be careful, but he was charming.

"Sure. There's a pretty good restaurant just outside the campus. A little pricey for most of us, so not usually too busy. I probably don't meet their dress code..." She half shrugged. "But if you don't mind overpaying, they'll probably let us in."

P.E. smiled as they walked by her office. But as Jason turned toward the foyer, Weezy caught a hint of the Look.

The Look was well understood by members of the IAC Tracker unit. Usually, it appeared right after a colossal mistake or as reinforcement of a very, very important point.

Puzzling.

***

Weezy and Jason walked across the NIH campus to Risotti's Grill. Mahogany, brass bar rail, table linen, people trying to look important, hushed conviviality. The maître d' gave Weezy's shorts and T-shirt a twice-over but acquiesced to Jason's "I'm sure you can find us a table."

Jason offered a glass of wine, which Weezy declined.

"So, what got you into the IAC?"

Weezy gave a brief tour through her résumé. Jason brightened at her mention of Boston.

"I have a lot of family in Boston. Fourth generation, but I heard quite a bit of Neapolitan dialect as a kid." He was a BC grad, and both were avid Red Sox fans. It was a friendly, relaxed conversation with no mention of the IAC or Weezy's work. Jason took the lead, telling of growing up in the crowded streets of the North End. Weezy watched him spin out a yarn featuring his Tante Agostina, whose English vocabulary consisted of "sooffabeech" followed by a string of Italian dialect so strong that Jason's mom covered his ears with her hands. True or not, it was a good story. As he became immersed in the telling, the Washington polish gave way to fluid hand gestures and a light Boston accent. His dark eyes twinkled as he explained what he thought Tante Agostina might have meant. Weezy found herself drawn into the story and drawn to the teller, as well.

The sandwiches came and they were quiet for a time, eating.

Weezy glanced at Jason. He was good-looking, fun to talk with. If he was hitting on her, it was a soft hit. Maybe he was working to increase his stable of sources who "are not allowed to speak publicly on the matter." But it wouldn't be all bad if he were hitting on her.

Jason put his sandwich on the plate. His laid-back demeanor disappeared, and the Boston accent was gone. "You said before that you're not the person to talk to about MedRecords, and you directed me to Annika Dreher. That makes sense if my focus was administrative issues, but they're not. I'm trying to chase down a rumor that someone's trying to break into MedRecords. Something in the system having altered a HealthScore, and this guy's on a tear to right what he believes to be a wrong. I don't want him to show up in the Senate committee meeting. That kind of case is right up your alley." He was an inquisitor now, friendly but serious.

"What do you know?"

Weezy pretended to think through her projects and hoped her face didn't give away her surprise. He must know about Joe. He had her so relaxed. She hadn't seen it coming. The bastard set her up That friendly smile now seemed sinister.

"Jason, there's nothing I know of that might be a 'gotcha' in a public meeting Sometimes, there are attempts to get into IAC MedRecord files. We generally know little or nothing of the motives of the people making those attempts."

"Nice general statement of policy, Louise. But I'm not asking you for motives or details, just a review of problems you're working on now that might surface."

Weezy looked Jason squarely in the eye and said, "None I know of."

Jason's friendly, conversational tone disappeared. "Well, I hope not. Thanks for taking the time to talk with me."

***

Jason focused closely on Weezy's reaction as he finished his question. "… that kind of case is right up your alley. What do you know?"

Charm almost worked, he thought. She trotted out the concentration line between her eyebrows a second too late. She knows exactly what I'm talking about. When she cleared her throat, he knew she was going to lie.

"Jason, there's nothing I know of that might be a 'Gotcha!' in a public meeting …"

He half-listened to the rest of her pro forma presentation of IAC policy. He suppressed the urge to say, "Now that you're finished lying to me, tell me about Joe Mayfield."

When she finished, he said, "Thanks for taking the time to talk with me."

They left the restaurant, strolling into the warm summer air.

Cordial handshake. He watched her walking away.

Time for plan B.

TWENTY-SIX

ON THE WAY BACK to N-Ops, Weezy replayed the conversation she'd just had. Squitieri knew about Joe, at least some of it, and he was trying to figure out what she knew. Was he trying to get out in front of what he thought might be a problem, like he said? How and why was he involved?

She paused at the door to P.E.'s office, unsure of what to do. P.E. had never been a confidante. Friendly, but too busy for chit-chat most of the time. P.E. didn't have the technical background for the hacker issues, but Weezy was in a quandary, needing someone to talk to about Squitieri. She leaned on the doorframe of P.E.'s office.

P.E. was giving Weezy the Look again. A warning?

"I just finished talking with Jason Squitieri."

P.E. interrupted...unusual for her. "Good. It's important to keep good relations with Thakur's friends, and MEP is a major player in healthcare nationally. It's also imperative not to give Squitieri details of projects, because that raises the issue of inside information. Technically, he's conflicted. He's CEO of US Health Audits, but he's also a board member of MEP and a confidante of the senator. Thakur has been a supporter of the IAC's involvement in medical information. There are plenty of people out there who think IAC is another example of government run wild, and those people would love to get information to smear Thakur and the MedRecords project."

Weezy fidgeted. "I wanted to ask you ..."

She got the Look again.

P.E. half-stood, assembling papers from several stacks on her desk.

"Louise, I'm late for a meeting. Can we discuss this tomorrow morning?" Not a question.

P.E.'s intent was clear. "Uhh. Sure. Tomorrow morning."

***

By 4:30, there were no hits on Weezy's electronic stakeout of the Mirror. She decided to pack it in for the day.

"G'night, Jim." The guard at the front desk eyed her and smiled. He had mentioned several times that they ought to get together, because he, too, was a computer guy.

Weezy waved and walked into the warm Maryland afternoon.

She paused, as she often did, to admire the beauty of the Bianchi. The cable was secured a little differently than usual, but she never was one for rigid habit. She shrugged, took out her key, unwound the lock, stowed it in her bag and was on her way.

The ride home was easy and pleasant. Sappho greeted her at the door with a laundry list of feline issues and commands. Weezy was spooning out Feline Delight when Bo knocked and entered.

"How are you doing? Haven't seen much of you for the last week," Bo said.

"Oh, I've been fine. Work, you know. Always busy."

Bo sniffed. "Weezy, you do know that all work and no play makes for a dull girl, don't you? I haven't seen that nice young man around recently. Derrick, isn't it?"

Weezy sighed. The social audit made her feel like a teenager. She closed the Feline Delight and turned to Bo, "I've been seeing Derrick, Bo. I've been swamped at work. There's this really interesting ..."

Bo's eyes gave her warning. Weezy hesitated. What was with the silent warnings today?

"... case my team is working on, trying to identify a bunch of hackers in Europe. Anyway, it's way more time consuming than I thought it would be."

"You need some time off work," Bo said. "Why don't you come over for a glass of wine?"

"That's very nice of you, but I really …"

"Louise, I won't take 'no' for an answer. We're going to trot over to the house, have that glass of wine, and you're going to use that fine mathematical mind of yours to help me determine my negotiating strategy with Clive. He's become more and more insistent on returning to the fold. He is apparently learning that concupiscence does not make for a satisfying relationship. Come on, girl!"

Bo turned and went out the door, giving Weezy no choice but to follow.

They walked across the yard to the back door of Bo's house and passed through the light and airy kitchen into the living room. Light was fading, and trees shaded the bay window. Bo usually offset the gloominess with flowers and carefully placed lamps. The lights were not on.

Bo poured wine. Three glasses.

Three?

"Sit. Relax."

There was a small movement in an overstuffed chair near the fireplace. Weezy realized another person was in the room.

"Louise," a familiar voice said.

"P.E.?"

Why was P.E. Smith sitting in Vivienne Beaumont's living room?

"Yes, Louise. We need to talk."

"Uh, sure. But what's going on? Why the mystery? I didn't know you two knew each other."

P.E. leaned forward in the chair and said, "Louise, Vivienne and I met in Washington. We've been friends ever since. Since you and I have a professional relationship, I have never mentioned the connection. Apparently, it didn't seem unusual that a perfect apartment just happened to become available right when you were moving to Bethesda from the Fredericksburg facility. But that's not the reason for meeting you here."

Bo whispered conspiratorially, "You're being followed, my dear."

A cloud of irritation passed across P.E.'s face, but she continued, "Something I don't quite understand is going on. I suspect it has to do with the MedRecords issue you're working on. In any case, Mr. Squitieri's visit seemed odd to me for a number of reasons. He showed up unannounced using the political sledgehammer of 'a question from Senator Thakur' to get into my office when I was elsewhere. He was all too interested in any problems related to MedRecords that might be lurking. Then he asked my analyst out to lunch."

P.E. took a sip of wine. "What did you tell him?"

"Nothing." Weezy exhaled, trying not to look defiant. "But he did bring up a good approximation of the Mayfield case. Somebody out there knows what we're doing. He caught me off guard. I didn't tell him anything, but I'm pretty sure he knew I was withholding information."

"All right. Good work." P.E.'s expression relaxed. "Make sure to follow IAC rules on confidentiality to the letter, starting today. Did you take Jason anywhere in the building, other than the tour of the bullpen?"

"No."

"Are you having any contact with Mayfield?"

Weezy looked the floor and exhaled.

"Louise? The truth."

"Yes."

P.E.'s jaw set. "Yes, you're in contact?"

"Yes, we're in contact." Weezy's admission came in a rush. "Public Internet, a secure platform. Off-the-grid phone."

Weezy realized she was more afraid P.E. would be disappointed in her than angry over broken rules.

P.E. examined Weezy with what might have been a trace of

sympathy.

"Okay. Until I get a sweep completed, I want you to keep all your communication within the walls of IAC. Nothing, I mean nothing, outside. Also, I want you to do nothing, I mean nothing, related to this case in your apartment."

"Why, P.E.?"

"Probably me being suspicious, but there are many ways to watch a person. Until we know there's nothing going on, we have to assume something's going on. Understand?"

"I do. But I need to stay in touch with Mayfield. I need to use the Internet."

P.E. considered, pursing her lips. "All right, I don't trust the public Net, but I may have a solution to the problem. When we took over the IAC space from NIH, I noticed a wall plate with a different connector than the ones we use now. I asked what it is, and the tech support guy said it was an old local area connector. When the tech team sweeps my office, I'll ask them to set one up for you to use if they can. Until then, you have to stay off the Net."

Weezy nodded.

"One more thing. Later this evening, your lights are going to flicker, go out, and then flicker again. Vivienne is going to come across to your apartment with a candle and invite you over while you wait for a truck to come from Commonwealth Power. They will sweep both the house and your apartment and "restore" your power. If they discover anything, they will leave it in place. Tomorrow, we will have run the regular semi-annual security sweep in the office. After that we will talk."

P.E. stood. "Louise, I'm not sure where this will lead us. Up until now, I have tolerated your disdain for rules and normal procedures because you are so good at what you do. But now, you need to follow my instructions to the letter. Do you understand?"

"Yeah, boss."

"Do you agree?"

"*Yes*, boss."

"Now, Bo and I are going to have a quiet dinner, discuss old times and that husband of hers, and then I am going to leave. I'd suggest you have a boring evening."

Back in her apartment, a cascade of small memories knit together...a black SUV crossing Georgetown Road in a hurry, a car going by the driveway slowly, her bike slightly out of place in the rack, Joe's warning. She told herself she was just being suspicious.

Later, the lights flickered and went out. A little too quickly, the flutter of a candle flame appeared from the back door of the house.

Bo's loving this, Weezy thought. Sappho did not. When Bo opened the door, cheerfully calling, "Louise, Louise, dear?" Sappho rocketed out.

"Louise, something terrible happened to the washer, and now all the lights are out. Louise, are you home? I've called the power company, and they promised to be out right away. Ahh, there you are. Come over to the house and we'll shiver in terror together." Bo played her part with panache.

Bo and Weezy walked across to the house. Sappho joined them, trotting high-footed through the gathering dew. As Bo opened the back door, a Commonwealth Power truck pulled into the driveway.

The two technicians were friendly, polite and surely not from Commonwealth Power. They walked through the house, discussing the wiring in the 120-year-old home. They did what appeared to be a perfunctory check of the garage and Weezy's apartment above it and got the power back on. They gave Bo what sounded to Weezy like a plausible explanation of a fused circuit breaker, packed up and left.

Weezy and Sappho turned in shortly after 11. Weezy had never been aware that there are so many night sounds in the old building. At 2 a.m., she fell asleep.

***

Weezy was at work early the next morning. Sure enough, the calendar on her monitor noted that the semi-annual security sweep of the office had been rescheduled for that morning.

The bullpen was in fine form, already fulminating. "Goddam spooks! No notice. Now I have to put everything on hold and wait for some mouth-breathing techie type to come through and pull my wire!"..."You said it, not me."..."You better deep-six the porn before P.E. sees it!"..."Yeah, you don't want her excited."

Everybody knew security sweeps were never "scheduled," but they provided a golden opportunity to bitch and moan, an important creative outlet in this corner of geekdom.

Weezy opened the Mayfield file. There had been a hit from her MedRecords portal sometime last night. Sign-ups for employees of a California public education group. Following the data was like threading through a minefield or playing an online war game. One careful step forward. Check for telltales. Another step. Time consuming. Weezy was lost in the back alleys of the system, with occasional interruptions by the security team, for three hours.

By noon the sweep was done. A note popped up on Weezy's number two monitor:

4th floor east conference room, 2:00 — P.E. Smith.

Weezy looked up to see P.E. leaving her office.

***

At 2:00, Weezy went to the conference room on the 4th floor. P.E. was already there. She did not look happy. "That smooth-talking bastard put an adit right on my desk!"

"An adit?"

"Asynchronous digital transmitter. Fortunately, it's only able to pick up audio and kneecaps because it's under the outer lip of my desk. The bullpen is clean. Oh, and your apartment is transmitting all sorts of data...video, audio, lord knows what else.

Your cat must have some Siamese in her, judging from the volume of her meow."

Weezy turned pale.

P.E. smiled. "Don't worry. No bedroom or bathroom data streams. So, unless you've been cavorting naked in the living room …"

"No, it's the thought of someone spying on me is more than creepy. How long?"

P.E. grimaced. "No way of knowing. Bo is not around all the time, but she's very inquisitive."

Weezy rolled her eyes in acknowledgment.

"… and she's seen nobody enter or leave. Of course, any professional would have been discreet. Have you had any visitors?"

"Not since last Friday…"

P.E. nodded, "Oh, yes, the 'nice young man' Bo mentioned. Derrick, is it?"

"Yes, Derrick."

"What do you know about him?"

"P.E., I doubt it's Derrick. He's a good friend. We go back to MIT. He has a small software company downtown."

"Okay. Well, anyway, we're going to treat this seriously. I say 'we' because I spoke with the FBI at length this morning. Weezy, I think your hacker is on to something considerably bigger than either of us originally thought. Something big enough that some pretty serious bad people might be involved."

Weezy bowed her head and chuckled.

What?"

"Mayfield told me the same thing. I blew him off. He's right…again."

P.E. continued, "The FBI is going to take you into protective custody while they investigate …"

"No!"

"Louise, this is not a negotiation."

"P.E., I understand what they're doing. Put me in protective custody and they simultaneously cover the possibility that I'm right and some bad guys embarrass the IAC by killing me...or that I'm part of the problem. But I have work to do. I need to be in the system, and I know without asking they won't allow a hot wire coming out of a nondescript bungalow somewhere in the country."

Weezy sensed the Look coming but continued. "You have to let me have a few more hours in the system." Almost pleading. "Someone has hidden a program in the Yak that captures certain names and dramatically reduces their HealthScores so that they get only low-cost, life-ending treatment. The trick is that the low scores never appear in the IAC's MedRecords files, so the IAC pays out as if these people were treated based on their original scores."

P.E. nodded, letting Weezy continue. "I followed the Mayfield file back. As far as the IAC system is concerned, Cynthia Mayfield had a high score for the disease she had. The system paid over $600,000 for cutting-edge treatment. If Mayfield is to be believed, she actually got only palliative care. He doesn't know the exact cost, but he thinks it was well under $100,000. Someone raked in over half a million on that case alone."

Weezy paused to let the numbers sink in.

"There's a program I call the Mirror that misdirects the system. I wrote a program that's watching incoming and outgoing traffic. Last night, four new individuals' data passed into the Mirror. Do the arithmetic: This could be tens of millions of dollars a year and hundreds of lives that might have been saved with aggressive treatment."

Weezy sensed P.E. coming over to her side and continued, "Now, I don't exactly know how the translation is done. I need to get into the Mirror without being detected, figure out what's going on and track down who is doing it. In other words, I need to continue to do the job you're paying me to do. If you want to deputize someone to work with me to be sure I'm not part of the scam, do it. But I need to stay on the job for at least several more days to zip this up. And I need access to the public Net, too."

P.E. folded her hands and stared down at the table.

After a moment, she said, "Why the public net? There's a lot of pollution out there. I don't want it to get into IAC on my watch. And don't blow me off on this. If what you say about the Mirror is right, someone got a pretty significant piece of software into the system. I'm sure you remember that the cyberwar started when a lazy employee left a backdoor open."

"I'm not a lazy employee."

P.E. pursed her lips and contemplated Weezy. "I can solve the public net problem," she said. "My suspicion about the old local network was correct. We can rig a connection out of the building on it. I'm going to document what we're doing, since it could cost me my job. I'd like to draw my retirement stipend when they've finished with me if this project explodes."

P.E's expression clicked a notch from stern toward concerned.

"Louise, I don't think you're part of the problem, but the FBI thinks you may be. This is a sophisticated hack, and their thinking is, 'who better than the person who knows hackers best?' That said, I think I can put them off for a few days. Just be very, very careful and spend a lot of time here. I don't like you living alone above Bo's garage. Do your work here, then we'll find a place for you to go until this is resolved."

"Thank you," said Weezy. "The FBI should consider that it may be a fancy program but doesn't have to be. A second-year IT student could probably write it. The hard part was getting it into the system. Yes, I could have done that, but if you assume for a minute that I didn't, there aren't too many possibilities. It had to arrive as part of something routine, something that's part of IAC's regular protocol."

P.E. thought for a minute, then said, "System maintenance?"

"Bingo! Hot damn, P.E. We'll make you a tracker yet!"

TWENTY-SEVEN

THE NEXT MORNING, WEEZY rode to work faster than usual. Was the internet connection P.E. had promised real? Would it work? She locked the Bianchi and race-walked through security.

"Slow down, miz Napolitani." But the security guard was smiling. "Anxious to run down those bad guys, right."

"Morning' Jim." She put on a smile. "Yup. Just can't wait."

Maddie Hollingsworth was already at her station, about twenty feet from Weezy's. Weezy waved at her and slipped into her chair. Her fingers flew through the morning protocol...iris scan...password. Then she paused, exhaled and typed

Open Olegarten Manufacturing

The public Internet came up cleanly, operating through wire unused for a decade.

"Hey, Maddie, I'm in."

" 'K."

P.E. hadn't forced Weezy to include an auditor, but it seemed like a good idea. Maddie joined Weezy, looking over her shoulder as Weezy tapped out a message to Joe.

Chester, you need to talk with me through our net connection. Phone contact is down.

A chime. HoHum signed into the chat room.

Hey Hotcakes! Where have you been? What have you been up to?

Weezy went on audio and said, "What's it to ya?"

"Somebody's been knockin' at your door."

"What do you mean?"

"What I mean is that as the semi-official poobah of security for Olegarten Manufacturing — may it live and prosper forever —

I cotched me some spurious queries tappin' on your door, trying to slip through unnoticed."

"When?"

"Couple days ago."

"Did you identify them? Did they get in?"

"Couldn't identify them. Came from the US of A, that's all I know. They were pretending to be you. Since it was pretty clearly not you, I redirected them to a dummy. They think they got into your secret site, and they believe you're a serious gamer who's also seeking...uhh...friendship online."

"Friendship online? Did you have to?"

"Well, I can hope, can't I? I know you work for some hush-hush government organization, so I had to give you a reason to be participating in a secret chat room, didn't I? By the way, who the hell are these dudes or dudettes, and are they going to compromise Olegarten?"

"Don't know for sure. They're only after me, though. Sorry to bring this on my friends."

"It's okay, Hotcakes. Those of us living in our basements with no social life whatsoever relish the challenges faced by human beings who have a life. Oh, by the way, will you marry me?"

Maddie bit her lip and grinned. Weezy shrugged.

"HoHum, you are sweet, but no. Not in this particular set of interstellar interstices."

"Okay, then how about some hot sex?"

"I'll pass."

Maddie covered her mouth with her hand, laughing silently.

A chime. Chester Burnell.

Weezy said to HoHum, "Gotta boogie, sweetheart. Got incoming I have to answer. And thanks for savin' my scrawny posterior."

"No problem. The sweeter the meat, the closer to the bone. Offer of nuptials stands."

Weezy went to "single line" and answered Joe.

"Joe, how are you?"

"Uhh...okay, considering. How about you? No Olegarten for what, a couple of days?"

"Long story," Weezy said. "Some bad people are watching me. I can't use the phone, but we have rigged an Internet connection here at work that I'm sure is safe. They probably picked up our last phone conversation. Most likely, they know where you were then, and Stevie Ray is compromised. They almost got into Olegarten, but our security caught them. They think they're monitoring me, but they're not."

"That explains a lot. They almost caught me."

"How? When? Are you all right?"

"I'm okay. It happened yesterday. I'm going toward home. Over the July 4th weekend, I went back to a place I'd been in May. A fine older gentleman named Mase runs it. I went down the road to a Laundromat. One of the guys I told you about from Orlando arrived, knocked Mase around. Mase played dumb and sent his grandson to warn me. Mase is okay, but hit a sweet, seventy-five-year-old man? These men are desperate and dangerous. Have you made any progress?"

"Yes, as a matter of fact, I have. Someone has managed to put a program that creates false scores into the system. I'm tracking it now, trying to run down how and why. The 'why' part is pretty straightforward. I believe someone billed $600,000 for Cynthia's care."

She paused, belatedly realizing matter-of-fact might not be the right tone.

"Sorry Joe. I didn't mean to dump that on you."

She turned on video. Joe sat on a bed in a shabby motel room. Well-used chenille bedspread, scarred bedside table, old TV, warped print of the Eiffel Tower slightly askew on the wall next to the window. Joe leaned forward, hands locked together, veins on his temples bulging. His mouth was distorted in an almost feral snarl.

"Joe...Joe, I put us on A/V."

She saw he was working to control his outrage. Maybe it was seeing Maddie over Weezy's shoulder. She gave a half-wave. "Hi. I'm Maddie. I work with Louise."

"There has to be one person I can trust with this inside IAC," Weezy said. "Maddie is that person. I'm tracking entries to the program I told you about...I call it the Mirror...coming in from California, so it's not something Florida Consolidated dreamed up. I need some time, probably a few days, to figure out who is doing this and who is affected."

Joe seemed to be thinking, gathering himself.

"That $600,000 is enough to put us both in danger. Now you're telling me it's much bigger than that."

Weezy had a flashback to the Underhill Diner, saw Joe across the table from her saying he would spend the rest of his natural life on this.

"I've contacted the few people I can identify who are affected by this," he said. "We have to get in touch with everyone else. How are we going to make sure that gets done?"

"When I know what's going on, I'm sure the FBI or NSA will go after the bad guys and fix the records and run down the people who might be getting bad treatment because of this."

"Okay." Joe said. "I might be offline for some time. If I go into the Net through wireless to Olegarten, it'll be easy to figure out where I am. Right?"

"Yes, that's true."

"Well, I'm out here in off-the-grid country. Not many signals to sort through to lock on to me. That's probably what happened yesterday. If I can't call you on the phone, how can we talk?"

Weezy turned to Maddie. "What do you think?"

"Joe's right," Maddie said. "Disposable phones can be traced. Ideally, find a place where Wi-Fi coverage is bad. Someone, probably a phone company, will offer wired services there. If you operate the old wired way, the last mile or maybe even several miles won't be exposed. Not a perfect solution, but better than nothing."

Joe seemed to reflect on the advice, then nodded, as if in conclusion of a thought. "Maddie, it's been good to meet you." He cracked a half-smile. "I think I see my way to a solution. Weezy, I'll be in touch."

"Be safe, Joe."

"I will. You, too." He smiled, and Weezy realized it was the first time she had seen him smile. The picture disappeared.

"Nice man," Maddie said. "Are you personally...you know...close?"

"No. Just a guy who stumbled on to a hell of a problem." But Weezy knew that wasn't true. Not since Underhill, not since she saw Cynthia through his eyes.

Maddie had gone back to her workstation. A muted "Bing" on Weezy's e-pad announced the feed from Olegarten delivering a message from Chester Burnell:

Think I have a solution to communication. See Panacea, FL.

***

Weezy turned back to her workstation. She tiptoed electronically back down the path to the Mirror. Slow going, when you have to be sure to leave no footprints. Finally, she was in the back alley of the IAC MedRecords files. She was tempted to add a dummy person and watch how Mirror handled it—like sending a canary down a mineshaft. But, if the canary dies, will someone find the carcass and get suspicious? She decided safe, slow and boring was best...a stakeout.

She put an invisible telltale on the portal...and waited.

Bored, she keyed Panacea, Florida. It was a kink in the Gulf Coast, tucked into St. Mark's National Wildlife Refuge in the eastern part of the state's panhandle. Protected by Tate's Hell State Forest on the west, the Apalachicola National Forest on the north and the Gulf of Mexico on the south and east. The main drag, the Sopchoppy Highway, passed to the north and carried the east-west traffic. The road to Panacea was a loop you would take only if you had business in the town or if you couldn't pass up visiting a place that might be, well, a panacea.

Weezy wrote a report on what she had done and what she suspected. P.E. read the draft, frowned, made a notation here and there, took out some of the technical detail. Peering over her half glasses, P.E. said, "This is going to the director, probably to the FBI and most likely to a couple of Senate committee chairmen. I can't be sure it won't be leaked. It's best for us to be conservative." Us. Relief flowed over Weezy. P.E. was on her side.

It took almost a week, but finally a tone from Weezy's console announced a hit on Mirror. It was early evening, and the bullpen was empty but for her. Sure enough, more California people, this time from a regional bank system. Twenty-plus that might die for no reason.

***

Weezy dozed lightly, half dreaming. She was in a computer game. The semi-conscious part of her brain realized she was working the problem of the Mirror and willed herself to remember what she was discovering. Finally, at 5:00 a.m., Sappho jumped on her bed, gave a her a friendly head butt, then marched several times across her bladder, making further sleep unlikely. Fully awake, Weezy struggled to remember what the computer game in the dream had been telling her.

After the bathroom, she walked out to the kitchen. She fed Sappho and was halfway through making coffee when she realized (a) she was on camera, (b) she was naked and (c) she couldn't react, even if some creep was watching. She started the coffee brewing, forced herself to walk, not sprint, back to the bedroom and got dressed.

She couldn't shake the feeling that there was a kernel of knowledge in the dream that would help her with the Mirror. She tried sitting and relaxing, emptying her mind. Whatever it was tortured the far edge of her consciousness. Something related to Joe, maybe? Something he said?

The coffee finished brewing. She went to the kitchenette, took down a mug. She poured. Liquid going from one vessel to another. Money is liquid, fungible.

"Follow the money." She slapped her forehead and slopped coffee on the counter.

Of course. That was what Joe said. The false bills get paid from somewhere. The bills IAC pays, they go somewhere. She didn't need to get inside Mirror. She only needed to follow the money.

Weezy tried to move at normal speed, hoping she hadn't telegraphed her flash of insight to an unseen watcher. She made a couple of sandwiches, packed them, an apple and a Thermos of coffee into her work bag and started off toward N-Ops. It was 7:00 when she arrived and signed in.

The bullpen was empty. Weezy opened Olegarten and composed a message to Joe.

Panacea looks like a perfect place for you. Getting more insight into what's going on in the Mirror. We are going to nail these bad guys. More when I know more.

She paused, realizing she had used 'we' again. But it was 'we' now. She pressed send.

Weezy signed out of Olegarten and into IAC. She followed the path she'd created into MedRecords. She found Mirror with its stack of patient files and went to Cynthia's. The payments for the low-level treatments and the hospice were all laid out, a total for Cynthia of $104,328, all going to an account in a New York bank called "Medical Disbursement Resolution." Payments from IAC coming into the account agreed with the numbers she got from Annika Dreher, $624,351. There were several other IDs in Medical Disbursement Resolution, so Cynthia's case was not unique. The transaction volume had risen rapidly over the last year, but the balance seemed to grow slowly. By far the largest amount of money paid out over the past year — some $7.1 million — was going to a bank branch in Reston, VA. It took her some time and a questionably legal trip into US Treasury records to find the account was registered to US Health Audits. The uncomfortable lunch conversation. Jason Squitieri.

Weezy found herself shaking, sweating. She shot out of her chair, stomping across the bullpen to P.E.'s office, angry that she had been attracted to Squitieri. Nobody home. Back at her workstation, she started a report summarizing her findings and outlining her suspicions. But P.E. always said, "Bring data, not opinion." Weezy steadied herself and thought through how to follow P.E.'s advice. Finally, she tracked back all the hits on the Medical Disbursement Resolution account and tallied them up. She then made a file of all 3,439 affected names, their organizations and which of them have had payments pass through the MDR account. Thirty people had been affected, the earliest two-and-a-half years ago. So this was not a long-term problem. Small relief.

She scribbled a note with her Resource Usage report asking for a meeting with P.E. She ate her lunch with the OddBalls and returned to the bullpen, hoping to see P.E. in her office. Instead, there was a note on her monitor setting up a 3 p.m. meeting in the fourth floor conference room. For the next two hours, she worked through the list of affected names, identifying those she thought had been given differential treatment. For seven of them, including Cynthia Mayfield, the record of payments had stopped.

***

At five minutes before 3:00, Weezy put her reports on a cube, grabbed her e-pad, and went to the fourth floor. P.E. was already in the conference room.

"Give me the short story." P.E. said as Weezy slid her e-pad across the table.

Weezy had mentally practiced her succinct treatment of the data. What came out in a rush was, "Jason Squitieri! He made half a million on Cynthia Mayfield, and seven-point-one million dollars went to US Health Audits out of the Mirror in the last year. He thinks we know what he's doing."

"Are you sure you told him nothing?"

"Yes, of course I'm sure."

"Don't get indignant, Louise. Give me what you know."

Weezy exhaled, composed herself, and moved into the report she had practiced.

"I think this problem is bigger than we thought. The Mirror's dummy name file has 3,439 names on it, and they come from several large businesses in Florida, California, and Pennsylvania. Of course, having your name in the file doesn't mean you'll get sick, but it means cheaper treatment if you do. Mirror has been operating for two-and-a-half, maybe three years. Twenty-three of the names got sick and then got reduced treatment. Seven of them show nothing for the last month. Mayfield's wife is one of the seven, and she died last February."

P.E.'s jaw set, reminding Weezy of her ability to intimidate even those several salary grades above her. Weezy continued, "The only good news is that Mirror is in startup mode."

P.E.'s sour expression didn't change. "So this is about money?"

Weezy nodded. "Yes, I think so. All the payments coming out of the Mirror go to an account in a New York bank. The Mirror pays the bills out of the account, and then charges IAC the much higher rates justified by the higher HealthScores IAC is seeing. If those were the only transactions, the account balance would quickly become pretty large. But over the last year, $7.1 million was transferred out to a holding account at US Health Audits."

There was a knock at the door. P.E.'s eyes flashed a warning. "Keep Squitieri to yourself."

The door opened, and a young man and a woman wearing Visitor badges joined them.

The woman nodded to Weezy, turned to P.E. and said, "P.E., how are you?"

P.E. stood. Weezy saw her making an effort to soften her expression.

The woman said, "P.E. Smith, this is Ryan Thomas, our public relations advisor. And this must be Louise Napolitani. I'm Michelle Barton." To Weezy, "P.E. and I have worked together often. I am IAC's legislative liaison."

Ryan shook hands with P.E. and nodded at Weezy, giving her the surreptitious looks-like-a-weirdo once over.

"You two seem to have uncovered a problem," he said. Turning to Michelle, "Needless to say, we want to solve the problem quickly, but we also need to get out ahead of any adverse publicity."

He turned back to focus on Weezy. She could see him calculating how foolish it would be to have Weezy represent the IAC in public, given the cargo pants, the T-shirt, and the hair, to say nothing of the 114 pounds. He turned back to P.E., "Let's cut to the chase. Who knows about this, and what's the timeline of your proposed solution?"

"I understand the problem in concept," P.E. said. "Louise knows the detail. Her first priority—" she gave Ryan a tight smile —"is solving this problem. Another staffer, Annika Dreher, knows there's an issue, but doesn't know many details. Another member of Louise's team has partial knowledge. At least one individual out in the public knows there's a problem but can't identify it as an IAC issue. I have made contact with a friend at the FBI on a confidential basis." Ryan frowned. "He knows some details of the case that exposed the issue," P.E. continued, "but not the breech itself. That's all, as far as I know. Oh, and whoever has read my note on Louise's June 23rd trip report."

Ryan turned to Michelle and raised his eyebrows. Michelle said, "The Director has seen the report. She, of course, is free to share it as she sees fit, with my help or not. However, she rarely goes around me on legislative matters."

"I've talked with the director," Ryan said, impatience breaking through his professional demeanor. "She's shared it with no one, except through you to Health, Ed and Labor."

"I've talked briefly with Chairman Thakur's staffer for health issues," Michelle said. "I have not shared the report, but I have given her a heads up that there may be a problem."

"When?" Weezy realized she'd said it out loud and three people had turned to her. She could see P.E. on the edge of giving her the Look, but her momentum carried her forward.

"When did you tell them?"

Michelle tilted her head, puzzled perhaps, or defensive. "Probably shortly before the July Fourth weekend."

Squitieri got that memo, Weezy was sure of it. She glanced at P.E. The Look had gone away, replaced by a subtler warning.

Michelle looked from P.E. to Weezy, saw nothing more forthcoming and continued. "There's a big up/down vote for a funding bill coming. If the "nays" grab on to the fact that there's a leak in the health care system, they will force Thakur to take the bill off the table. We don't want that to happen. It would be more than a delay. There are members who don't like having a government agency in charge of private personal data. They would gain leverage they need to hurt IAC."

Weezy's anger boiled up. They were covering their butts.

They weren't even considering the people who may die.

She saw anger in P.E.'s eyes, too.

Oblivious, Ryan produced an e-pad and dictated. "Bullet one. Minimize communication until full understanding of problem. Bullet two. Talking points for Director. Include number of people in system, medical costs processed, number of mistakes as in 'fewer than one in a million.' " He stopped to think, then turned to P.E. "You can get me the data, right?" P.E. nodded. Then he turned to Weezy. Speaking slowly and with emphasis, he said, "This must not get discussed publicly before we know the details. Understand?"

The gratuitous "understand" popped the cork for Weezy.

"Yes, I understand. And I don't understand any better when you speak slowly. It's true that the details are not all clear, but we know that a lot of people are in harm's way right now. Also, the government has been defrauded of millions of dollars. I know this is a sensitive issue, but like P.E. said, the focus needs to be first on stopping the process and notifying the people whose scores have been changed. And catching whoever who did this. Papering over your butt is way, way down the list."

Ryan's eyes shot up from his pad, his mouth agape.

Weezy continued, "This will come out. There's no way around it. You can manage how it comes out. Let us catch the perpetrators. We need to let the affected people know that we care for them and the safety of their personal data. Then we'll be both honest and get credit for doing the right thing."

The room was silent but for the white noise of the air conditioning. Ryan turned off his e-pad more firmly than necessary. He glared at Weezy, nostrils flaring, opened his mouth to speak, then clamped it shut. He turned to P.E. and said, "I have read your summary and the most recent report. Not many people are affected yet. Your analyst ..." he cast a sidewise glance at Weezy, "said this is really just starting up. All we need to do is change the numbers back to the right ones and send 'em a nice letter explaining there was mistaken data entry...Oh, so sorry."

He turned back to Weezy. "I understand you're the best tracker we have. I'm sure you're very good at what you do. You may not have gotten the message, but I didn't come here for advice on how to manage the potentially negative publicity this could generate. So, let's keep it simple. You keep doing your job. Keep your head down and work the system until you hear from P.E. what the next step is. Like they say out in the real world, 'asses and elbows.' And do not, under any circumstances, give interviews or otherwise discuss this outside your office. Understood?"

Weezy gave him her "jackass" look, mixed with a hint of resignation and turned to P.E. for confirmation.

"Louise, Ryan is right," P.E. said. "We have to hold on to this until we understand it. I agree with you that our first priority is to figure out Mirror in detail and to notify the people affected. But for now, speak only with me on this matter."

"Yeah, boss," Weezy said. Then she turned to Ryan, "Now I have an assignment for you." His eyebrows rose. Clearly this slip of a woman...girl, really...was not supposed to assign anything to anyone. He cocked his head, a half smile playing at the corner of his mouth. Weezy continued, "You need to come up with a fancy way of notifying the next of kin of the people that die while you're covering the organization's ass."

The nascent grin disappeared. Ryan stood, shoving the chair backward into the wall. He said to P.E., "If I hear a breath...a hint...that Ms. Napolitani has spoken of this, I will have both of your jobs." He turned, almost running into Michelle Barton, who stepped aside to let Ryan lead out the door. She glanced back at P.E. and Weezy and smiled an apology as she left.

P.E. shook her head and sighed. "Louise, antagonizing a PR guy is foolish. And, yes, he can cause us a lot of trouble, which would slow us down. Follow his advice. Head down, keep working on Mirror. I am worried that you're living alone and riding back and forth from home to work." She produced her own e-pad and tapped on it. "I want you to have the name of my FBI contact, just in case. Millard Williams, but call him Mel. He's in Washington. I sent his information to your e-pad. If I'm not around and you need help or fear for your safety, call him. He understands the outline of the problem, and he'll get you help faster than the local police." Her expression softened. "I want you to finish your work on Mirror, and then we are going to put you out of circulation for a while. For your protection."

Then she smiled, her eyes resting on the recently slammed door and said, "And mine."

TWENTY-EIGHT

MOST PEOPLE ARE ON the grid all the time and don't care that their life can be inspected by algorithms, government sleuths, and hackers. But there are still places unconnected to much of anything if you look hard enough.

Sitting in his motel room, Joe did a coverage search for Wi-Fi. Weezy's colleague Maddie was right, there were holes in network coverage. Of course, each provider claimed "near 100 percent" Wi-Fi coverage in the panhandle of Florida. But maps showed a lighter coloration all through the curve where the panhandle joins the dangling participle of the rest of the state, hinting at poor coverage. Complaints in chat rooms validated the suspicion.

Joe traced the map back to the places he loved as a young man. Almost anywhere along what the Florida Tourism Bureau called the Nature Coast would probably work. He remembered fishing in the Apalachicola as a kid, when the family had moved near Tallahassee, and he remembered the town of Panacea.

A "for sale by owner" search didn't show much. Finally, he saw an ad he liked:

Sgl. Wide 52', hookups, LP gas, ideal fishing & hunting. Rent to buy. R. Spencer. There was a number, which he called from one of his disposables. A gruff male voice answered, audio only.

"Yeah?"

"Mr. Spencer, you advertised a mobile home available for rent?"

"Uh-huh?"

"Yes, the fifty-two-footer you say has hookups for electricity and LP gas. You know, the one you say is ideal for hunting and fishing?"

"I don't say squat. Ain't mine, and I wouldn't buy it. Hold on …"

Spencer didn't bother to cover the phone. "Rosie...Rosie? Man wants to talk with you 'bout your uncle's trailer."

A silence, then footsteps shuffling.

"Yes?"

"Hi, I'm John," Joe said. "I see you're offering of a trailer to rent."

"Oh, yeah, well it's still available."

"Great. You said it's great for fishing and hunting, and I'd like something I can use on weekends and vacations."

"You from around here?"

"Well, not too far. Lived in Tallahassee when I was younger. Orlando, now, but I'm on the road a lot. Always loved the Apalachicola, though."

"It ain't a mansion, but my uncle lived there for twenty-three years. It's a rent to buy unless you want to buy it straight up. I own the land, and I want to keep it that way. That a problem?"

If she owns the land, that should keep my name off county records, Joe thought. Bet she wouldn't spend the money on a lawyer to register the rental contract. Perfect!

"Not a problem for me. I'd like to see it. I'm out near New Orleans now, coming back toward Orlando. Can we meet early next week?"

"Fine by me. Gimme a call at this number. We can meet at the place."

"I'll call you on Tuesday morning."

He called up a map of the region. His GPS didn't give a precise location of the trailer, a plus. Must be up Joe Mack Smith Extension, a dirt track that ran off of Joe Mack Smith Street north of the town and east of Tate's Hell.

So he was going to go to hell down a path named after Joe Mack Smith. Perfect.

***

The next Tuesday morning, Joe called Rosie for directions.

"You come through Sopchoppy," she said. "Go 'bout four mile east, and you come to the Coastal Highway and a sign toward Panacea. Turn south a mile or two. I ain't so good at distances."

"Tell me the address...I can find it from that."

"It's got no address I know of. Can't find it on your phone. But it's pretty easy to get to. Come south on Coastal, hang a right on Joe Mack Smith Street. Follow straight on 'til it turns to a dirt track. That's Joe Mack Smith Extension. Keep on less'n a mile. You come to a bobwire fence. Then there's an open field. After that, on your left, is the trailer. White with a green awning."

Joe followed her instructions. Where the Joe Mack Smith paved road turned south, a sandy track went straight. Finally, he passed by the barbed wire and saw the trailer. An old red pickup truck was parked in front. As Joe approached, the door of the pickup opened and a none-too-friendly-looking man got out. Joe stopped the Element fifty feet behind the old truck, opened the door, stepped out and froze. The man carried a none-too-small sidearm.

The man took in Joe's surprise and smiled a none-too-friendly smile.

"Can't be too careful out here in the country. Woman out here alone, might be raped and killed and nobody'd know it." He thrust out his chin. Joe couldn't tell whether he expected confirmation or argument.

Joe said, "Well, I can't disagree. But I've always found the people around here to be friendly. 'Course, I can afford to be open-minded. Not likely anyone's going to rape me."

A half laugh, half whinny issued from the man. "You're right about that. Rosie's in the trailer cleanin' up. You can go on."

Joe knocked at the screen door. A voice from the depths of the trailer said, "Yeah, come on in."

A middle-age woman appeared down the narrow hallway, cigarette dangling, damp graying hair framing her face. Sweat beaded on her brow. The smoke from her cigarette made her right eye squint. She inspected Joe suspiciously with the unimpaired left.

"I been cleaning up. Uncle Fred was a slob, and I ain't had the chance to work the place over since he died."

Joe had entered a small living area. The furniture must have been assembled over a half-century or so. A recliner that was much too big for the space. Old TV. Kitchenette to the right, melamine counter etched with cigarette burns. Small gas stove. Ancient refrigerator. A narrow hallway leading toward what must be a bedroom currently filled with Rosie's imposing figure. The stale air hinted that Uncle Fred had been a smoker and a beer drinker.

Rosie continued, "Electric's up and paid for. Stove runs on LP gas, which you got to buy. Don't know how much is in the tank. Coverage for phone and such ain't so great out here. Fred had the TV hooked up, but I turned it off a ye—uuh—a while ago. You'd have to turn it back on."

Joe said, "I'd probably do that. Can't be on vacation without watching football, can you?"

Rosie shrugged, "Not much of a TV...prob'ly forty years old. 2-D. You'd want to bring your own."

Joe nodded Yes and said, "So, how does this 'rent-to-own' thing work?"

Rosie said, "Pretty simple. You rent. I keep track of what you paid. If you buy, the rent you paid goes toward the price. Only thing is, we have to agree to the price right now, and I have the right to sell even though you're renting. And you pay eight hundred dollars one month in advance."

"I'd like to go ahead," Joe said. "I can pay you in cash."

He filled in his name as John Maxwell. "I'm going to give you a post office box in Orlando, because I'm moving to a new place. That okay?"

"I think it's okay, but I want to talk it over with Reggie." She crossed the living area, went down the steps and out to the truck. A short conference ensued. She came back across the yard and said, "Reggie said it's okay, 'long's you pay in advance."

Joe finished filling in both copies, signed them, kept one, and paid. Rosie counted the cash, reorganizing the bills so they all faced the same direction.

"Okay, then," Rosie said, "I expect a call before the tenth of next month. Don't be comin' round without callin' first. We got unfriendly dogs, and Reggie ain't all that hospitable, either."

Joe mumbled his thanks. Rosie took a swipe at her brow, tapped the ash off the cigarette, passed Joe a rusty key and said, "Well, all right, then." She turned and walked to the truck, raised her herself into the cab. She and Reggie drove off, leaving Joe to reconnoiter.

He pushed the recliner into a corner and opened all the windows that weren't stuck or nailed shut. The kitchen occupied the front of the trailer. The middle was the living area and the back had a small bedroom, a smaller bedroom and a tiny bathroom with a shower stall. Joe unloaded the Element and moved into what was undoubtedly advertised as the master bedroom. He gave thanks that he was just over six feet, not taller.

In the living room, he put Cynthia's guitar on its stand. Maybe he'd finally have time to learn to play. He took Lucky Monkey out of his box and put him in the corner of the kitchen counter, having a fleeting feeling that the lar liked this place. In the bedroom, he stripped and crossed the hall to the shower. The water smelled sulfurous, not unusual in this part of Florida. There was an aged, cracked remnant of soap, no shampoo.

Much refreshed, he put on a T-shirt and shorts and drove into the town in search of soap. He discovered a general store that also sold groceries. He bought hot dogs and canned mixed vegetables, as well as a small, wax paper wrapped "ho-made" pie. Back at the trailer, Joe tried the compact stove without success. Outside, he found the LP gas canister, which seemed full, but the hose was not connected. He decided not to fuss with it and used the microwave to make a simple dinner. The pie more than justified the rest of the meal.

The tin box of the trailer was still hot, but it was cooling down outside. A light breeze out of the south teased the dirty curtains, bringing a hint of saltwater.

He put a pan of water on the stove to boil for tea. No flame. Rosie had said there was gas, but maybe not. Outside, he tilted the gas canister. Full, but not connected. He decided not to fuss with it, returned to the kitchen, and heated water in the microwave. Tea in hand, he went outside again to sit on the steps and enjoy the cool breeze and scent of the forest. The silence of the Florida dusk brought back memories of drifting on the Apalachicola, and he felt at home. Birds talked quietly, settling in for the evening. Tree frogs began their nightly chorus. In his mind, Big Bill Broonzy was singing about going to the river, taking his rockin' chair.

It wouldn't be so bad to disappear. He fell into a reverie of canoeing on the river, fishing, and talking with the nice lady at the grocery ("Well, you know, I realized there's more to life than grinding it out for a big corporation.") But the old Joe, the concrete-sequential, plan-your-work-and-work-your-plan Joe, wouldn't leave him alone. How the hell was he going to disappear? What about the apartment? MedRecords? His promise to Cynthia's memory?

***

A few days later, Joe navigated the rutted track that led to Rosie Spencer's trailer. It was a quarter mile down the dirt road that fronted the single wide he had rented. The Spencer trailer came into view, shabbier than Joe's and nearly hidden by big live oaks and jack pine. Two large dogs loped toward the Element. They didn't bark until they got right up to the car, then their greeting was a ferocious warning, not the inquiring bark of dogs anticipating a whole new bouquet of smells. Reggie sauntered down the path, his sidearm very much in evidence. He spat a stream of tobacco juice and glared at Joe with a ferocity matching that of his dogs.

"What you want?"

"Uhh, Reggie...Mr. Spencer...I went to get the TV hitched up, and the company said it was easier to keep it in Rosie's name. So she's going to get a bill for my setup. I thought I'd better pay before she gets surprised by the bill."

"Uh huh."

"Shall I stay in the car? I'm guessing your dogs are not very friendly."

Reggie gave a squint that might pass as a grin.

"Annabelle. Scooter. Down."

The two dogs seemed disappointed but settled, hackles down and ears at attention.

"My, those are impressive dogs. What breed are they?"

"Them's crossbred Shepherd and Doberman. That way, you get the size of the Shepherd and the meanness of the Doberman all wrapped up in one pretty package."

Another squint-that-might-be-a-grin, but Reggie's features softened as he gazed at them. Pride.

"They're brother and sister. Litter mates, otherwise they'd prob'ly tear each other to pieces. Didn't have Scooter cut, so's he'd keep the fire in the belly. Had to have Annabelle spaded, though, 'cause I don't want pups all over the place."

Joe said lamely, "Well, you're well protected out here."

"Yup. Sure's hell keeps people who got no bi'ness out here from gettin' nosy."

Joe wondered idly what business Reggie had going that he didn't want people investigating, then realized he really didn't want to know. He saw Rosie appear at the door of the trailer and start out toward them, her scuffs raising puffs of dust. Dry summer, so far.

Reggie had run out of things to say. To break the silence, Joe said, "On the map, and it seems like we're right up against the edge of a state forest called Tate's Hell."

Reggie's stare said what's-it-to-yuh?

"Well, I mean, a place doesn't get a name like that without a story. Seems like nice woods to me, not Hell."

Reggie seemed to relax a fraction. Yet another squint. "Yup. Well, seems like, back just after the War 'Tween the States, there was a farmer up the way called Cebe Tate. A pan'ter was carryin' off his livestock, so he took off with his gun and a coupla dogs to hunt the pan'ter down. Disappeared for a week and ended up layin' in a field up near Carrabelle. He said to the people who found him, 'My name is Cebe Tate, and I come from Hell!' Then he died. Forest is still too thick to get into 'less you know what you're doin'." It was clear that Reggie knew what he was doing and knew Joe did not and never would.

Rosie arrived, looking nervous as she passed the dogs.

"Rosie," Joe said, "I told Mr. Spencer...Reggie...that I had to get the TV restarted, and it was simpler to leave it in your name. You'll get a bill for $155.40 in a couple of weeks. I wanted to get ahead of that, so you're not surprised."

Joe dug in his pocket, brought out eight twenties and handed them over. Rosie counted them, lining them up again, and said, "Guess that's okay. It's more'n we pay, though."

"Well, I realized that I have to get to the Internet even when I'm on vacation," Joe said.

She shook her head. "Yeah, that's okay by me, long's you pay in advance."

Reggie decided their business was concluded, turned back toward the trailer, calling the dogs.

"Annabelle. Scooter. Up!"

The dogs rose gracefully, fanned out to Reggie's right and left and trotted up the path with their master.

Rosie turned to watch the trio. "Reggie sure does love them dogs," she said wistfully.

TWENTY-NINE

THE MORNING DATA DUMP from FBI headquarters was uninteresting, as usual. Henry Barber would rather have been doing something other than answering inane questions with insipid responses. The news aggregator that Jennifer Rowland set up was nearly blank. No news may have been good news, but it was also boring.

Henry sighed and turned to the stack of folders that probably contained the secret of success of a locally prominent financier promising unrealistically high rates of return to his well-heeled clients.

A soft "Bing" on his monitor announced a call from Mel Williams, Federal Crimes division.

"Barber here."

The picture popped up. Mel Williams...sure. Good guy. Academy, '09. The track star.

"Hey, good to see you, Mel. What's up?"

"Henry, I'm following up a call I had from an old friend, P.E. Smith. You might remember her as Priscilla. She was at headquarters after you left for Florida. She went on to become a director at the InterAgency Channel. She's running the group they call trackers. They're the folks that protect the Yak against hackers. Anyway, she called a couple of days ago with a problem involving a company in your neck of the woods. Florida Consolidated Energy."

"Really? Yes, well, we do have an open investigation of FCE. Does this have to do with wire fraud?"

"No, as a matter of fact, it has to do with falsified medical records."

Jennifer Rowland had come over to stand behind Henry,

listening with furrowed brow.

Henry glanced at Jennifer, then said, "Uh, oh...Mel, this is Jennifer Rowland. We're working on this together. Jennifer is way ahead of me on the technology we're all supposed to be using these days. Jennifer, Mel is in criminal investigation in the Washington office. We go back to the Academy."

"Hi, Mel."

"Nihow. I'm surprised you've managed to tether Henry to a desk. He was the best of us at the financial stuff. But he always wanted to get out in the field, kick butt and take names."

Jennifer chuckled. "Not much has changed."

Henry shrugged, trying to appear innocent, then continued, "So, on this medical records case, let me guess. An employee is maintaining that his wife's records were changed?"

"Yes, that's right. Do you know about it?"

"Yes and no. We got drawn into an odd meeting over at Florida Consolidated two months ago. Had to do with illegal money transfers. When I met with company officials, they tried to blame a man they had just fired. But they fired the guy because he broke into their personnel database. He was apparently concerned that his wife's HealthScore was changed."

"No follow-up on the MedRecord issue at that point?" Mel asked.

"Nope. We had to stick to the money issue," Henry said. "The MedRecord thing was the most interesting part of the story, particularly after the head of Human Resources drowned under suspicious circumstances. But the locals and FBI brass get their collective knickers in a knot if we start freelancing on the interesting stuff."

"Know about that," Mel said.

"As it stands, the local police down here are investigating the drowning. I don't think they've made any progress."

"Well, that's interesting, Henry. It seems like the medical

records problem is real, and far wider-spread than Florida Consolidated. Priscilla thinks it's a fraud that has resulted in several deaths already. Someone or some group is trying hard to cover it up, which might explain the homicide."

"Can you get us leeway to follow up?"

Mel grinned. "I believe 'constructively interpreting your assignment' is what I'll say to the brass. We're going to put the IAC tracker who discovered the problem in protective custody. We understand she has talked to the man you said was fired by FCE. I'd really like to find him. Among other things, he apparently managed to hack the Yak, which is how the tracker became involved. Does anyone know where he is?"

"We don't know," Henry said. "But I have a hunch we may be able to get to him through people he worked with. Why don't we try that angle?"

"Great idea, Henry. Let's stay in touch. Seems like there's more here than meets the eye."

***

For several days after the meeting with the PR people, Weezy stuck to her agreement with P.E., fuming at the vapor-brained PR guy, mumbling to herself. The OddBalls watched from a distance. Such mumbling was usually preface to an entertaining eruption.

She was leery of penetrating Mirror, but there was enough electronic traffic associated with a bank account that she felt safe examining it. Mirror paid the lower-cost bills from the actual treatments immediately. REDIRECTR then generated false bills for much larger amounts to the IAC.

When she was finally satisfied with her understanding of the Mirror, she drew an interactive process diagram, which she tucked away in secure IAC files and the Mayfield folder.

Then, she fiddled. If Mirror paid real bills quickly, but there was a delay in payments from IAC, she could drain Mirror's bank account by setting the HealthScores back to what they should be.

People would start to get the treatments they should get, Mirror would pay out the higher real bills, and Mirror's bank account would go negative. The PR flacks could do their dance of seven veils all they wanted to. Meanwhile, she could fix the problem, at least going forward.

She took a day to write what she called Mirror Two to accomplish this. She slapped the program, inactive, right next to Mirror in the IAC. No risk of being activated by chance. Just insurance. The feds might whisk her off to Timbuktu, for all she knew.

Toward the end of the day, Weezy felt satisfied. She toyed with writing a note to P.E. but decided against it. P.E. had left in the morning for a meeting in Washington, and Weezy didn't want to put Mirror Two in the formal record yet.

Her monitor showed an incoming message. It was a memo to P.E., with copies to the director and L. Napolitani. She had never been copied on a memo to the director. It directed P.E. to "Stop all research on the MedRecord Project" and "All materials, reports and files are to be collected and sent to Ryan Thomas."

The OddBalls got the eruption they had been waiting for.

***

Weezy was contemplating what to do next when a muted "Bing" announced a hit from Joe's avatar Chester Burnell.

Open Olegarten Manufacturing ...

She went on as Hotcakes, and Joe responded almost immediately.

Hotcakes, progress report?? Video Okay?

Weezy glanced around the open bullpen. No one seemed interested in what she was doing. She turned the monitor audio lower.

Sure.

A video window opened. Joe wore a T-shirt, looking warm.

He said, "My new place" and moved the camera around so Weezy saw the inside of the Panacea trailer.

"Not a palace, but like your friend said, off the grid. I have a wired connection to who-knows-where. Probably shouldn't stay on for long, but I'm relieved to have found a place where I can relax for a while."

"That's great, Joe, and I do have a report. I have figured out how the scam that killed Cynthia...and it is a scam...works. I'm uploading a flowchart. Please, puhleeze, don't do anything but read it. My boss and I have written a report that's going through the system. I think I can catch the bastards that did this. I've identified at least one of them."

Joe blinked several times and then looked directly into the camera. Intense. Almost as if he'd jumped through the wires right to her desk. "Louise, thank you. Thank you. I wish I could say it better, more eloquently. Thank you."

Weezy realized she was crying.

In the silence, another window opened on Weezy's monitor, showing a text from P.E. Smith's private phone.

"Ge <missing> Ou <missing> Ow"

Strange. Bad reception, apparently. "Hold one minute, Joe."

She tapped the message playing across the monitor to open video. A breaking up picture. It was P.E., disheveled. The inside of a car. Something on her face. *Blood? Blood!* Eyes rolling back. Weezy saw P.E. was saying something. She replayed the message. Questions she hadn't time to answer crowded the edge of her consciousness.

Weezy focused on P.E.'s lips, trying to pick out consonants and vowels. She was saying, "Get out now."

The video disconnected.

"Get out now? Why are you saying, 'Get out now'?" Joe asked from his window, brows furrowed. "What's wrong? You look like you've seen a ghost."

Weezy stammered, "Oh God, Joe. That was my boss, the only other person who fully understands what I'm doing. I just got a call from her. Breaking up. Something's terribly wrong with her. An accident maybe. There was blood. She said, 'Get out now.'"

"What can I do to help?"

Weezy was trembling.

"How the hell do I get out now?"

She saw Joe was forcing himself to stay calm. "Where are you now?"

"I'm at work at the IAC."

"Do you have to go home?"

"Yes." Sappho, Bo, Joe's cube, clothes, money. "I really do have to."

"Can you get home safely?"

"I'll have to work on that, but I think so."

"What worked for me was to travel by rail. Buy a ticket with cash, if possible. Do you have someone who can go to the main train station and buy a ticket for you?"

"I think so." Bo would do it in an instant.

"Okay. The safest place to go is somewhere in the ten percent of the country where you can get off the grid. Don't go home to your family. They'll find you there. The safest place I know is right here in Panacea. You have seen the trailer I rented. Nothing is associated with my name or any one of the avatars. You could come here if you feel comfortable moving in with someone you don't know very well. You could have your own bedroom. Or we could put you up in the motel up the road."

Relief. A good, practical, plausible solution. Go see a...friend.

Weezy's head spun. "This is all happening so fast," She said. "I know I don't have time to think it through the way I should, but give me ten minutes and I'll be back to you."

"Sure. I'll go offline now."

"And Joe, thanks for the offer. It means a lot."

"No problem. I owe you."

His face disappeared.

Weezy felt a sudden rush of wanting to remain rooted right in the bullpen. Two of her team were at the large display, studying a map tracking a hacker from somewhere in Eastern Europe. Adam was at Maddie's console, pointing at the status board. Low light, familiar furniture...but mainly, friends. Safety.

P.E. said "Get out now," but it was safe inside the IAC. Twenty-four-hour security. She could sleep here, order in food, get Bo to feed Sappho for a while. Maybe...she sighed.

But P.E. said, "Get out now." Weezy thought of P.E.'s face, eyes rolling back into her head, hanging on to the last shred of consciousness to deliver the simple message. Of course, she had to go.

Maddie caught Weezy's look. She interrupted Adam and came to Weezy's console.

"What's wrong?"

Weezy opened her mouth to speak, knew tears were starting.

"Weezy, what's wrong?"

"Something happened to P.E. Something bad." Weezy keyed a repeat of the video.

Maddie watched, color draining from her face. She watched again.

Then, in a rush, questions. "Do you know where she is? What's she saying? Car accident? Must be. She's in a car. What's she saying?"

"Get out now."

Stricken, Maddie asked, "Does it have to do with the MedRecords project?"

"Yes. It must."

"What are you going to do?"

"I just talked with Mayfield. I think he has a safe place. Maddie, I don't want to put you in danger..."

Maddie put her arm around Weezy. "Adam thinks he's joking when he calls me Mad Dog. I want to help run these bastards down. Let me."

Another friend.

"Thanks, Maddie. I need to call Joe back. He gave me a plan. I had to have a few minutes to think it over before deciding. If you're willing to help, I'll make the call."

"Do it. You have to believe P.E."

Weezy keyed Olegarten, and Joe answered immediately.

"Thanks for the offer, Joe. I'm going to take you up on it. You met Madeline Hollingsworth last week." Joe nodded a greeting to Maddie. "She's the only person besides P.E. who understands the project. She will be our contact here at IAC. I'll leave a note on Olegarten when I have plans made. Okay?"

"Okay. Good luck...I mean, stay safe." There was something more than polite concern on Joe's face.

Weezy signed off and turned to Maddie.

"If I'm going to get out of here, I have to bring you up to speed."

Weezy showed Maddie her files. She copied the Mayfield folder onto a cube for herself, a violation of IAC protocol Weezy knew P.E. would approve of under the circumstances. She explained Mirror Two and how to activate it. They made a plan to get Weezy out of the building into Maddie's car. She told Maddie about the meeting with Michelle Barton and Ryan Thomas, the data from Annika Dreher, and the reason for the security sweep. Lastly, she explained the US Health Audits connection.

"You mean, the dreamboat who took you out to lunch?"

"That's the man."

Maddie shook her head sadly, lapsing into her Georgia voice, "Well, I declare. Bad things sometimes come wrapped in pretty packages, don't they?"

***

Maddie, given the task of being Weezy's contact and confidante, took over the business of getting Weezy safely out of the IAC. Over the course of an hour, cash appeared ("Who uses cash anymore?" Adam asked.) and several burner phones were procured. Weezy was sidelined to "make plans" and the OddBalls were warned to stay away from P.E.'s office.

"I'd sure like to shut down that adit," Weezy said. "That must be how the bad guys knew where P.E. was."

"Strike that," she said. "I want to take the transmitter out before I leave. It probably doesn't transmit very far, so I need to find the relay transmitter, too. Any idea how we can find it?"

"Adam's our best hardware guy," Maddie said. "Let's let him have a run at it." Maddie went off to get Adam started.

Adam quickly found the relay transmitter in the men's room. He tried to make it seem like no big deal, but he was clearly both relieved and proud of himself. "Always the first place to look, because you can be in there and nobody wants to know what you're doing."

Maddie went to the parking lot and met Weezy at the north entrance to the building, on the opposite side from the bike rack, and drove her home. The side streets were quiet as dusk fell, and they saw no followers. She said, "Nice digs!" as she turned into the driveway of Bo's house.

Weezy handed Maddie one of the disposable phones and said, "Just in case. I'll try not to use it unless I have to."

"Keep in touch," Maddie said. "I'll get to you through Olegarten and let you know as soon as I know anything about P.E." She leaned over to Weezy and gave her a long hard hug. "Be careful," she said. "We're with you in spirit." Her eyes sparkled with unshed tears. Weezy patted Maddie's arm, trying to look brave and strong. Then she was out of the car, across the lawn, and knocking lightly on Bo's back door.

Bo answered almost immediately. "About time you got home.

Sappho has been asking after her dinner rather stridently!"

"May I come in, Bo? Quickly?"

"Of course, dear, but you really should feed that awfully demanding feline of yours ..."

Weezy slipped by Bo into the kitchen.

"I have to leave here for a while. A week or two. Maybe longer. And I need your help. P.E.'s been in a terrible accident."

Weezy told the story while Bo listened in stunned silence.

"I must call Walter."

While Bo called P.E.'s husband, Weezy crossed to her apartment and climbed the stairs. She forced herself to behave as if everything was normal. Day at work, home for dinner.

She fed Sappho, then said, "I hope you enjoy your dinner, my beautiful feline. I am going to enjoy mine, because Bo has invited me over for a light supper," hoping the unseen watcher didn't sense her manufactured nonchalance.

Sappho seemed to sense something was amiss because she stopped eating and followed Weezy across the yard.

Bo waited at her back door.

"I talked with Walter, and it's serious. She was driving back from Washington and got run down right after she got off the beltway. Crazy person trying to pass. Ran her into a retention pond. The car was destroyed, and P.E. would have drowned but for the quick action of a firefighter on his way home from Chevy Chase. The young man was a quarter of a mile behind her and saw her car go in. He dragged her out of the car, but she's in bad shape."

Weezy absorbed the news. At least P.E. was alive. Bo was on the verge of tears, though, looking old and frail. It wasn't fair to ask for her help.

Bo seemed to sense Weezy's conclusion, sat straighter and said, "So, what are your plans? How are you going to get out of here?"

Weezy gave her a quick rundown.

Bo zeroed in on the issue of tickets. "How are you going to get the train tickets?"

"Well, I'm going to ask a friend to go down ..."

"I'm a friend."

"No, Bo. You're already too exposed. We now know these people are vicious."

"Louise, I'm the obvious choice to get the tickets. I use the train all the time. I can whisk in, use my imperious manner, and buy tickets with cash. You can get from BWI to Union Station in Washington every hour. I'm sure there's a train to Atlanta several times a day. In fact, there's no time like the present. Speaking of cash, you'll need some. I'm old enough to remember the days of carrying cash, unlike you younger folks who swipe for everything. Hold on." She reached into a cubby above the kitchen counter and pulled out her purse. She dug into it and produced a stack of bills, which she handed to Weezy. "Are you packed?"

Weezy started to shake her head, but Bo continued, "We know that someone may be watching the apartment. If you drag a suitcase out, they'll know exactly what you're doing. I don't know how you have been doing your laundry...if you have been doing your laundry...and the watcher probably doesn't either. So, if you load a laundry basket up with what you need to take and walk it over here, the watcher will think you do your laundry in my house. We'll then pack you up, I'll drag the suitcase out as if I'm going on a trip. We'll drive to the station, I'll get your ticket, and you'll take the train."

"Bo, that's a wonderful plan, but it will be quite obvious to anyone watching that you are involved."

"So?"

"So, I don't want to put you at risk."

"I didn't finish the plan, Louise. I will also buy a ticket. At the same time you go south, I shall go north to New York for a few days. You will have to have your friends take care of Sappho. I'll take in some theater. Clive is up there now, you know, spending lonely nights at the New York Athletic Club. Perhaps I'll give in to his increasingly desperate entreaties to 'have dinner and talk.' I think I have him exactly where I want him." She sniffed. "And he claims to be the experienced negotiator. Hah!"

THIRTY

JOE WAS ON THE road to Tallahassee to pick up Weezy when one of his phones rang. He dug into the ditty bag on the front seat and fished out the one that was flashing. The ID said Maggie McTillis. How had she gotten the number? Oh, yeah, that last call so long ago. Let her leave a message.

The ringing stopped. Joe pulled onto the shoulder. No cars around. *Missed call* popped up the phone's display.

Of course. Disposable. No messages.

Joe hesitated. Someone could be tracking Maggie's phone.

He stared at the number, torn. He stared at the number, torn. At least he was a few miles away from the trailer.

He dialed and Maggie answered.

"Joe?"

"Yes, Maggie. You called just now?"

"Yes, Joe, and I'm so glad to hear your voice. Are you all right? Where are you? Oh, I suppose I shouldn't ask."

"I'm okay, Maggie. I've been staying off the grid, and I'm not in Orlando. I've been checking out this medical records issue, and there is something to it."

"Have you been using avatars? Did you send a message to Susan Rodriguez?"

"Well, yes, I did...almost a month ago. I've stayed away from the avatars recently, though. There's a person...I met a person who works in the system, and she is running it down far better than I could. But there's somebody out there who wants this whole issue to disappear, and me with it."

"That's why I'm calling," Maggie said. "The FBI agent who questioned me back when Laura died stopped by my house last night. He wants to talk with you about the medical records issue.

He also said he thinks you aren't safe. I said I would get in touch with you if I could and ask you to call him."

"I have to think on that, Maggie," Joe said. "So far, there are very few people I can trust. No offense to your judgment, but this whole MedRecords thing has been crazy. Just give me his number."

He paused, remembering Weezy's comment about the loyalty of a "woman you used to work with" and said, "Thanks Maggie...for believing in me."

***

The new train station in Tallahassee was quiet on a Saturday. The combination of heat and humidity had driven most people indoors, and the normal flow of traffic from the state capitol was small on the weekend. Joe spotted Weezy as she got off the train. She scanned the platform and saw him, gave a half-wave.

Joe went to her and put out his hand. She hesitated, then shook.

"Do you know any more about your boss?"

Weezy shook her head. "Only that she's in the hospital and will survive."

When she didn't continue, Joe said, "My home is pretty basic, but the country's beautiful. And Panacea is the best place I know to be overlooked. I hope so, anyway."

Weezy looked at him obliquely. "And where is Panacea?"

"We'll go thirty miles south to the Gulf coast. I grew up canoeing and fishing along the rivers that drain into the Gulf. My place is not far from the town of Panacea, but you can't find it in an address search." He realized he was talking too much, but kept on, wanting to fill the gap, hold off the hard reality of their situation. "I took your colleague Maddie's advice and had my phone and Internet wired, because Wi-Fi reception there is spotty. I'm guessing the signal comes out of Tallahassee. Lots of traffic on the grid there because it's the state capital."

They had arrived at the Element. Joe put Weezy's bag in the

back and they got in. BeeBee, the voice of the navigation system, said, "Where to?" Joe said, "Panacea, Joe Mack Smith Extension." BeeBee said, 'Cain't find that location, exactly."

Joe turned to Weezy. "See what I mean?"

"Where did you get the nav system?" Weezy said with a grin.

"The voice came with the car. The former owner probably recorded herself. Reminds me of New Orleans."

"I hope she's not transmitting," Weezy said.

"Nope. I disabled that part of the system long ago."

Joe glanced at Weezy. "I feel bad that you got wrapped up in this. After we talked, I realized I was selfish. Selling Panacea because I want to get a chance to understand what's been done and what to do about it. It wasn't fair of me to put you at risk to pursue my own vengeance. The FBI probably would have put you into witness protection, or something like that."

Weezy gazed off into the middle distance for a moment. Then, picking her words, said, "My boss, P.E., used to work at the FBI, and she contacted them. You're right...they wanted to take me into protective custody. But then I wouldn't have had full access to the Yak to work the problem. That was back right after the July Fourth holiday. I've been figuring out the Mirror ever since. You know about that." Joe nodded. "Then, yesterday, P.E. got run off the road. She didn't say, 'Call the FBI.' She said, 'Get out now.' I hope I'm doing the right thing," she said, clearing her throat to cover the quaver in her voice.

***

The road from Tallahassee south passed down the east side of the Apalachicola National Forest. Pines and live oaks closed in on the road except where modest houses and trailers interrupted. Bird calls, heat. Weezy felt the tension flowing out of her. She wanted to plan her next steps, but the heat brushed aside the efforts of the air conditioner, and the rhythm of the old car kept time with a song Joe had on the system, scratchy recording of a man singing about the

Yellow Dog and the Southern.

She woke with a start as Joe turned off the main road. "Joe Mack Smith Street," he said. "Seems like every place here has a story, and I'm sure there's one for this street." Nice houses, a residential neighborhood. It didn't look far off the grid to Weezy.

Joe Mack Smith Street curved left. Joe continued straight on the unpaved extension. White Florida sand, lush underbrush closing in as they penetrated the edge of the forest. After what must have been less than a mile but seemed like more, they came to an open field, barbed wire on one side and an old trailer on the left.

"Home, sweet home," Joe said with a smile and a shrug. "Be it ever so humble...and it is...there's no place like a single wide in the forest."

Weezy revised her opinion about being off the grid.

***

Joe moved to the smaller bedroom, giving the larger, more private master bedroom to Weezy. She argued, but not too hard. She dropped her bag and went to the living area, where Joe had set his e-pad on the table that folded out of the wall opposite the outside door. She spent a few minutes making absolutely certain his e-pad was clean, then plugged hers in and tested the connection.

"Looks good. Now, I need a shower."

"Water doesn't smell great, so I got the only soap the store had. Hope you're partial to Hidden Grotto Mist. Take any towel in the cupboard under the sink."

"I'll make it work."

Joe took a seat and began working at the e-pad. The trailer walls were thin, and Joe heard Weezy humming, splashing and then the water being turned off.

The bathroom door opened inward, and Joe glanced up from his e-pad. Weezy emerged through a cloud of steam, still humming, gazing out the side window while drying her hair, pensive. Naked, but for panties that made the term "briefs" seem an understatement.

Small, firm breasts, flat everything else except a delicious, tight derriere. A second or two passed before she gasped and covered as much as the small towel allowed, turning away from Joe.

"What the hell are you gaping at?" she said, glaring at him over her shoulder, shock turning to anger.

"Sorry, I ..."

She turned toward the bathroom, indecisive, then stomped the few steps to her room.

Ten minutes later, Weezy emerged, mouth set into a line, eyes angry.

"Goddammit. I live alone. I don't have to worry about some guy gawking."

"I, I'm...Sorry. You surprised me." Then defensively, "Any man would look at a beautiful woman."

"Don't get any ideas ..." Slightly mollified.

"No."

Later, they ordered dinner from Pelican's Roost, the local restaurant. Joe said to Weezy as they entered, "This is the South. If it can be fried, they fry it, and it's generally delicious." They carried out fried chicken, okra (also fried) and hushpuppies (ditto, of course). On the way back to the trailer, they added a wax paper-wrapped strawberry-rhubarb pie from the general store. Dinner was awkward, each of them thinking about Weezy's nakedness in a different way and each a little embarrassed. Maybe because of that, they retreated to family stories.

Weezy told of growing up in the North End of Boston, her mom Maria and dad Louis, and the trips to the fish market where he worked. She explained the way he assessed the quality of a catch, priced it out, sold off the parts he couldn't use in the space of five minutes. Joe listened, understanding that they were both giving the brutality and fear of the current situation a time-out.

Joe took her cue and related his childhood in Illinois, grandparents he loved, his dad's rigidity and aphorisms, the hard transition to Tallahassee when he was a teenager, football success bringing social acceptance, and his love of the rivers around Panacea.

Light was fading, and they had given the ancient air conditioner a well-needed rest and opened the entrance door to capture a cross breeze. A light chorus of tree frogs started up, interrupted occasionally by a diffident-sounding hoot owl. Weezy came back to their situation, explaining how Revelator identified Joe and how she found the Mirror. She described meeting Jason Squitieri, the intended cover-up by the PR people and P.E. Smith's sudden, terrifying call to "Get out now." Then she was silent.

Joe, channeling a feeling he found hard to express, gazed out the open door to the field across the way. "This old music I've been listening to, the music Cynthia loved so much, really speaks to me. I keep hearing Robert Johnson's 'Cross Road Blues.' He's just trying to flag a ride, but when I listen to the song, it's as if all the stuff I always thought was the purpose of life...you know, a job, getting promoted, making money...sits on the surface. But the crossroad is always down there. Do I grieve for Cynthia and then get back to those surface things, or do I go deeper? I keep choosing a path, following it, and finding myself back at the crossroad again. Trying to flag a ride out of this horrible situation."

He saw a wry smile on her lips. His fixation with the blues must sound odd, maybe pompous. Or sorry-ass maudlin.

"What?"

"I was thinking it sounds like trying to drive in Boston...no matter where you're heading, you always end up in Kenmore Square."

Before he could get offended, she shrugged. "You're facing the moral compass issue over and over again. I think your compass points you toward the right thing to do." Then, with a twinkle in her eye, "If you want to get out of Kenmore Square, one thing you can't do is follow the street signs. You've got to believe your compass."

Joe started to answer, but Weezy continued, "My choice is easier than yours. I decided to go up against the Yak by coming down here. I could have let it go...called the FBI...let them stow me in a safe house, do their job and maybe catch the bad guys. But they didn't protect my boss, and the higher-ups in the Yak have decided to kill this project. That's truly scary...scary enough to kick my butt right out of the crossroad and execute my plan."

She stopped, grinned, then said, "And I sure as hell don't plan on ending up back in Kenmore Square."

THIRTY-ONE

THE EARLY SUN SHONE brightly, humidity in check for the moment and temperature not yet risen to the point of engaging the air conditioner. Joe and Weezy sat on the stoop of the trailer watching a pileated woodpecker methodically work his way up a dead tree. Reggie's sun-bleached red truck had passed by, leaving a suspension of fine, white dust that the sun captured in gold-orange striations. Weezy bent over her e-pad, and the light caught her face, making Joe remember a picture...Leonardo...no, a Caravaggio Madonna. One of Cynthia's favorites. Angles, softened by shadows. Beauty without pretense.

Joe broke the silence.

"Last night, you said you have a plan."

"I do. Well, half a plan."

"Care to elaborate?"

"Sure," Weezy said. "Remember how I told you I found the Mirror?"

Joe nodded.

"Before P.E.'s accident, I wrote a program that will destroy Mirror. If I turn it on, this horrible scam implodes. Problem is, I know the person at the root of this, but I can't figure a way to get at him. If I call the feds, they'll tell me I don't have enough evidence for them to investigate. The minute I destroy Mirror, the owner will disappear, along with seven million dollars and those thugs trying to erase you. And the thing is, the longer I hold off, the more likely he'll add more names and kill more people."

She shut off the e-pad and put it aside.

"I got a call yesterday from a person I worked with," Joe said. "She passed along a contact at the FBI. They apparently know about me, probably you, too, and they—"

"Why didn't you tell me?"

"Weezy, I had to decide what to do. So far, the people who care about me all seem to want me dead—except maybe you and the person who called me."

"What do they know?"

"I'm not sure. There was an issue of someone stealing from Florida Consolidated. You mentioned that when we met."

Weezy nodded.

"My friend in Florida Consolidated said I'm not a suspect any more. Sounds like she thinks the FBI agent is a good man. But this is a high-stakes decision for me. Now I've dragged you into it. Who knows? Maybe they want to locate me so they can arrest me. Maybe something worse. Did I mention that the head of Human Services for Florida Consolidated died under suspicious circumstances?"

Weezy watched the woodpecker for a bit, then said, "The FBI won't stop the MedRecords scam as quickly as we can. We understand the problem. We don't have to do an investigation to figure out what's going on while someone like Cynthia gets poor treatment. But..." she turned to face Joe, "you have handed us the last half of my plan. Our plan."

"How so?" Joe asked.

"Between the two of us, we have enough evidence to get the FBI working on Squitieri and your friends Snake and Big Louie. And we're tucked away in a single wide in the Florida forest. Let the FBI track down the bad guys. We'll expose the scam."

Joe leaned over to trace lines in the sand with a twig. After a minute or so, Weezy's foot began to tap.

Finally, he said, "My immediate reaction is to turn the whole thing over to the authorities, shrug it off and get on with my life. The team player in me believes the team does better than the lone cowboy." He tossed the twig. "I sit here coming up with a laundry list of reasons to do exactly what I did when Cynthia got sick: go through channels, rely on the folks designated to solve this kind of problem, cooperate." He gave a sour smile. "Only problem is, I did that once before, and my wife is gone. I failed to save her because I played by the rules."

"No, goddamn it Joe, you didn't fail," she said fiercely. "The rules failed you. That's why I come down on the side of solving this problem ourselves. We are in a better position than anyone else to know how to do this. The OddBalls can help, and we won't bend to political pressure like the brass at the Yak. Let's square our shoulders and leave that crossroad you were talking about last night." She put her hand on his shoulder. "Let's stomp on this problem and the really, really bad people who created it." As if to add an exclamation point, she leaned on him to stand up, turned to step up into the trailer, then stopped.

"Joe, quit trying to be a nice guy. You didn't cause this, and it's not fair that you and I have to solve it. But that's the way it is. Let's hit back. Let's hit 'em hard!" She looked at Joe for support or disagreement. Getting neither, she said, "I'd better get on with setting up some gear before it gets too hot in that tin box."

"Gear?"

"Yeah. Computer stuff. I want to set the trailer up to watch us, but only if we need it."

Then she was gone into the trailer, and Joe heard equipment moving, hammering, cupboard doors opening and closing, and a muffled *damn*.

***

Joe sat on the steps, knowing he owed Weezy an answer and not wanting to give it. So many unknowns. Was the FBI trustworthy? Could Weezy stop the Mirror? Would shutting down a piece of software stop the people behind it? He concentrated on the woodpecker, knowing he was delaying. Finally, the woodpecker finished his work and flew off. The sun had risen above the tree line. Hot day coming. Joe stood and stepped into the trailer. Weezy was on her back, working some wiring under the sink, "Harvard Sucks" T-shirt rising above a delicately tattooed pattern around her belly button.

"Okay. Let's do it."

Weezy pulled herself out from under the sink. "Wondered how long it would take you to see reason," she said with a shake of her head.

Weezy's e-pad was on the same cable as Joe's. She had installed the tiny camera from P.E.'s office above the kitchen sink. The relay transmitter was tucked into a cabinet. Weezy wrote software that directed her e-pad to turn on the camera and transmit to the Olegarten website if the e-pad went off for more than ten seconds. She tested the system by signing into Olegarten.

Hotcakes to HoHum: You out there?

HoHum responded almost immediately

Hotcakes, Nihow? Decided to take me up on that offer of matrimony?

Weezy went to video.

"Not yet, but I need your help."

After a brief pause, HoHum's video came up. It really did look like he was in a basement. He had a round face, manicured beard, and was trying unsuccessfully to both slick down his Einsteinian tangle of hair and brush crumbs off his T-shirt, which advertised AKG headphones.

"Of course, what do you need?"

"This is going to sound weird, but I'm in a tight spot. Don't want to burden you with details, but it's possible that some bad folks are interested in what I'm doing at my day job. I've gone off the grid, but I'm nervous that they may find me...us. So I put up a surveillance camera. I'd like to have it transmit to you if anything goes wrong. Then, at least, there will be a record ..."

"Well, number one, I would love to have details. Details are exciting. Number two, what should I do if there's a problem?"

"I'll send you some contact information that will include a coworker I trust at the IAC and possibly an FBI name, too. Not sure about the FBI yet. As to details, the scam is a nationwide medical payments rip-off, and that there are some people seriously angry enough to kill to protect it. If I tell you any more, they might find you." She gave him her pixie grin. "I have to keep the possibility of your proposal alive, you know."

HoHum responded with a radiant smile.

"Now that I've seen you, it'll be hard not to jump in my mono and ride right out to, lemmee see here..." He squinted at another screen "...somewhere in Wakulla County, Florida."

"Damn, you figured it out that fast?"

HoHum beamed. "Looks like you're using a wired connection. Smart call. And the owner of the cable, Rosalind Spencer, can't be found on GPS. Not bad. Not bad at all."

"Puhleeze don't pass any of that on."

"No worries. Better test the video link."

"Gotcha. I'm going to sign off, and your link should pop up shortly."

She shut down the monitor, waited half a minute, waved to the camera, started the monitor again, and went back to Olegarten.

HoHum came up on video.

"Worked like a charm. You're livin' in an old single wide."

"That I am. Well, HoHum, my friend, I hope you won't see the camera go on, because if you do, I'll be in trouble. But for now, gotta boogie."

"Glad to see you finally in the flesh, Hotcakes. Your name is aptly chosen. The offer stands."

Weezy blew him a kiss and signed off.

Joe had been standing in the doorway of the kitchen, watching the interchange.

"Pretty good friend, huh? I thought you said Olegarten

doesn't do video."

Weezy shrugged, "I've known him for four or five years, but I have never opened video with him before. Net jocks like HoHum are mostly motivated by curiosity. The adit gives him a way to check us out. Best satisfy his curiosity so he's less tempted to watch us secretly."

Weezy dug into her ditty bag and produced a phone. "Disposable" she said in response to Joe's raised eyebrows. She clicked the phone on and moved it around, looking for a signal. "Never going to work in our humble, metal framed abode. Where's the best place to get a signal?"

Joe thought for a moment, then said, "There's no high ground around here. We may get better reception in town, near the water."

They drove through the middle of Panacea to the public boat ramp. Weezy got a good signal there and called Maddie.

"Weezy?"

"Can you talk?"

"I can. I'm right here in the bullpen, but nobody's around."

"Have you heard anything about P.E.?"

"P.E.'s going to be all right. I talked to her husband. She was badly hurt, but she'll be okay. I told Walter you're in a safe place, and he said he'd pass that on to P.E."

"That's wonderful. I mean, it's wonderful under the circumstances."

"Weezy, I'm here on a Sunday because I'm using your Internet connection, as well as the Yak," Maddie said. "I've been researching Jason Squitieri. Surely the right guy. He founded a company called US Health Audits, and ..."

Maddie briefed Weezy, fleshing out the bits Weezy had told Joe.

Finally, Maddie said, "There's an ongoing connection with Ricky Thakur, the senator who has been a strong supporter of healthcare reform. Squitieri started out working for MEP, the advocacy non-profit, and he continues to represent them to the government. In fact, he's going to present to the committee Thakur chairs a week from this coming Tuesday. You might want to take that into account when we plan how to disable Mirror. 167 new names were added yesterday."

"Could you see the channel adding them?"

"I wish. But it was coming from within the system...a normal log-in. Not much help, I know."

Weezy stared out over the Gulf, thinking, then said, "Maddie, can you find out who signed into, I mean physically, N-Ops yesterday? Shouldn't be too many on a Saturday. The person doing the additions must work inside N-Ops unless he or she has a secret connection to the outside like our Internet line."

"Makes sense." Maddie said. "I'll check it out."

Thinking of the 167 names added to Mirror, Weezy glanced at Joe, who had been following her end of the conversation, and said, "Better activate Mirror Two."

THIRTY-TWO

ZIMMERMAN'S PRIVATE PHONE BUZZED, alerting him to a message.

He scanned the squad room, then checked his phone. Louie.

He stepped into the men's room and called back.

"What you got?"

"Last couple of days, I'm getting signals from over near Tallahassee going into the Olegarten site on the Net. Seems like all from one place."

"Did you get a location?"

"Yep. It's a brick building, out here on the edge of Tallahassee. Nobody in it I can see. No car, no nothing."

"Louie, check it out. It's probably serving a phone company tower."

Zimmerman heard Louie's shoes crunching on gravel, then the swish of grass.

"Uhh, it said Westel. 'Telecomm we can all rely on.'"

Zimmerman's shoulders slumped. "Should've guessed it."

"Guessed what?"

"Mayfield is either pretty clever or he's getting good advice. He's using a wired connection. You've arrived at the place where the wired connection goes wireless. You better hang tight. I'll see if I can figure out what area that brick box serves, and then...well, then you'll have to start looking."

Louie was sweating. The humidity hung over North Florida like a blanket, too early yet to have burned off. An inspiration struck.

"Zimmerman, how about we use a drone? It'd check every house in the place, cross-reference against addresses, maybe find Mayfield that way?"

Zimmerman sighed. "Louie, that'd get the attention of three kinds of law enforcement and the Yak, and ..."

"Yeah, but boss, what if you call it a 'police action' and ..."

Zimmerman was momentarily tempted, but said, "Not a bad idea, Louie, but too risky. Permits are hard to get now that General Motors screwed it up for everyone by taking drone surveys of which cars people had in their driveways. I'm afraid you're going to have to canvass the area the old way."

Zimmerman hesitated, conjuring up a vision of Big Louie doing anything that required finesse. "Louie, I'm going to come out and help you. I can't get there before Saturday morning, but you should start checking the communities in Wakulla County. Don't question anyone, just scope them out."

"Yeah. Okay."

Zimmerman understood from Louie's relieved tone that he'd made the right call. Now, he thought, all I have to do is report to the Ice Goddess.

***

Big Louie felt pretty good. For the better part of three days, he'd busied himself driving main roads and back roads, looking for places with no obvious address. He copied the coordinates and pictures into a list of what he called "places of interest." That had a nice cop-like ring to it. Maybe Zimmerman would be impressed.

He'd worked from north to south, west to east. It was early Thursday afternoon. He'd left Medart headed toward Panacea. He hummed as he drove, worrying a big piece of Fat Yankee Jerky around like the chaw of tobacco he used to enjoy. The breeze off the Gulf made the afternoon tolerable. He lowered the window to take in the sound and scent of the country. A slight salt taste in the air quickened memories of days spent at the Jersey Shore as a kid.

He checked his map. There were a few houses along the way, all of which got a check on his log as "not likely" because they had mailboxes.

On the right, he saw Joe Mack Smith Street. These hicks came up with weird names. He made the turn. A couple of blocks with nice houses. One with a pool. Horse corral. They all had addresses. He marked them "not likely." As the paved road curved left toward the town, Louie noticed a dirt road branching off. He slowed, checking his map. The dirt road drifted along for almost a mile, then stopped. He saw no addresses. He punched the map application to get satellite view. A little wheel spun on the screen. No picture. Weak signal. Might be nothing but pasture, but if there were houses, they'd be candidates for sure.

He turned onto the dirt track and drove nearly a mile. He was about to turn back when he saw a barbwire fence, then a trailer on the left. White with a green awning. He slowed down. No cars or signs of activity. Hard to tell whether it was occupied or not. Louie marked it down as a place of interest.

The road continued on, forest closing in. Nervous, he chewed the jerky faster.

Then, after a short distance, another trailer, almost hidden in the trees. A weathered red pickup truck marked the end of the road. Louie stopped to take coordinates and picked up his list to mark "place of interest." His skin tingled. There was a presence at the open window. A warm breath? He slowly turned and found himself eyeball to eyeball with a large dog, ears erect, snarl rippling his jowls revealing canines that appeared to Louie to be an inch and a half long.

Shit!

He inhaled, causing the wad of jerky to lodge in his throat, doubled over in a coughing fit, banged his head on the steering wheel, hacked out a fragment of the jerky. Finally he sat up, breathing hard. There were now two dogs, paws neatly aligned along the edge of his window. A man wearing a sneer and a large-caliber sidearm had come up behind them.

"Whatchou want?"

"Jee-zus!"

"You ain't gonna find Jesus around here unless you really piss me off." The man patted his gun. "What's the matter with you, man? You're sweatin' like a whore in church. Dogs make you nervous, do they?" A malicious grin. Then, again,

"Whatchou want?"

Louie's vital signs sloped back toward normal, and he reverted to his tough-guy attitude.

"Just drivin' down the road, enjoying the pretty country you got here." He tried a hard-eyed stare back at the man. Neither dog seemed impressed. At least, that's how Louie interpreted the low rumble. "I saw a trailer a quarter mile back. That occupied?" A more insistent rumble. The dogs appeared to be getting impatient.

"That's none of anybody's business 'cept mine." The man's hand rested on the holstered pistol. "This here's a private road. Why don't you turn around and drive your sorry ass outta here?"

Louie considered challenging the man. But the unblinking stare of the two dogs and the sidearm convinced him that it was, indeed, a good idea to turn around and make his exit.

***

As Louie negotiated the dirt track past their trailer, Joe and Weezy were on the Wakulla River. Earlier that day, Weezy stood up from the e-pad and stretched, doing a half twist to relax her back. Joe said, "Maybe we ought to take a break. Rent a canoe. The rivers here are breathtaking in a quiet kind of way."

"I'm game," Weezy said. "Ought to give the connection a rest anyway."

They found the Wakulla County Visitor Center at the edge of town. A friendly volunteer told them where to rent a canoe.

At the dock, Joe selected a paddle for him (up to his nose) and one for Weezy (to her collarbone).

"Have you ever been in a canoe?"

"Camp, a couple of times," Weezy said "Pretty tippy, as I

remember." Joe saw she was trying to appear nonchalant.

"This old aluminum gal is pretty stable. Step into the middle and you'll be fine. Take the bow position."

She gave him a quizzical look.

"Up front." He offered a hand. She took it and stepped in. He felt electricity in the touch and wondered if she did, too.

For Joe, managing the canoe was a welcome return to something he knew and loved. To Weezy, it was a surprising pleasure.

While Louie drove away from Reggie and the dogs, Joe and Weezy were sharing a bottle of water in the shade of a bald cypress leaning out from the bank.

Weezy leaned back, stretching shoulders and back. "This is the first time I've relaxed since P.E.'s accident. Seems like it's easier to see the big picture out here, too. Easier to believe that things will work out."

Of course, she hadn't seen Big Louie.

***

Joe and Weezy arrived home as dusk was gathering the trailer into its shadows. They unloaded fried chicken from the restaurant and another of those wax paper-covered "homade" pies, together with a bottle of wine from the grocery's limited supply.

Reggie's red truck came down the road and wheeled onto the stubble of grass in front of the trailer. He jumped out, slammed the door, came stomping toward them.

Joe said, "Evenin'." More a question than a greeting.

"Tell me what the hell's going on here." Reggie's cheeks were mottled with trying to hold in his anger.

"What do you mean?"

"What I mean is why's some guy in a big black vee-hickle comin' 'round here askin' questions 'bout who lives in this here trailer?"

"When?"

"Today. Afternoon."

Joe glanced at Weezy. Reggie watched, shook his head and said, "You two are up to sumpthin', and I bet it's no damn good. Now, I really don't care whether you two are shackin' up, but I do care if your husband ..." Reggie gave a sidelong glance at Weezy, "...sends some investigator to nose around my property, pry in my business. That's got to stop."

Joe saw Weezy's color rising. Boston scrappy fixing to confront redneck macho. She said, "We are not...are not...shacking up."

Reggie shot her a dismissive "Yeah, right" smirk.

"I said, I don't care 'bout that. But I do not like snooping of any kind. People come around here without me knowin' what they're doin' makes me nervous. I get nervous, I might perforate their sorry ass. That'd get Sheriff McCutcheon on my case again, and I do not want that. You don't want that either, believe me."

Joe knew it was his job to mediate.

"Reggie, we don't want to cause you any trouble. Ms. Napolitani and I work together. We work with, uhh, patents and industrial designs." He smiled toward Weezy, who didn't seem as surprised as she probably was.

"Anyway, the only thing I can think of is that someone wants to know what we're doing is trying to find us. If someone's after us, they want the information we work with. They wouldn't bother you."

"Anybody comin' 'round my property without a reason bothers me."

Joe shook his head. "What I mean to say is they wouldn't be at all interested in your business."

"You didn't hear me the first two times, maybe. I don't want nobody comin' out here lookin' for you unless they're droppin' by to explain how you won the lottery. And don't you be callin' in the law to investigate, neither."

"No, I wouldn't do that, Reggie."

Reggie, not knowing exactly how to break off the conversation, pursed his lips and said, "Okay, then." He turned on his heel and stomped back to the truck.

Inside the trailer, Joe and Weezy set out dinner in silence. They sat.

Joe picked up a hushpuppy, added a drop of hot sauce, then said, "It may be nothing."

Weezy shook her head, nostrils flaring, " 'Nothing' is when I get a hang-up call. Getting accused of shacking up by some mouth-breathing redneck who thinks I'm a brainless bimbo, that's not nothing."

"I mean, Reggie is probably not the most reliable observer of other people's intentions," Joe said, then bit into the hushpuppy, and chewed. "Could be a lost tourist. Might be someone taking a drive in the country."

"Not down this road, Joe. Not in that big black vee-hickle Reggie mentioned." Weezy was cooling down. "We have to assume it's someone interested in you...or me...or us."

Joe considered, then said, "We should pass that file of names off to the FBI. If it's true that someone's after us, we may not be in a position to be on the Net. I know. I had a hard time getting connected safely while I was traveling. We need someone with major resources and a lot of time to help find and warn the people the Mirror is manipulating."

Weezy was thinking, giving Joe most of her attention, but not all.

"That's probably a good idea, Joe. It gets us on the right side of the law. We have to stop this thing. And it'll kick the IAC out of its 'bury the problem' mode. They may not be able to figure out what to do, but I can."

***

Open Olegarten Manufacturing

HoHum from Hotcakes: You there?

Hotcakes from HoHum: For you, always.

Weezy switched to video. HoHum wore the same AKG T-shirt from four days ago.

"I have a request."

"For you, Hotcakes, anything. Well, almost anything."

"Okay. You remember our last conversation about the project I'm working on?"

"Sure."

"Well, I need some help. Your help, as well as someone who looks ..." How to phrase this? "... very establishment."

"You mean...uhh...someone other than me?"

"Probably."

"So, Wall Street Ivy League, maybe? Middle America? High-tone lady lawyer? Church lady? We've got 'em all in the circle of Olegarten friends."

Weezy tilted her head, considering. "Middle America person-you-would-trust," she said finally.

HoHum scratched his mane, then apparently was struck by inspiration.

"Jake! You want Jake."

"Really? Have you ever seen her?"

HoHum nodded, "I have. She's a nice older lady. Grandmotherly."

Weezy exhaled, relieved. "Perfect. Now here's the idea. First off, can you hack into a Senate conference room video system?"

"Does a bear defecate in the greenwood? I mean, do members of *Ursidae* evacuate their—"

"HoHum? C'mon!"

"Of course I can. Absolutely."

THIRTY-THREE

HENRY BARBER READ OVER the message from Joe Mayfield as he sipped morning coffee. Jennifer arrived as he read it the second time.

He handed his e-pad to her.

She read a few lines, and her eyes widened, "Ohmigosh. This is the guy they blamed the FCE transfers on, isn't it? Why's he getting in touch with us now?"

"After we talked with Mel, I visited the person that worked most closely with Mayfield at Florida Consolidated. I had a hunch that she might be able to get in touch with him. She must've passed my message along."

Jennifer concentrated on the rest of the note, then said, "Hell of a story. Looks like you were right to contact her, Henry. Mayfield said the attachment has the list of people affected. Let's open it."

"Sure. Go ahead."

Jennifer tapped the attachment, and a long list appeared. She scrolled through it slowly. "Holy Fu—" Blush. "3,500 people from several big companies. Pennsylvania. Here's Florida Consolidated. A California bank. This is a big damn problem."

Henry shook his head in frustration. "Sure wish I knew where he is. He wants to talk by e-note. That's baloney. I don't like it."

"Henry, we do know where he is, at least approximately. He had to send this from somewhere, and we have state-of-the-art tools to find him."

"So...figure it out."

She grinned. "Thought you'd never ask." Ah, the confidence of youth, Henry thought.

Jennifer disappeared to her desk and returned in five minutes.

"Where is he?"

"Well, he's somewhere near Tallahassee."

"What's that mean?"

"It means the signal is coming out of a phone company tower at the southern tip of Leon County. Most likely a wired connection somewhere in Wakulla or Jefferson county."

"Hmmm. Wakulla...Wakulla County. Carrabelle, Sopchoppy. Wait a minute, that's Sheriff Mike McCutcheon. Great. He's a top-notch officer. Met him at the Academy."

"What's an FBI Academy grad doing in the Big Bend of Florida? Seems like a big step down."

"Not for Mike. He was one of the best of the class. Spent ten years being a cracker-jack field agent. But he was born around the Big Bend, and he loves the country. Hunting, fishing, outdoor life. That, plus the fact he wasn't one for the organizational minuet...he never would kowtow to the brass."

Henry was searching his address file for Mike as he talked.

"Been sheriff for eight or ten years. One of the best-run departments in the state. It seems like Mike knows most everyone in the county. He'd be the person to find Mayfield."

Contact information popped up from Henry's file. Florida Sheriff's green, gold star badge. There was a hint behind the formal pose of an interesting person, someone ready to tell you a funny story or buy you a beer. Someone you'd trust in an emergency.

"Let's give him a call."

Henry pressed Send. The video of the Wakulla County Sheriff's Office immediately came up, and a friendly synthesized voice listed out five options for the call. Henry interrupted at number two, "Mike McCutcheon, official business, from Henry Barber, Florida FBI."

A pause, a flicker, then the inside of a patrol car appeared with an amused Mike McCutcheon at the wheel.

"Henry Barber, you ol' sumbitch! How come a serious FBI

financial expert is callin' out to Wakulla County, or are you just passin' through God's country and want to share a beer?"

"Mike, I'd like nothing better than to share a beer, but I'm calling on business."

"Aw shucks. Well, then, let me pull over."

Mike checked his rearview mirror and wheeled over. A bump or two, a radio call blared something unintelligible. Mike reached up and tapped it into silence. All business now.

"Mike, I'm here with my associate Jennifer Rowland, and we're working on a really strange case. Do you have a couple of minutes for a briefing?"

"Shoot. Mind if I record?"

"No problem. I'm calling you because a person related to our case but not a suspect is probably somewhere in Wakulla County. He's being tracked by people we suspect in two homicides, and we think they'd like to make him a third." Mike nodded. "The man's name is Joseph Mayfield. I'm sending you a picture and some background data. An accountant, basically."

Mike interrupted, "So we know why you're concerned, right? Birds of a feather..." The same big aw-shucks smile Henry remembered.

"Well, he's...or he was...a real accountant, working at Florida Consolidated Energy here in Orlando. His wife got sick, and he believes someone changed her HealthScore, which resulted in reduced treatment. She died this last February." Henry stopped, swallowed.

"Anyway, this Mayfield hacked into the IAC, apparently to try to figure out how the score got changed. He took the case to his personnel director, who agreed to follow up. They fired Mayfield, and right after that the personnel director drowned. All evidence points to homicide. Mayfield said he's being watched and followed, and that appears to be the case. When he got fired, he was also a suspect in some wire fraud going on in his department, and we were involved in that investigation. He's no longer a suspect in that case, but he doesn't know that. He may be afraid to come forward for fear of being arrested."

"So, what's that got to do with Wakulla County?"

"Well, Mayfield went on the run shortly after he was fired in late April. We lost track of him. He managed to make his electronic footprint almost disappear. But then, a couple of weeks ago, I got a call from Mel Williams up in Washington about this HealthScore issue."

"Curly hair, quiet black man? Track star before the Academy?"

"Yep. The same."

Mike nodded, "I always liked him when I was on the street. Straight-up guy. Supported the FBI's working staff. No kiss-ass."

"That's the man. Anyway, he was passing along a message from P.E. Smith. She used to be FBI. She went on to work in the IAC, and she called Mel because it appears that the same people that are after Mayfield are monitoring her lead tracker, Louise Napolitani. Apparently, Napolitani met up with Mayfield, did some research, and found out the problem is real and much larger than just Florida Consolidated."

"And Mayfield inexplicably decided to take some time out to do some fishin' in Wakulla County?"

Henry chuckled. "He sent us a message yesterday with information that this problem is big and bad. Jennifer tracked the signal to a tower in Leon County that covers Wakulla. I'm sending you the location of the tower, and a map of the area the tower serves. Jennifer said...Well, you talk to Mike, Jennifer."

Jennifer leaned over Henry's desk. "Mike, Joe Mayfield is probably using a wired connection. I sent you a map of the area where he might be, along with the message Mayfield sent to Henry. I searched for his name and several aliases he may be using...I sent those, too...and saw nothing out of Wakulla. No credit card charges, no electronic motel sign-ins, no phone use in his name or the aliases. But there's a fair amount of traffic from unregistered phones —"

"Uh-huh," Mike said. "That's because there's a fair amount of non-domestic tobacco grown in the state and federal forest, and some coming in over the water. Not legal yet in Florida, but nobody's gettin' put in jail for it anymore. Lots of those folks use disposables—"

Jennifer continued, "—so I haven't been able to tie any of them to Mayfield."

Mike took out a stick of gum, concentrated on unwrapping it, folded it over, and popped it in his mouth. He chewed for a few seconds, then said, "You know, if I were a smart guy trying to stay away from the electronic grid, I might choose Wakulla County. We're seventy percent forest, and a quarter of the dwellings don't have a proper address, mostly P.O. boxes or General Delivery. And it's still mostly a cash economy."

He chewed, cogitating.

" 'Course, a guy has to eat, has to find a place to stay. Good news is there aren't a whole lot of places to do either of those in Wakulla County."

Mike turned to the camera, chewed a couple of times. "See, that's why I'm out here in the palmettos and cypress trees. I get to do the interestin' stuff, and you have to make the balance sheet balance. I'll scout around."

***

Liza Franklin was sweet on Mike McCutcheon. When she saw the green, white and gold cruiser pull into the Pelican's Roost parking lot, she took a mental inventory of the pies available and then quickly inspected her hair and lipstick in the mirror behind the cash register.

"Liza, oh my. You are looking great. How are y'all doin'?"

Liza gave him her friendliest smile, one she hoped carried

extra promise without being too obvious.

"Why, Mike, I'm doin' just fine. What brings you to Panacea this fine afternoon? Care for coffee or sweet tea? Got some berry pie and some pecan here, too."

"Liza, I'd love a cup of coffee, but better make it to go. I'd much rather keep company with you, but I'm on the job. I wonder if you've seen this man?" Mike showed Liza the picture of Joe Mayfield that Jennifer sent up from Orlando.

Liza leaned down to inspect it, squinting without her glasses. "Why, yes, Mike. I'm sure I have seen him. Nice man. Must be staying near here because he and his lady friend carry out dinner most every night."

"Lady friend?"

"Yup. Cute li'l thing. Not from around here, though. Talks kinda funny, like New York or somewhere up north. Wearin' a T-shirt from one a' them fancy schools. But, like I said, cute li'l thing. Are they dangerous?" Liza conjured up Bonnie and Clyde, a movie she loved as a kid.

Mike shook his head, "Not at all. Maybe witnesses in a federal case, but not dangerous."

Liza thought for a minute, then said, "Mike, I don't know if it helps, but I hear Rosie Spencer rented that old single wide of her uncle's to a guy from downstate. I wonder if that might be the same man you're interested in."

"You mean the place next to Rosie's out on Joe Mack Smith Extension?"

"Uh-huh."

Mike collected the cup of coffee and said, "If you see them this evening, give me a call. And don't mention this conversation, if you know what I mean."

"Wouldn't think of it," she said.

After Mike left, Liza fell into a daydream that featured seeing the man, calling Mike, being held hostage, Mike rescuing her, being meltingly grateful, thinking of his strong arms wrapped around her, and...and....

"Ma'am? Ma'am?"

The reverie shattered. The man with the angry wife and sullen kid from booth five wanted to pay.

***

Later that day, the man in the picture Mike showed Liza came into the restaurant. He ordered chicken for two, to go. Liza was tongue-tied for a second, then almost stuttered. "Be with you in a sec, hon." She walked as slowly as she could manage, which was nearly a trot, back into the kitchen.

She glanced through the order pass-through at the man as she took her phone out of her handbag. He looked puzzled. He probably expected the relaxed, friendly Liza, the one with the voice a half-octave lower.

Her hands were shaking, and she dialed Mike's number wrong. *Damn!* She dialed again, and Mike appeared in the small window.

"Mike, Mike. That man you showed me today? He's right out in the restaurant. Right now. Wants chicken and coleslaw, extra hushpuppies."

"Okay, Liza. Thanks for calling. I'll be over shortly. Just relax, now."

"He's not dangerous, is he?"

"No, Liza, he's not dangerous. Don't you worry. I'll be there shortly."

"Okay, Mike. Hurry. Please!"

Liza put in the chicken order and forced herself to walk out front again, playacting a toothy smile. "It'll be ready in ten minutes. Why don't y'all have a seat? You want a glass of tea or coffee?"

The man sat down. "Yes, a glass of sweet tea would be nice. Thanks."

Liza turned into a model of efficiency and impersonal goodwill, hoping Mike would arrive sooner rather than later.

The chicken order came up faster than Liza wanted it to. Still no Mike.

The man finished his tea and stood as Liza brought the bag to the front.

"There's no hurry. I can refill that tea if you like." Liza was beginning to enjoy playing her role.

The man said, "Thanks, but no thanks. You folks make delicious chicken, but it's best eaten hot. Gotta get home."

"You must be new here. I don't recollect seeing you until a couple of weeks ago. Where you stayin'?"

She saw him go on guard.

"I'm not local," he said. "In town for fishing and relaxing."

Liza realized he was being evasive, but politely so. Not much more she could do. She looked past the man through the window to the parking lot, hoping to see Mike's cruiser. No such luck.

"Well, come back to see us often."

"I will do. Your food is great."

Liza waited until he was out the door and moved to the window.

She dialed.

"Mike! Mike!"

Mike answered right away.

"The guy left in a dark green sorta van goin' north on Coastal Highway. Not a Florida license. Not Georgia, either."

"Liza, thanks. I'll find him. You've been a great help. I'll see you soon."

Very soon, she hoped.

***

Joe parked the Element under the big live oak that partially shaded the trailer. He knocked lightly, then entered. Weezy was at the e-pad.

"Dinner is here. Chicken again, this time with extra hushpuppies."

Weezy moved the e-pad to the counter, and they opened the brown sack.

Weezy took out the wax paper bag of hushpuppies, put out plates, then glanced at Joe and stopped what she was doing.

"What's wrong?"

"Probably nothing. Maybe I'm just jumpy, but all of a sudden, the waitress at Pelican's Roost is trying to get me to tell her where I live. I've been in there, what, five or seven times and she's never been interested before."

A flash of headlights let them know a car had turned into the front yard.

Joe peered out the window. "Damn, I hope it's not Reggie again."

Weezy grimaced. "Yeah, the paranoia does not go well with his big pistol."

"I don't think it's Reggie."

The shadowy form approaching materialized into a large man in a sheriff's uniform.

"Good evening. Joe Mayfield and Louise Napolitani, am I right? Michael McCutcheon, Wakulla County sheriff. May I come in?"

Weezy looked perplexed. Joe's heart sank, but he said, "Sure, come in. And, yes, I'm Joe Mayfield and this is Louise Napolitani."

McCutcheon took off his hat and stepped into the trailer.

"Sorry to disturb your dinner. Pelican's Roost makes great chicken."

Joe nodded understanding. That was why the waitress seemed nervous.

"I got the message you sent to Henry Barber in Orlando," Mike said. "Used to work with him. He gave me a pretty good run down on what you're doing."

"Why are you here?" Weezy asked. Joe saw she was readying an interrogation.

"Good question. You are what the FBI likes to call 'persons of interest.' I think Henry needs to talk to you about a homicide, and he's quite worried that you may be in danger. So why don't you two give me a detailed rundown of what's going on?"

Joe hesitated, wanting to believe he really was here because of the note to Barber.

Joe turned to Weezy, raised his eyebrows. There was a moment of hesitation, then an unspoken agreement. Joe started at the beginning, back when Cynthia was fine and he was grinding it out at work. Mike listened, interrupting occasionally to ask a question, as Joe told the story of Cynthia, the avatars, being fired, Big Louie and Snake, and his trip. He finished with finding Panacea and Reggie's report that a guy visited a couple of days ago. When they got to the part about Mirror, Weezy took over and described discovering Joe. After a couple of minutes, Mike stopped her.

"Hold on, missy." He unwrapped a stick of gum, popped it into his mouth. Chewed several times. Gave them an aw-shucks grin. "I used to chew tobacco, but you're never gonna get kissed by the finer class of women if you're chewing tobacco." His eyes twinkled.

Then he asked Weezy, "So how the hell did that program get into the IAC operating system?"

"That's the most important question right now," she said. "That's why we're in Panacea." She told about P.E.'s accident and her message to get out, but without mentioning Squitieri or the apparent decision by IAC brass to bury the issue.

After an hour, they were finished, and Joe asked the question hanging in the air.

"So, what's your position in all this?"

Mike shrugged. "Well, there's no warrant out for your arrest.

'Course, what you're doing down here is probably illegal, but it's probably also temporary from what you've told me. So let's just say you have a few days to resolve this. I'm going to tell my buddy Henry Barber that we've talked and see what he wants me to do."

Mike chewed a couple of times, thinking, then said, "I'm concerned about the men you call Snake and Big Louie. Reggie Spencer is paranoid to the point of being delusional, but far less dangerous than he thinks he is. If he's suspicious of this guy he talked with yesterday, it may mean nothing at all, or it may mean something. I want you to be able to get in touch with me. Phone probably won't work out here, but if you send a text, I'll see it." He handed his card to both Joe and Weezy. "And...don't hesitate to call."

Weezy brightened. "Thanks for the offer. If you see a video come on from inside this trailer, that'll mean we're in trouble."

Mike leaned his head toward the kitchen. "You mean you have that adit on a dead man switch, right?"

Weezy startled. "Is it that obvious?"

"Nope. It's pretty well concealed, but I've had a good hour to scope this place out."

Joe said to Mike, "I hope the bad guys are less observant than you are if we ever need that switch to trip."

Mike stood, gave a half-salute and moved to the door, fitting on his hat as he stepped into the Florida evening. He turned back to then, serious. "Stay safe. Call if you need me."

Joe and Weezy discovered that Pelican's Roost chicken was delicious even when cold.

THIRTY-FOUR

THE ODDBALLS GATHERED AROUND Madeline Hollingsworth's station at N-Ops. It was Sunday evening, and the four of them were alone in the bullpen. "Time to pull the trigger," Maddie said. Two members began tapping at e-pads. Maddie watched her monitor as the commands flowed into the system.

"Mr. Williams, I've dropped the dummy dataset into Mirror." She listened for a confirmation, then nodded to the group. "Done and done."

"The FBI's on it," Maddie said. "Let's get here early tomorrow morning."

***

Buzz Gray was the kind of man who didn't often get the Monday workday blues. His job as Controller at US Health Audits was not demanding — in fact, his main problem was the long, boring afternoons. This Monday morning had included leisurely coffee at HeartyJoe, where he read the financial news (so everybody would think he was a heavyweight) and checked out the ladies coming in and out of the shop.

Finally, he went into work, expecting a relaxed morning. He fired up the accounting computer. The top of his message queue had one marked URGENT.

"Overdrawn?" Across the room, both analysts' heads popped up. Buzz realized that he said it out loud. He was more puzzled than concerned. $348k in the bank on Friday. Overdrawn Monday morning?

He switched to CitiBank and went to the account. Citibank was right. The $348k disappeared Sunday afternoon in a flurry of several dozen payments. Buzz realized he should have figured this out before now. But Jason was, as usual, gone, and he had taken off a little early on Friday. Well, a couple or three hours early.

Another $200k-plus was queued up to pay, with no cash to cover. Pretty big haircut to undo Friday's investments, but that was a smaller problem. He switched over to the investment account to start the process and...it was gone, too.

Buzz suddenly felt ill. He'd call the bank and bitch and moan, but that would buy him four hours at best. Where the hell did the investments go? He hadn't bothered to check that account since last financial close. Hand shaking, he scrolled down to the last entry. He saw incoming cash from his automatic sweep on Friday afternoon. There was one more transaction, a transfer out to a bank in the Seychelles, authorized by Jason Squitieri.

When the hell was he going to mention that?

Buzz knew he had to call Jason, who was somewhere out in the California bio corridor. He rehearsed what he would say, leaving out the part about leaving early on Friday. He hoped Jason wouldn't answer. Then he could shovel the manure into Jason's lap without getting a tongue-lashing on the spot. Three hours earlier in California. Maybe he'll be on his morning run.

Buzz was in luck. The phone explained that Mr. Squitieri was not available and beeped. Buzz dictated: "Jason, the operations account for Phoenix is overdrawn as of this morning, and there's 200k waiting to be paid. The bank will cover temporarily. I'll say a transfer's missing or some other BS. It'll take 'em a couple of days to figure it out. I hope we'll be out of the bind by then. Give me a call with further instructions."

Reciting the plan made Buzz feel better. He and Jason had done this dance with the bank several times before. Buzz clicked Off, terminating the call. The coffee was giving him heartburn.

He hoped Jason had some answers.

***

Annika Dreher was in a hurry. The Director pulled their quarterly meeting forward to 10 a.m., and she had only ten minutes to polish her report and maybe check her hair and lipstick. Then there were two people at her door, a woman—Madeline what's-her-name from the Tracker organization—and a man she had never seen. The man, buzz-cut, serious, government-issue, said, "Annika Dreher?"

She began to stand. The man displayed a badge. "FBI. Stay seated, please. Hands on the desk."

"What is this?"

Maddie, not meeting Annika's eyes, said, "We think we have the MedRecords issue figured out."

The agent said, "What monitor are you using, Ms. Dreher?"

"Uhh, three, I think, or four. Why?"

He tilted his head and said, "Check three and four," then waited for a response.

Annika, beginning to rise from her seat, said, "You will explain what you are doing. I am calling security." She reached for her e-pad.

The agent squared his shoulders. "Sit," he said. Annika hesitated. He took a half step toward her. "Now. This is a national security matter, ma'am. Sit down, keep your hands on the desk and follow instructions."

He tapped his earpiece, listened, then asked her, "Where is monitor eleven?"

"At the far end of the work area."

"Who uses it?"

"It's a maintenance port. Any analyst can use it."

The agent cocked his head, again listening.

"Is Megan Hernandez authorized to use terminal eleven?"

Annika startled. "Megan? No. She moved to Cincinnati a year ago."

The agent said, "Well, the system says Megan is doing some nasty things on terminal eleven right now." He turned to Maddie. "Please make sure no one uses Ms. Dreher's terminal." He turned toward the door. "Ms. Dreher and I are going to see why Megan is trying to kill people."

"Mein Gott." Annika's face turned ashen. "From inside."

***

Tommy Fischer had been at his desk early, processing MedRecord transactions that came in over the weekend. By shortly before 10:00, he had finished most of them, and people were going on coffee break. The large room of gray carrels was nearly empty. He signed out of his terminal and went to one at the far end of the work area to do what he logged as a "maintenance check." This morning he chose Megan Hernandez from his collection of identities and signed in. He shouldn't get anything new today, but Jason was out in the bio corridor...there might be something tomorrow.

He was surprised to see a new entry, EXELbiosys, 600-plus names. He pushed back from the monitor, elated. Maybe those big promises would finally come true. He opened a small disposable phone and tapped out a confirmation to Jason. As he pressed Send, he realized a man was blocking the entrance to the carrel. Annika Dreher was standing right behind him, mouth agape.

"I bet you aren't Megan," the man said.

Annika turned to the man, eyes wide, and said, "This is Tomasz Fischer. He's one of our systems analysts."

"Annika?" Tommy said. It came out as a whine, because the adrenalin rush had started. "Who is this?"

In answer, the man produced an FBI badge. "Come with me, please."

"What for?"

"Thomas Fis—"

"It's Tomasz," he stuttered.

"Okay, Tom-ahzz," the agent half-smiled. "You are under arrest for criminal use of the IAC and conspiracy to commit murder."

***

By afternoon, Jason Squitieri had finished two important sales calls along the bio corridor in Silicon Valley.

When he opened his e-pad, listened to the message from Buzz, he was concerned, but not particularly worried. Probably just a timing effect. He'd said that to his employees often enough that he had come to believe it.

The message about EXELbiosys coming up in the system was baffling. He hadn't called on them; in fact, he'd been with a major competitor of theirs that afternoon. He called Tommy Fischer from a disposable. No answer, so he left a message asking Tommy to get back to him. Then to the airport. Presentation tomorrow to Thakur's committee. Pain in the ass, particularly since they pulled it forward from last week. The redeye is the redeye, no matter how fancy they try to make the accommodations. He hoped he could sleep.

THIRTY-FIVE

"LOUIE, WHADDYA GOT?"

Zimmerman pulled up a chair in the log cabin-themed restaurant in Sopchoppy, Florida. The decade-old country hit playing too loud for eight in the morning, and Zimmerman almost had to shout.

Louie mopped up egg yolk, bowed his head in greeting, and continued to chase the remnants of breakfast around his plate. "Like you said, I scoped out pretty much the whole county. Here's my e-pad. See the list called Places of Interest? Well, those places have no address I can see. Got pictures of most of 'em. When I saw a car or truck that looked like what I think Mayfield's drivin', I took a picture of it, too. Not many of those."

Zimmerman nodded approvingly, "Not bad, Louie."

While Louie finished his breakfast, Zimmerman tapped away at the e-pad, converting the coordinates into stars on a map of the county.

"Damn, they're spread all over the place. We'd better narrow this down."

He glanced up from his e-pad. "Let's see your list. You got pictures of the places, too, right?"

"Most of 'em. Missed a couple." Louie thought immediately of the dogs, the guy with the gun and the deserted trailer, where he had been too much in a hurry to take a picture.

Zimmerman stood and stretched. "Well, no time like the present," he said, anxious to get going. Louie paid his bill, picked a toothpick out of the dispenser next to the cash register, took a handful of complimentary hard candies, and followed Zimmerman into the bright sun of the Florida morning.

They spent the next two days driving the county roads,

checking out Louie's Places of Interest, talking to gas station attendants, drinking countless cups of coffee and (in Louie's case) sampling several kinds of pie. Nobody had seen Mayfield or a squarish, green car with a Louisiana license.

On Monday morning, they were on the Coastal Highway, going south toward Panacea.

"What have we got around here?" Zimmerman asked.

"Uhh. Not too much. Coupla houses at the edge of town, couple way out in the sticks."

In the town, they passed a small grocery and Pelican's Roost restaurant.

"Wanna get some lunch?" Louie asked hopefully.

"Naw, it's early yet. But we should check the restaurant, see if they know anything."

***

Liza watched the black SUV pull into the parking lot. Unusual these days. Two men got out and came into the restaurant. Nice looking guy built like a weightlifter. Slightly shorter guy, shaved head, not nice looking.

"Good mornin' gentlemen. You here for lunch? Or you can still get breakfast. We got specials listed on—"

"No, not for lunch," the good-looking one said. "Just a couple of questions." He reached into his pocket. "Have you seen this man around here recently?"

He put a picture on the counter. Same man Mike was looking for. Liza froze. She stared at the picture, buying time.

"No, I don't believe I have."

Good Lookin's eyes rest briefly on her, evaluating.

" 'Course, this time of year, there are a lot of people in for the fishing and canoeing and such, but no, I don't believe I've seen that man."

Liza felt like she was babbling and shut up.

"Well, thank you, ma'am," Good Lookin' said. "Appreciate

your help."

***

Liza watched the men get into the SUV as she tapped on her phone. "Mike, honey, two scary guys just came in. Didn't want lunch. Wanted to know if I'd seen the man you're lookin' for. I didn't tell 'em, but I think they knew I was lyin'. I mean, I tried my best, but my knees were shakin'. I mean, I was scared. But, but I got their license plate, at least part of it."

"Liza, I'm going to come over," Mike said. "Just to make sure everything's all right. You've done a great job."

"I'll save a piece of that berry pie you like so much."

***

In the car, Zimmerman turned to Louie. "Did you see the way that waitress choked when she saw the picture of Mayfield? I think she was lying. Let's concentrate on this area. What about these places in the sticks?" He opened his e-pad, pointed to three locations Louie marked as Places of Interest. Louie furrowed his brow, trying to remember.

"Lemme see. This one here has a sorta barn, but no mailbox. Not too likely, but I marked it anyway. This one here," he pointed to a new picture, "is kinda old and fallin' down. No mailbox. Didn't seem like the kinda place a city boy would go, but I marked it, too. This one here," pointing to the star at the Spencer single wide, "This one was occupied. Has a couple of big dogs and a crazy redneck that carries a .45. Right before that place is another single wide that looked empty. I marked it but didn't get a picture...looks like the red neck's place. We'd have to approach them very, very careful."

Zimmerman stared at the map, irritated, then sideways at Louie. "Well, then let's go be very, very careful."

Zimmerman and Louie quickly eliminated the first star on the "sticks" list from Panacea. As they drove by, several children ran out of the house, around the yard, and back into the house. No one was home at the second house. Zimmerman said, "Might be at work. Probably not the place we want. Let's check it later."

As Joe Mack Smith Street curved back toward town, Louie pointed out the extension. "That's where I ran into the guy with the dogs. Trouble is, if we go down there with this vehicle, we can't turn around until we get to the place I marked. If it is what we're looking for, they're not gonna be surprised."

Zimmerman thought the situation over, then said, "There's no way in or out, other than that road, right?" Louie nodded. "And you weren't sure the first trailer was occupied, right?" Louie nodded again. "We could spend the rest of the day diddle-dickin' around and end up with nothing," Zimmerman said. "We have nothing so far, and we're pretty much at the end of your list, unless you missed something. I guess we have to go in and check it out."

He wheeled the SUV into the entrance to the Extension. Crushed rock soon gave way to gray sand and coquina. After a slow half-mile, Louie said, "The first trailer is up on the left."

"Okay, why don't you check out whether anyone's there," Zimmerman said. "I'll hang back and wait for you. Take a look and come right back."

Ten minutes later, Louie trotted toward the SUV. He got in, slightly out of breath, sweating. "Damn, there is someone in there. It's closed up, but I heard the air conditioner running. There's some kinda car parked around the back now that was definitely not there when I came the first time. I think it's dark green like the one we've been tracking."

"Okay...we probably don't want to drive by them, so we'd better back out of here and set up a stakeout." Zimmerman put the SUV in reverse and backed up until there was a big enough break in the foliage to let him turn around.

"I'm going back to watch for some movement," Zimmerman said. "See whether it is Mayfield." They had done this a couple of times over the last two days. Last time, Louie had to stumble through underbrush, then sit around for an hour while gnats swarmed, mosquitoes feasted and ticks did whatever they do. Then the itching, and Zimmerman finally yelling, "Louie, for chrissake, quit fidgeting."

Zimmerman took water bottles, binoculars, a small camcorder, and a fanny pack. He turned to Big Louie. "Go back and hang out where you can't see the entrance to this road. Pick a place where you won't draw attention. Can you do that?"

"Yeah, Paul. I can do that." His attempt to inject sarcasm into the answer made it come out as a whine.

Zimmerman left the car, closing the door quietly. He watched the SUV disappear and faded into the brush, like he'd learned in Ranger training. He found a sheltered place, hunkered down, and trained the binoculars on the trailer.

Holding the mic from his e-pad close to his throat, he whispered a message to Tosheka:

"Ms. Jackson. Paul Zimmerman here. We may have located Mayfield outside Panacea, Florida. I'm currently watching his suspected residence, so I can't talk. When I can verify it's him, I'll let you know."

Almost immediately, a text flashed: How long?

He texted back: On location here. Will give it two hours, then go in.

The answer came back: Why not go in now?

Zimmerman half shook his head. *Amateurs!*

Don't want to alert local cops. Best way is to wait for him to go out, break in, and take him when he returns.

Okay, but get back to me as soon as you know.

Zimmerman tapped out Will do. Some of the outcomes of his contract work were unpleasant, but necessary. He didn't have the mean streak that occasionally got Big Louie in trouble. But he didn't look deeply into his soul when he needed to eliminate an obstacle in the way of a client's plan, either. Particularly when it paid well, like this job. Mayfield probably wasn't a bad guy. If he'd toed the line, he probably would have come out okay. To reduce the risk of further introspection, he pumped some thrashmetal into his ear buds and busied himself with the binocs.

It turned out to be a longer wait than he'd hoped. The two hours passed and then two more, giving a variety of insects plenty of time to locate and dine on him. Big Louie texted "You OK?" after an hour. Zimmerman tapped back, "K." Tosheka's messages began arriving on the mark of two hours. Zimmerman ignored them. If she wants a professional job done, he thought, she should let the professional alone.

***

Joe stood up from the armchair, needing a break from cross-referencing tables of data for Weezy.

"Chicken or fish?"

Weezy sat back from her e-pad and stretched. "Either one's fine. Surprise me."

Joe chuckled. "I could order the steak, but it would be fried, too."

"Yeah, and it would probably be great," Weezy said. "Never make fun of good food."

"One of these days, I'll have to fire up the stove," Joe said. "My waistline can't take this good restaurant food much longer."

He picked up the keys for the Element and left the trailer.

***

Zimmerman watched an old, red pickup roll by the trailer, middle-aged woman driving. He knew he'd have to do something soon, stood up to get the blood circulating, stretched carefully. As he was starting to move, the door of the trailer opened. A man stepped out. *Mayfield!* For a second, Zimmerman thought Mayfield had spotted him. But of course, he couldn't have. Mayfield walked around the trailer and got into the car Louie saw earlier. He backed up and turned onto the unpaved track.

Zimmerman tapped his call button, "Louie, it is Mayfield, and he's on the move. Dark green Honda Element. Tail him and tell me when he's coming back to the trailer. I'm going in."

Before he went, Zimmerman called Tosheka. "I've verified it's Mayfield. He just left an old single wide trailer. I'm going in, and I'll take him when he returns."

"Good," Tosheka said. "Let me know the outcome."

"Will do."

***

After Joe left, Weezy continued working on the Mirror's data she had downloaded in Bethesda. The whirring and creaking of the old air conditioner was mesmerizing. The data seemed to blur into a continuous string of numbers. Her mind wandered.

Joe. What a surprise. He seemed so ordinary, but he wasn't at all. She wondered what it would be like to make love to him. Even as a daydream, the thought surprised her, but she realized she'd had it before. He said she was beautiful. Not in so many words, but with his eyes. He was attractive. He would be a sensitive lover.

She allowed the reverie to go on, imagining the situation, perhaps an involuntary touch as he glanced over her shoulder at the e-pad. A mutual recognition. He would be afraid of hurting her at first, until he learned how strong she was.

There was a small click at the door, interrupting her daydream.

It seemed as if he'd only been away for a few minutes.

She turned to the opening door, smiling.

***

The sun slanted toward the horizon, casting shadows across the dry stubble in front of the trailer. Zimmerman heard only birds calling and the trailer's A/C unit wheezing. At the door, he worked the cheap lock expertly. Alert, he opened the door quickly, even though he knew the trailer was empty.

A woman!

She had her back to him, working at a small table across from the door. She said, "Joe? Back so soon?" as she turned toward him. A split second passed. She stared, eyes wide, mouth open.

She bolted out of her chair as Zimmerman stumbled into the trailer.

He reached for her, grabbed her left arm. She hit him hard, harder than a slender woman should be able. He stopped, then reached for her. She tried to get her knee into his crotch. It nearly landed, but he wrapped her up almost like a lover would, much stronger, feeling her breath rush out, seeing the hate in her eyes. She passed out, and he put her on the chair she'd risen from, feeling her litheness and wishing, for once, that the task at hand did not have to be done quite yet.

THIRTY-SIX

WHEN WEEZY CAME TO, she was tied to her chair with plastic cable binders. Sore, but not hurt. The big guy was at her e-pad, scrolling through file lists. She hoped he couldn't read code or see the hole in the molding covering the adit.

But he was looking at the e-pad...which was on...which meant the camera was not on.

Big Guy saw she was awake. Weezy stared at the e-pad, hoping to make him think she was trying to send a warning through its camera, but he was preoccupied. He turned to her and snapped a couple of pictures with his phone. He said, "Lion" and looked expectantly at the phone's screen.

"Got me a surprise here."

A woman's voice crackled. "You're breaking up. Where the hell are you?"

Big Guy shook his head in irritation and stepped out of the trailer. He held the door open so he could keep an eye on Weezy and tapped the phone.

"Better?"

"Slightly." Loud enough for Weezy to hear.

"I said, got me a surprise. Got into Mayfield's trailer, and there was a spitfire of a girl waiting for me. I'm sending the picture, but it's slow uploading. Wi-Fi here is pretty spotty, which I suppose is why Mayfield chose it."

Long pause.

The person on the other end of the line said something Weezy couldn't follow, finishing, "I need to consult on this."

Weezy did not like the sound of "consult."

"Better do it quick," Big Guy said. "Mayfield will be back any minute."

The voice said, "Zimmerman, you're telling me to make it quick when you have not even responded for the last two hours?"

"I am. But you can get back to me when you want to. It's your party."

Big Guy's phone beeped, and he clicked on a message.

"Louie said Mayfield is going to be here in ten minutes, maybe fifteen."

The woman said, "I'll get back to you."

***

Zimmerman stepped back into the trailer. He switched into tough cop mode.

"What are you doing here, ma'am?"

"Seems like I should be asking that question of you, dumbass."

He stifled the urge to give her a short explanation upside the head. Instead, he asked, "Did you know you're in the company of a criminal, and that you are at very least an accessory to violation of the National Data Protection Act?"

The woman did not look intimidated. "To answer your question, yes. I do know that I am currently in the company of a criminal who is going to have a hard time explaining why he broke into a private residence and assaulted a federal agent."

She said the last several words pointedly in the direction of her e-pad.

Zimmerman shook his head. Sometimes people were so transparent.

He went to the e-pad, found the wired connection and ripped it out of the wall, watching her cringe. For good measure, he rolled the e-pad up and leaned down hard until a muted "pop" indicated the demise of some critical element.

The woman looked horrified.

***

Thirty seconds later, all hell broke loose in several parts of the country.

In Nebraska, a loud alarm went off in the basement of the Suttermeier farmhouse. Marge Suttermeier ran to the head of the stairs.

"Herman?"

No answer.

"Herman, something's making a terrible racket in the basement. Herman?"

She made helpless circling movements with her hands, and then trotted to the back door.

"Herman? You out there?"

"Yeah, Ma?"

HoHum was on his weight bench, inside the main door of the barn. He was relaxing after several sets of crunches. He had begun his biannual effort to make himself a better, healthier, more exciting man.

"Herman, something loud is going off in the basement."

HoHum jumped up from the bench and pounded down the basement stairs.

In Orlando, Jennifer Rowland was on her way past Henry Barber's office to go to the fitness center and then home. Henry's monitor screen came to life, catching her eye. She saw the young woman from IAC staring defiantly off-screen, dropped her gym bag, sat down at Henry's desk and began a series of texts and calls.

At the IAC bullpen, Maddie Hollingsworth's private phone buzzed on her hip. She flipped the cover, gasped and went to a monitor, where she projected the Panacea feed on to the OddBalls' overhead screen. She called out, "It's started." Then, in a small voice, "Weezy's in trouble."

Mike McCutcheon didn't see the story playing out on his cruiser's video until some minutes later because he was on Billy DeFore's doorstep. He was explaining to Billy that "correcting" his wife with a belt was not only against the law, but it would never, never be tolerated in Wakulla County while Sheriff McCutcheon was around, and, yes, you call all your pissant friends and tell 'em to vote me out of office, but I do want you to be sure you heard me and, yes, your wife is going to stay at Priscilla Day's as long as she needs to and, yes, that might just be forever if she's a sensible woman and yes, Priscilla owns a Browning over and under that's only a 20-gauge but knows how to use it and uh-huh, I'll string up what's left if you go anywhere near Priscilla's.

When McCutcheon caught the rerun five minutes later, he called his deputy. "Frank, I need you to get to Joe Mack Smith extension in Panacea right away. Lights, no siren."

"What's up?"

"Looks like a hostage situation in a trailer down by Spencer's."

"Lemme guess. Reggie's blown another brain circuit?"

"Nope. More serious than that. I'm tracking it, but I'm up in Crawfordville. I'll stay in touch."

"Gotcha."

Unaware of all the attention, Paul Zimmerman lifted Weezy and her chair to position her away from the trailer door. He leaned his weight on her pinioned wrists. The fierce glare she directed at him said she was not going to admit how much he was hurting her.

"Now, I'm going to appeal to your reason, young lady. I'm going to say this nice and slow, so you can see my lips move: This Mayfield that you're living with is a criminal. I need to interrogate him. If you raise hell and tip him off, my associate and I will have to capture him the hard way, and that won't be pleasant for him. If you both cooperate, we will have a conversation and probably hand you over to local authorities. Do you understand what I'm saying?"

***

Weezy thought, Yes, I understand what you're saying, dumbass, and I hate it that I can't do anything about it.

"Yes."

There were a couple of minutes of silence, during which Zimmerman checked out the living area, peered at lucky monkey, ran a finger over the guitar strings, not making eye contact with Weezy.

Interrogation? Right. So why wasn't he interrogating her now? He didn't break in here to take a deposition. He didn't need to "consult." He already knew the answer, and it wasn't going to be "Turn them over to local authorities."

She wasn't scared, just mad as hell that she and Joe let themselves relax into this. Playing secret agent. So exciting. So childish. So stupid.

***

Joe parked the Element behind the trailer. He lifted two bags containing a dinner of fried chicken, cheese grits, okra and two large cups of iced tea from the car and walked around to the front of the trailer. Concentrating on keeping the packet of fried okra from spilling, he opened the trailer door with one hand and sidestepped in, bringing with him the warm, lush air of the Florida evening laced with the round, brown smell of fried chicken. He was halfway in when he saw Weezy tied to a chair, then Snake. Snake rested a paw on Weezy's shoulder, the same big hand that escorted him out of Florida Consolidated.

Joe's rage took him by surprise. He moved toward Snake, who reached back in a swift, practiced move and produced a Glock.

"What do you want?"

Snake's face held no expression. "Put the bags down nice and slow." He watched Joe put them on the counter.

"You have been causing a great deal of trouble, stealing information with this illegal operation of yours. You've complicated it by dragging in this lady," he said, giving Weezy a proprietary pat. "That makes the problem even worse. We need to talk our way through it so we can come to an understanding on how to go forward." Snake's phone buzzed. He answered and, keeping his eyes on Joe, listened.

"Yes, I have both of them here," he said. "We were having our discussion. Yes, both. I am sure."

The person on the other end said something short and broke the connection.

Snake turned to Joe and motioned toward the desk chair with the gun, "Sit." His hand tightened suggestively on Weezy's shoulder. She winced.

Joe, eyeing Snake, took the seat next to the ruined e-pad.

A vehicle pulled up outside. Shortly, Big Louie appeared at the door.

"These are the guys I told you about," Joe said to Weezy.

"I figured. The one you call Snake is named Zimmerman, and Big Louie's name is Studt."

Zimmerman glared at her. "Lady, you're too smart for your own damn good."

"Whoever-you-are Zimmerman, you talk too loud. That doesn't make me smart, just observant."

Paul Zimmerman motioned with the gun to Louie. "Bind him to the chair." Louie took two plastic binders out of the fanny pack Zimmerman left on the counter.

"Feet, too," Zimmerman said.

Louie fished out another two binders and leaned forward to secure Joe's right foot.

Zimmerman's voice curdled with anger. "Hands first, for chrissake!"

Joe's adrenalin surged. He projected himself forward, his forehead smashing into Louie's nose. Joe kept his legs moving, pushing. Like football. Momentum carried them across Weezy, into Zimmerman.

Joe saw Zimmerman's hand grab Louie's collar, jerking him

aside. Joe twisted toward Zimmerman, bloodlust rising, saw Zimmerman take a step back and swing the Glock. Then a sharp "tock," like a wood bat hitting a baseball. Then black.

***

Hazy, gray images. Pain. Voices. Cracked linoleum coming into focus, blood.

"Shit goddamn son-of-a *bitch!*"

Joe's brain tried to assemble pieces into a picture.

Louie's voice. "He broke my *nose! Waste the motherfucker!*"

Another voice, Zimmerman. "Here's a towel. Get him up into the chair."

"Shoot him" came out as a muffled whine.

"Damn it, Louie. Can't do that. Get him in the chair."

Then, "You, Mayfield, get your ass into that chair unless you want to see your chickie short a finger or two."

A boot prodded him. Strong hands pulled him to his knees. Weezy's face was white with fear. Something drip-drip-dripping. His blood.

"Stand up."

Joe tried to stand, but the room spun and he began to fall.

Grabbed and pushed into a chair, he saw Louie, a kitchen towel held to his face, blossoming red. Louie dropped the towel and leaned toward Joe, eyes ablaze with animal hatred, dripping blood and snot.

"This time, secure his hands first, dumbshit!"

Louie dropped the towel and pulled the restraints painfully tight, mumbling, wheezing and dripping blood on Joe.

Joe's humiliation stoked his rage, and he screamed at Zimmerman. "Is this some kind of joke? Do you know how much trouble you're in?" The room spun. Joe leaned forward, stomach churning, then forced himself to straighten up. He tried to stare Zimmerman down, but the room kept going out of focus.

"Beating up an unsuspecting accountant is one thing, but

you're working for people who are in the business of killing by the hundreds. The FBI has enough information to put your bosses away for life. You too, if you keep this up."

Zimmerman gave a puff of a laugh and turned to Louie. "You know, I need some coffee. It's been a long day and listening to this high-tone bullshit has gotten me drowsy. You want some coffee?"

"Huh?" It was clear Big Louie had no idea what Zimmerman was talking about.

"Some coffee."

Zimmerman stepped into the kitchen, rummaged around without taking his eyes off Joe, came up with a saucepan and filled it with water. He put the pan on the stove and turned on the burner. Nothing happened.

"Something wrong with the stove?"

"We haven't used it," Joe said.

Zimmerman motioned toward the door with his head, "Louie, see if you can turn on the gas. Should be around the front of the trailer."

Louie, still obviously mystified, said, "Yeah, okay."

Holding the towel to his face, he went down the steps and turned toward the front of the trailer.

Zimmerman twisted the burner to full open.

"Yeah, I sure do need a cup of coffee."

***

Five miles away, Mike McCutcheon called his deputy, Frank Sayos, "How far are you?"

"Fifteen miles. Making good time. Lights, no siren, like you said."

"Better hit the siren and the accelerator, Frank." Mike said. "We need to get there fast."

Mel Williams was watching the feed from Mike's e-pad from his Washington office. "What's the rush?" he asked. "They're not going anywhere."

"They're going to blow the place up." Mike's voice rose above engine and road noise. "Gas leaks are a pretty big problem with these old trailers. Bottled gas piping gives out, propane creeps in through the flooring too low to be noticed until someone decides to enjoy a smoke, and 'Boom!' Maybe they think that being country folks, we won't examine the corpses too carefully, because being fried while attached to a chair is more than a little suspicious."

In Bethesda, the OddBalls stood in a semi-circle, watching the overhead monitor. Maddie had called the FBI when her phone alerted her. Then they watched and waited. Adam, always clever and sarcastic, broke the tension. "Gee, exciting show. All we need is popcorn."

Maddie glared at him with such ferocity that he took a couple of steps backwards and said, "You have Weezy's phone number. Call her up. We can at least slow things down. I can't stand waiting around for something bad to happen."

"Shush!" There was a loud noise coming across the feed. Garbled speech of some sort. All four OddBalls concentrated. As they watched, the big guy in the trailer blanched and picked up his gun.

***

Big Louie rocked the propane tank. There was plenty of gas, but the hose wasn't attached. He knew the routine from a childhood spent in a similar trailer, but the fading light and his throbbing nose made the job harder than it should have been. He tried a third time to get the threads to mesh correctly with the tank's spigot.

"Why the hell does he suddenly want coffee, for crissake?" he mumbled. "We should just do 'em and get the hell outta here. Why do we need to have a friggin' kaffe klatch?"

The threads meshed. Louie twisted the connector home and put a hand on the tank's valve.

Bang! A crash and the sound of a big-block engine revving. He turned toward the sound and harsh light blinded him. Through a cloud of dust, a loud squawk, then painfully amplified, "This is the Wakulla County Sheriff. Come out of the trailer, hands showing. NOW!"

Louie was stultified. His lower brain briefly considered the fight-or-flight question and opted for flight. His feet were moving well before his upper brain engaged.

He ran away from the trailer, through the fading light and into the shadow of Tate's Hell. Louie was a city boy, not used to finding his way through the thicket of roots, saplings, and vines. A protruding root of an oak tripped him, and he fell hard. He lay on the ground, dazed, nose bleeding again, cracked rib on fire.

He rose to all fours, more careful now. In the protective cover of the forest, nobody could see him. His confidence rose. "Just gotta pick my way," he whispered. But there was something in the ground, a gentle thrumming. Then a small movement in the darkness. A flash of white? An exhalation of breath, a soft, eerie rumble? Fear flooded Louie as he strained to see into the darkness. He had heard that before. Where?

The light from Reggie's big EverLight Sonolaser hit him like a fine left hook, and he was eye to eye with the predatory stare of a German Shepherd-Doberman who seemed to know exactly where her next meal was coming from.

"Get up, you miserable sumbitch!"

Big Louie felt very small, afraid to move.

"I said, get up, goddammit!"

Louie stood slowly, embarrassed.

"Aw shit, Annabelle, looky there. This piece-o-crap, big black vee-hickle-driving city boy done pissed hisself."

Reggie reached down to touch the dog's head softly, lovingly. She lowered her ears to accept his congratulation on a job well done.

Then Reggie drew his .45.

***

"This is the Wakulla County Sheriff. Come out of the trailer, hands showing. NOW!"

The volume of the command seemed to rock the old trailer. Bright light blasted through the window, casting Zimmerman's face and chiseled upper body into sharp relief, making him a comic-book illustration. He reached for his gun.

After a brief silence, Weezy's voice. "Come down here nice and close, so you can see *my* lips move, dumbass. Ever since you smashed my e-pad, Sheriff Mike McCutcheon, several people at the FBI and my friends at the Yak have been watching this play out. So, there's no way out for you. Only minimax regret. Want me to define that for you, or can you figure it out for yourself?"

Zimmerman blanched, scanned the trailer, saw the adit peeking through the kitchen cupboard molding.

"You goddamn little bitch. You suckered me."

She gave him an infuriating grin.

His instinct was to crush her throat. No, rip out the adit, then crush her throat. Mayfield must have seen it in his eyes, because he said, "Weezy, don't ..."

Zimmerman willed himself to slow down. Think this through. He could play the cop card. It was just a job. This bohunk small-town sheriff would understand.

He put the gun on the counter. In Bethesda, the OddBalls heaved a sigh of relief. In Kansas, HoHum did, too, and sank back into his chair. His feed through Olegarten to "a few close friends" also yielded sighs of relief from five continents, in eight languages.

Zimmerman began building his case. It wasn't going to be pretty back in Orlando, but this sheriff might back him up if he played his cards right. Really, not such a big deal.

He produced a clasp knife, held it up to show what he was doing. "Let me release these folks."

He'd explain that he was a professional moonlighting for some heavyweight, nasty corporate types. They told him to do anything he needed to protect their data from this hacker who's trying to get back at them for having been fired for, let's say, incompetence.

He freed Weezy's and Joe's wrists and stooped to release their feet.

And the girl? Oh, yeah, this Mayfield turned her...somehow, how would Zimmerman know? She was helping him. Zimmerman had an idea of what they're trying to steal, but no details. His job was to help the clients get it back.

He put the knife on the floor. Tight story. What had he missed?

Louie—where the hell was Louie? Must've run off. So much the better. Lay off the bad stuff on him. Not a perfect story, but he had to tie the ribbon on the package, even if he was wrapping up dog crap.

Zimmerman half-smiled at his quick analysis. The gun was on the counter, and …

He glanced at the counter. No gun.

He turned toward Joe and saw the gun.

It was shaking, even though Joe held it in both hands. The business end of the .45 was a whole lot bigger than Zimmerman ever imagined.

Joe said nothing, but Zimmerman knew he was a dead man.

Suddenly, Weezy was between them.

"Joe, no! It's not worth it. He's not worth even a little bit of Cynthia. Joe …"

She wrapped Joe up in a hug.

The door of the trailer opened, and Mike McCutcheon said, "Lady's right."

THIRTY-SEVEN

JASON SAT IN THE Senate committee chambers, bleary-eyed. Staffers gathered, laying out agendas and water bottles. He hadn't slept well on the plane, worrying in spite of himself about the cash shortfall and the failure of Fischer to respond. But he had put together a fine, reliable holographic show. The right amount of data, blended seamlessly with human interest stories designed to target the emotions of each committee member. He had made a quick stop at his apartment to change into an expertly tailored suit, a crisp shirt, and a muted tie. Old school. Impressive.

Members of the committee arrived over the next ten minutes, and the noise level began to rise. Handshakes, hearty laughter.

In a hospital bed near Bethesda, P.E. Smith pushed the switch to raise her bed so she could see the wall-mounted screen. The pain was better, but the meds made coherent thought difficult. She remembered that Maddie called. When? Yesterday? Maddie had insisted that P.E. watch a Senate meeting, but why? A few minutes ago, a nurse's aide had appeared with a slip of paper and fiddled with the monitor's controls and left. The monitor now showed a hearing room, one she knew well from the battles for IAC funding. It was nearly full, senators she recognized from the Health and Human Services Committee taking their seats, staffers stopping their conversations.

Sen. Thakur entered the room from a side door. He took his position as Chair and called the meeting to order. He smiled toward Jason, acknowledging him. The first two items on the agenda passed quickly, with sponsoring senators given time to make brief statements that would generate valuable news coverage in their respective states. The third item listed was "Medical Equity Project: Extending Horizons; Results"

Jason readied himself. Thakur stopped to confer with his Chief of Staff, who spoke quickly, pointing at a recessed monitor. Committee members on either side studied their own screens, also apparently puzzled.

Thakur paused, then said, "The next item of business is the continuation of work done by the Medical Equity Project, with which I think you are all familiar. Somebody on the Internet is telling us all to attend to this presentation, because our constituents will be following it closely. I certainly hope so, because this is important work."

He cleared his throat and continued, "Here to present today is Mr. Jason Squitieri, whose work on this project dates back to his tenure at MEP."

In Panacea, Joe and Weezy leaned toward the screen of Joe's e-pad. Weezy reached to take Joe's hand.

Jason stood to address the senators, clicking the remote to turn on the Holographis machine that had been placed between the committee and the speakers' table. "The battle to include all Americans in our national health plan is almost complete." A hologram rose from the machine, projecting a quick sequence of healthy families, a pregnant woman consulting her doctor, a pharmacist talking with an elderly woman, fading to a colorful bar graph.

"Twenty-five years ago, four of ten Americans went without health coverage…"

A magenta "354" appeared in the upper right of the hologram. Jason paused. He didn't remember a number there.

"… The Affordable Care Act of 2010 began progress toward complete coverage, but even today, the job is unfinished." The magenta number jumped to 819 and began pulsating.

"As many as 4.5 million people are still not covered under any program." The Holographis projector showed a chart detailing the groups not yet covered, overlaid with pictures…older folks staring anxiously out at the panel members, children in pain, an earnest Latino family, a silver-haired grandmother. "Many of these people—" Jason hesitated. He didn't remember putting the grandmother into the presentation. He cleared his throat. "Many of these people—" he clicked "Forward" on the hand control. The image of the grandmother enlarged to fill the screen. Jason clicked Pause. The woman reached out of the hologram and fiddled with something. The hologram wobbled. A window appeared showing a gear-stuffed basement and a wild-haired man surrounded by displays. The man glanced out at the crowd, said, "Oops!" and disappeared. The hologram dropped down to rest on the floor. It seemed as if the woman was addressing the senators from a kitchen table. In the foreground was a coffee cup that said, "Gramma Rocks!"

"There, now," she said. "We won't be interrupted." She took a sip from the cup, paused, and looked around the chamber, her attention coming to rest on Jason. She pointed at the magenta number, which was now over 3,000.

She said to Jason and the room in general, "The number you're seeing on your holo is the number of people linked into this channel. Most of them are people Jason Squitieri—" she focused her gaze on Jason, not seeming so grandmotherly anymore "— planned to let die using a program to steal millions...ultimately billions...of medical payments intended to save the lives of desperately sick people. He calls it Phoenix, and he installed it in the Yak using political leverage with the chairman of this committee." She paused. As the first shock passed, Jason punched the off button on the Holographis remote. Nothing happened.

Several committee members' hands shot up. Apparently the tripwire of desire to jump on the bit about Sen. Thakur overrode protocol. The grandmother continued, "Senator Thakur was probably unaware of what you were doing, Mr. Squitieri, but several hundred employees of companies and insurance providers are, let's just say, compliant if not complicit. They surely understand parts of your vile program, and they must know it is wrong. Yet, no one has spoken up. So I am here to represent the people you are willing to let die." Jason realized he had been repeatedly punching the Holographis 'off' button and the MEP staffer sitting next to him was staring at him.

The holographic figure turned away from Jason toward the committee members. "I have no doubt most of you will be surprised that the IAC has been hacked. That single intrusion is no reason to compromise the capabilities of the finest, most secure data system in the world. The problem was potentially huge and has already claimed the lives of a brilliant artist, an honest employee at a company infiltrated by this odious software, and more than a dozen others unlucky enough to get sick while their HealthScores were under Mr. Squitieri's control. But it has been nipped in the bud. The people who are supposed to protect the system did their jobs admirably, even at risk of their lives, even when their management...mostly appointees of this committee...refused to take action." She peered over her glasses. "You have some work to do there."

The woman shook her head, then continued, "In the end, the protections you insisted on building into the system worked. You can be proud of that. And, here in America, we don't hide problems. We expose them. We expect you, our leaders and representatives, to solve them."

In Panacea, Joe turned to Weezy to say something and couldn't find words. He nodded Yes. On their e-pad, a window showed HoHum in an Apple T-shirt, fingers flying across the keys of his terminal, muttering "Bandwidth! I need more bandwidth." The magenta indicator in the Holographis projection in DC showed 5,474 connections.

Several members of the committee, particularly those who had been critical of Sen. Thakur's commitment to funding the IAC, motioned for time to speak. Thakur, nervous, ran his hand over his hair several times, seeming to preen for the camera. He covered the mic, leaned back toward his chief of staff. She had gone pale under her carefully nurtured tan. She leaned toward him and whispered. He nodded, turned back to the mic, and said, "This meeting will be in recess."

At Florida Consolidated, Tosheka Jackson was unaware of the Senate meeting. She was making sure her files gave no clue of her activities or location when she disappeared. Jason had said only five days to go. She might have to pull the plug sooner. Too many questions, particularly after Milt James. The elevator door across from her office opened, and a red-haired woman stepped out and strode toward her door. Tosheka had seen her before, she was sure.

Then, approaching obliquely from the staircase, the nice FBI agent. Tosheka stood as they converged on her. She flashed a wary smile. "Henry? To what do I owe...?"

The red-haired woman showed a badge and said, "Tosheka Jackson, you are under the arrest for the murder of Milton James and conspiracy to murder Laura Raskin."

"That's preposterous! You have no evidence!"

The woman gave Tosheka a knowing smile and said, "You must have enjoyed doing in Mr. James, because you left some of your DNA on his hip bone."

Back in the committee chamber, Sen. Thakur pounded the gavel, calling for a recess. The projection of the polite grandmother remained in place despite efforts by several staffers to shut down the Holographis machine. It was a portable, with no plug to pull and apparently under the unerring control of a man with a mass of curls and an Apple T-shirt. The holo image sipped her coffee.

Jason Squitieri told himself that his best course of action was to make a quick exit under the cover of confusion. Leave quietly, grab a cab, disappear. He had enough cash stashed to make a new start, and he had always been good at making lemonade out of lemons. He collected his e-pad, gave a tight smile to the woman next to him, rose and turned to leave. A serious, fit-looking black man blocked his passage. A badge. FBI. The whole getaway dream evaporated. The grandmotherly figure in the holo turned toward Jason, taking the focus of the camera with her. She watched him being handcuffed by two burly federal marshals. She took a sip from her Gramma Rocks cup and said, "Bravo!"

The Holographis machine was heavy. It took two staffers to drag it out of the room, trailing the projection of the kitchen table and the grandmother, which made for an embarrassing video when it went viral.

The blogosphere lit up, each one of several dozen bloggers trying to weigh in quickly, piquantly, quotably.

In Panacea, Weezy shook her head. "Dumbass."

***

Later that day, Mike McCutcheon and his deputy Frank sat at a back table at the Pelican's Roost. Liza brought coffee to top them off. She put a hand on McCutcheon's shoulder while she poured. Everybody in town had heard about the big to-do out at Spencer's last evening, some more or less accurately. Mike was a hero. Liza said, "Can I get you boys anything?" clearly hoping for a conversational opening.

Mike smiled up at her, "No, thanks." Frank shook his head "no."

"Well, just let me know," she said, and walked away.

Frank said, "That's, what, the fifth time she's filled our coffee? Mike, she's sweet on you. You'd better decide to propose to Prissy Day and put Liza out of her misery, or put the move on Liza, or move out of the county."

Mike chuckled. "And I thought law enforcement was complicated ..."

Frank laughed, then said, "So, what's the plan now?"

Mike said, "FBI is sending agents out to acquire Zimmerman

and Studt. Thanks for managing them so well. I've been underwater since last night. This Mayfield and Louise Napolitani thing is a much bigger deal than anyone thought. Mel, Henry, and several other division heads in the FBI have been all over this. This morning, they snagged the guy who started it, and there's a murder back in Orlando that may involve Zimmerman and Studt. Somewhere in the process, word got out to the press. I started getting calls from reporters and bloggers on my personal phone in the cruiser last night. So much for "unlisted." I'm sure the office is crawling with media types. That's why I asked to meet here."

Frank regarded his coffee cup, shook his head, and said, "What the hell are we going to do with Reggie Spencer? I mean, he was certainly within his rights to draw down on Studt, but now he's parading around town like a banty rooster. You'd think *he's* the hero of this whole thing. He said to Jim Osborne, 'Hell, I saw this comin' long before the po-lice figured it out. That guy Studt came nosin' 'round my place coupla days ago, and I knew he was trouble right away. Looked pretty tough 'til he saw Annabelle and Scooter.' "

In Frank's retelling, Mike saw Reggie's sneer.

"I asked him if he really meant to shoot Studt in both kneecaps and then let Annabelle do what she wanted with him afterwards. He said, 'Naw, I was playin' with him. I mean, I had to get him to ee-vacuate both receptacles, if you know what I mean.' "

Frank winced. "Of course, I knew what Reggie meant right away when I finally got Studt out of the woods. He wasn't really talking, just whimpering and trying to stay away from Spencer's dogs. But then I had to put him in the cruiser. Been airin' that poor vehicle out for eight hours, and it's going to take a lot more than a dozen of those deodorizer pine trees to get me back in it again. We stripped him at the jail, gave him a shower and a set of grays. Not too worried about suicide...he was shaking too hard."

"But he's okay this morning, I guess." Frank smiled. "Woke

up hungry, asking for breakfast."

"And Zimmerman?"

Frank snorted. "Pain in the ass. Apparently he's an Orlando cop. 'Doing investigative work on the side.' He paces in the cell talking to himself as if he's studying for a leading role in some Shakespeare play. Cell's side-by-side with Studt's, so he must think he's coaching Studt on the story without being too obvious. Studt appears to be more interested in breakfast."

Frank gave a sour smile. "Zimmerman asks for a private conference with me, acts the sophisticated city cop talking intimately with the dumb country cop, a part he's probably also rehearsed carefully. 'My associate has a crazy streak, you know. This really started out as investigation only. The client wanted me to investigate the theft of intellectual property, a complex matter. But I needed some help and Studt is, well, unpredictable. Did some things that weren't authorized.' Then he gives me the just-between-us, you-know-what-that-means look. Sleazy bastard."

Mike laughed and started to respond. A young, blonde, well-dressed woman clicked across the terrazzo floor, making for the ladies' room, stopped, her eyes widening and mouth forming an "o." Recovering, she smiled, turned, and clicked quickly off toward the front of the building.

Mike shook his head. "Dammit, Frank, we've been spotted. Liza's tried to run interference, but I guess you can't hold back a lady who says she needs the facilities. You better duck out the back...lucky you're not in the cruiser. I'll have to face the crowd and play my role, just like Zimmerman. 'Cept mine is the aw-shucks, friendly country cop, and I won't have to be playin' it in front of a federal judge."

THIRTY-EIGHT

Joe and Weezy had paddled a couple of miles up the Wakulla river and were being pulled slowly by the current.

Weezy let her hand drag in the cool water.

Joe leaned back on the small rear deck of the canoe, resisting the temptation to scratch the row of stitches on his scalp. Popcorn white puffs of cloud made luminous by the deep azure of the Gulf dotted the horizon. He felt a familiar stab of pain. Cynthia. But now he welcomed it.

Weezy half turned back toward Joe...slowly, having learned her normal antic motion didn't go very well with this particular watercraft. "What's next for you?"

He sat up, leaned forward and rested his forearms on his knees.

"I was thinking how nice it would be to drift out into the Gulf, find an island, disappear. Maybe learn to play the guitar better. But every time I get to thinking that way, my realistic side snuffs it. I need to put my life back together. Get a job."

"Joe, c'mon. Your old life is gone. You're RazorBlue now, not middle management Joe Mayfield. I mean, how they gonna keep you in the treasury department when you've seen New Orleans and confounded Phoenix? Right?"

She gave Joe her pixie grin. "You know I'm right."

"Great thought, but I've got to be practical. I need a job."

"So, play by the rules. Use 'em to get a job you'd really like."

"I have no desire to go back to Florida Consolidated and ..."

"Joe, damnit ..." She turned fully toward him, forgetting to mind the balance, and grabbed the gunwales as the canoe rocked.

"For being a smart guy, you are sometimes such a dumbass.

You're the one who's always following rules. Follow 'em now! I mean the real rules, the slide-into -second-with-your-spikes-up rules. Florida Consolidated owes you a generous...scratch that...a princely separation payment and a gold freakin' plated recommendation. They will grasp that pretty quick when the media figures out who RazorBlue is. So, take their settlement. Or get a lawyer and triple it. Figure out what you'd really like to do and do it. Underneath all that 'ordinary guy' B.S. you like to trot out, there's a really smart, not-very-ordinary guy. Cynthia saw that. I see it."

She colored a bit and gazed down into the water.

"You're right, as usual," Joe said. "About the rules, I mean. But I'd like to stay here for a while to let things settle out." Weezy had half turned away. Sunlight danced on the water and caught her face. The Caravaggio Madonna again.

"Will you stay with me for a while?"

Weezy turned to Joe. A smile he'd never seen before.

"Yes, Joe. I'd like that."

Acknowledgements

They say, "Never ask your wife for critique," and that's generally a good rule, I guess. Not for me, though, and not for this book. Beverly Boden Rogers is a fine writer, a punctilious editor, and the source of many improvements to the story. She encouraged me to write and gave me the time and support to complete the effort. Noel Neff copy edited an early manuscript; readers Ned Froelich and Bill Baldwin corrected errors in the final version.

Many others helped along my twisted path to authorship. Arthur Dewing, my first creative writing teacher, conducted his classes with delicacy of judgment, instinctive tact, and a "keen discernment of the capacity of the student," as a colleague put it dryly. Cape Cod Writers Conference instructors Bret Anthony Johnson and Steve Ulfelder helped me understand technique, as did The Loft in Minneapolis. Michael Remer described how a smart guy without a lot of computer expertise would best hack a system. My critique groups, Crème de la Crime, Plymouth Writers, and Minneapolis Writers Guild have given me valuable perspective on the craft of writing. I am especially grateful to Karl Jorgenson, Tim Mahoney, and Miranda Kopp-Filek for their insight.

Coming in 2019 --- the second in the Joe Mayfield - Weezy Napolitani series

Skins and Bone is a thriller with an eye to international finance, European elegance, and simple greed.

Joe Mayfield lands his dream job: Move from Florida to New York, go to work for the respected investment bank ZCG, fly with the finance eagles—and be a short train ride away from Weezy. ZCG uses complex financial derivatives it calls 'Skins' to craft protection for firms working in politically unstable regions...but disaster seems to follow Skins creation, and someone is raking in millions. Joe, curious, begins to dig. Murders follow. Undaunted, Joe and Weezy dig deeper. A financial conference in Vienna and a sumptuous cruise down the Danube to Budapest provide the opportunity for the man making the millions to eliminate Joe and Weezy.

Join my mailing list at *johnbairdrogers.com/contact* for updates and advance purchase discounts. I am happy to join book club discussions via Skype or Facetime. Contact me at john@johnbairdrogers.com.

WITHDRAWN

CPSIA information can be obtained
at www.ICGtesting.com
Printed in the USA
FFHW010101241118
49524174-53900FF